Only Ever Friends

Only Ever Friends

SHAELA KAY

 Blue Water Books
Richland, WA

For Sally,
because I couldn't do this
writing thing without you

Chapter 1

W hoever said that money can't buy love was never
given a diamond ring from Tiffany's.

Not that I needed it. I'd have been happy with a fifty-cent
vending machine knock-off if Derek gave it to me on one knee
and asked me to marry him. But that's me, not Derek. Derek is
two dozen roses and a reservation at Top of the World. Derek is
a private gondola ride and éclairs at The Venetian. Derek is
romance. Derek is perfection.

Derek is Tiffany's.

"Oh Amie, you look beautiful!"

I turn to see my best friend, Tara, walking into the room
behind me, late as usual. It doesn't bother me this time. Today
is only the final fitting, so it's not like she's late for the actual
wedding.

Yikes. I hope I didn't just jinx myself.

"Traffic?" I ask.

"Like you wouldn't believe," she says, dropping her bag
onto an empty seat. I turn back toward the triple mirrors, my
hands running down my side once more. The ivory gown is

1

heavily beaded, perfectly fitted to my form. Derek picked it out of course, because I have absolutely no fashion sense. He said the mermaid silhouette would compliment my curves, and he's right. I look like a goddess.

"Dang, Amie. That dress!"

"Right?"

"Wish I could find *me* a filthy rich fiancé to pay for my dream wedding," she mumbles, fluffing out the train so the gauzy fabric trails off the step.

"Whatever. You've already got your knight in shining armor. Now it's my turn."

"Hmm. I guess Jeremy *is* kind of dashing."

We burst out laughing, because her portly, balding husband is anything *but* the handsome dreamboat we were both convinced she would someday marry. After all, Tara was the prettier between us. She'd always had her pick of dates for Homecoming and Prom, while I sat at home with my two other best friends, Ben & Jerry. But Jeremy came charging in on a noble moped and swept her off her feet our second year in Vegas. Turns out she finds brilliant statisticians with a dry sense of humor *extremely* attractive.

"So did you bring the veil?" I ask.

Her deer-in-the-headlights look threatens to burst my euphoric bubble, but I manage to keep my smile in place.

"You forgot," I say, just as she blurts, "I totally forgot!"

"I'm so sorry," she gushes, "I was running late and meant to grab it on my way out, but I completely spaced it."

I sigh. "That's ok. Can you get the pearls from my bag?"

She digs through my purse, finally pulling out a faded, blue velvet bag. She unties the string and tips the strand of pearls into her hand, dropping the bag back into my purse.

I step off the pedestal and turn my back to her, holding up my long, brown hair so she can place them around my neck.

"Are these new?" she asks.

"No, they're my 'something old.' They were my mom's, but I had them restrung."

"Ah. That explains why the spring on this clasp is so tight. I can't quite—oh, there."

She steps back and I let my hair drop. It's almost halfway down my back, which is longer than it's been in years. Ever since I turned twelve and cut my hair for the first time, I've kept it just brushing my shoulders.

"What's your 'something blue?'"

"Sapphire earrings. Derek got them for me."

She rolls her eyes. "Figures. And the dress is your 'new?'"

"Yes. And if you can remember the veil," I give her a pointed look through the mirror, "I'll have my 'something borrowed.'"

It's silent for a moment, my thoughts on the wedding I've been dreaming about since my childhood. I stare at my reflection, trying to marry the image of the three brides staring back at me with the little girl from my memory, dressed up in her mother's old wedding gown and worn-out high heels. Somehow I can't seem to do it.

"When are your parents flying in to town?" Tara asks.

"Monday. That way they can be here all week."

"And they're leaving...?"

"Sunday. Derek and I will have brunch with them before taking off."

"For Fiji." Her voice says I'm-so-jealous but her face says I'm-so-happy-for-you.

I squeal, unable to contain myself. "Can you believe it? In two weeks, I'll be in *Fiji!*"

The nostalgic sound of Monica's *Angel of Mine* cuts into our conversation, and I nearly trip in my haste to get to my phone in time. My cheeks protest as I pull them into another mammoth grin. "Hey babe," I say into the phone.

"Amie?"

Amie? He never calls me Amie. It's always Baby, or Beautiful. My smile falters. "Yeah?"

"We need to talk."

————

The restaurant he takes me to is nice, just like all the others he's taken me to. Real tablecloths, real candles, real expensive. Because that's Derek. He holds the door open and pulls my chair out for me, because that's Derek, too. And when the waiter comes, I don't even open my menu. Derek always knows exactly what to order.

This time, though, he dismisses our server without ordering anything. My stomach flips.

"I've been doing a lot of thinking."

Oh, no.

"And... well, maybe we're jumping into this a little too quickly."

I blink.

"Too quickly? Derek, it's been three years."

"I know." He leans back and his Armani suit jacket falls open. "But I've got my own firm to build up now, and you've still got another year before graduation. Maybe we should, you know, wait for things to settle down."

4

I can hear what he's saying, but it still doesn't register. "So, like, what. You want to call off the wedding?" It comes out in a puff of laughter, because he can't be serious.

He can't be serious.

But when he doesn't laugh with me, my gut flips inside-out and suddenly I'm sixteen again, about to pass out after donating blood for the first time. My face gets cold and my lips start tingling and my ears are ringing and Derek is saying something but I can't hear what it is because he doesn't want to marry me.

He doesn't want to marry me.

"Amie? Amie?"

Derek's concerned voice finally reaches my still-ringing ears. I lurch to my feet. "I'm going to be sick," I mumble, trying to stop the room from spinning.

"Baby, sit down. Here, have some water."

I sit automatically, fighting the urge to throw the glass of water he offers me right in his face. He launches into a prepared speech about how much he loves me and what a great person I am and how someday I'll make someone really happy. He's using his lawyer voice, like I'm an incompetent member of one of those juries he despises so much—the kind he has to convince to see things his way. At last he's finished, and he gives me a sad, half-smile.

"Do you know what I mean?"

I rub my temple and nod, even though I have no idea what he actually said. He helps me to my feet and out to his car, where we ride in silence back to my place. The neon lights of Las Vegas flash past in a dizzy kaleidoscope of color, and I feel sick again. I almost wish I could throw up right here, all over his leather seats.

We pull up in front of my apartment, but Derek doesn't

5

cut the engine. Even though it's only May, the thermometer on the console reads 82° and he's not staying. He's not coming in tonight. I stare at my hands, waiting for him to say something.

"Baby, I'm sorry."

I nod, my nose prickling with the tears I'm trying desperately to hold inside.

"Are you going to be ok?"

"I don't know," I answer, my voice cracking like a 12-year-old Boy Scout's.

He reaches over and squeezes my hand. "You'll be ok," he says, confident.

I nod again. *I'll be ok.* My heart disagrees, considering the vice-like grip those two letters have around my chest. But my head is calm. *Derek is right. He's always right. I'll be ok, somehow.*

He walks me to the door and waits for me to unlock it before brushing a kiss on my cheek. "See you, Amie."

I nod—I've been a Bobblehead all night—and go inside. I stand in the dark until I hear the purring thrum of his Mercedes as he drives away. Slowly, I drag myself down the hall to my room and flip on the light.

My eyes are assaulted by the very thing that caused so much joy this morning—was it really only this morning? It seems a lifetime ago that I was standing in Belladonna Bridal with Tara, laughing about her follicly-challenged Prince Charming.

But at least she has one.

I stare at my dress, hanging in its custom muslin bag on my closet door. It represents so many things that for a moment, I'm blindsided by all that I've lost. So many hopes. So many dreams. So many hot fudge sundaes, passed up just to fit into a size 4 again.

My knees buckle beneath me and I collapse on the floor, gasping for breath. The tears come hot and loud, like the locker room showers that pelt your skin with tiny, wet bullets. I fumble for my phone, desperately trying to find Tara's number before my vision disappears.

Somehow she understands enough of my blubbering to realize something terrible has happened, and she's pounding on my door within twenty minutes. By the time I finally let her in, she's already on her phone, Googling how to pick a lock.

"Oh, Ames."

She comes inside, hugging me so tight I get hiccups. "I'm so sorry. This sucks," she says.

I Bobblehead back at her.

I can't make myself go into my bedroom again, not with my dress hanging there to mock me. We head for the tiny living room instead. I lie on the floor while she strokes my hair, just like she did years ago when my first boyfriend broke up with me. We were seventeen then, and as much as she *wanted* to empathize with me, Tara had no idea what it felt like. She'd always been the dumper, not the dumpee. And this? This is a million times worse.

Minutes pass. Hours. Months. I've been curled up on this scratchy carpet for decades. But somewhere between my-life-is-over and he's-not-good-enough-for-you, my tears dry up. I feel like a wrung-out sponge, full of holes.

Finally, Tara clears her throat. "So, what are you going to do?"

"I don't know," I say, sitting up. "Ugh." My head feels like a balloon about to explode, so I go into the kitchen for some

Aleve. I grab a bottled water from the fridge and down one of the little blue pills.

"Do you think he just needs some time?"

"I don't know what to think about anything."

"Yeah." She bites her lip.

I come back and plop down on the couch, wincing when the movement sends shards of glass shooting into my brain. "Derek would know what to do. He always knows what to do," I mumble.

"Well, he's the one who made this mess, so we're not asking his advice about anything anymore." She starts gathering the puffballs of used tissue that litter the floor. "What if..." she starts to say, but then she shakes her head.

"What?"

"Well, what if you go home for the summer? It might be good to get away from... all this."

We both know she was about to say *Derek* but neither of us acknowledge it. It's enough that we know.

"School doesn't start again until the end of August," she says. "When are you supposed to go back to work?"

"The guys at Beckett & Jones knew I was planning to start my internship late this summer. I could probably just cancel it..." My voice drifts off like a lost puppy.

Tara offers me a half-hearted smile. "It might be a good idea. You haven't been home for ages. I bet your parents would love to have you visit."

"Yeah."

Tossing out the tissues, Tara grabs a water from the fridge. She stays in the kitchen, putting away the dishes and tidying things up. Watching her reminds me of when we were roommates, back before she fell in love and married Jeremy. I miss having her as a roommate. Sure, we had our differences and minor annoyances (could you PLEASE just shut the cupboard doors when you're finished?), but when you've been friends as long as we have, you learn to overlook things. She was the sister I never had, and I was the sister she wished she could trade her three younger sisters *for*. After high school we never even considered going our separate ways, and since I got into UNLV, she tagged along to find a beauty school to attend. We've been through so much, she and I. I couldn't bear the thought of living with someone else after she ditched me for The Great Baldini. So I didn't.

With the kitchen cleaned, she comes back and sits beside me. I lean my head on her shoulder, and she rests hers on mine.

"None of this makes any sense," I whisper.

"I know, Ames."

"I love him."

She wraps her arms around me. "I know."

"And he loved me."

Silence.

"I was perfect for him. I was everything he ever wanted. Wasn't I? Wasn't I everything he said he ever wanted?"

"Yeah."

The silence stretches between us, the rock in my chest growing heavier and heavier until it's crushing me with its weight, eking out the tears that I thought had all dried up.

Chapter 2

When we were sixteen, Tara and I made a pact that we would be each other's Maids of Honor when we got married. I kept my end of the bargain a few years ago when she married Jeremy, and together with her mom, we made it a lovely wedding. If it hadn't been for us, Tara would probably have been married without flowers, without a cake, and in some run-down old church because she'd forgotten to book a venue. But, knowing Tara tends to miss things, we took care of all that for her. Don't get me wrong—she'd sell her left kidney to help a friend in need. But if that same friend asked her to pick up a gallon of milk on the way home? Or meet her at the airport Friday at 9pm? There wouldn't be any milk and her friend would have to call an Uber because Tara forgot. Again.

So naturally, I'm hesitant when she offers to take care of all the cancelations a few days later.

"I don't know," I hedge. "Derek made most of the arrangements."

"So I'll call Derek. I've been meaning to give him a piece of my mind, anyway."

I flinch. "Please, Tara. Don't."

She sighs, crossing her arms. "Fine, I won't. Even though he deserves it."

"Thanks."

I turn again to the book in my hand. It's a tattered, secondhand copy of *Anne of Green Gables* that I've read so many times it's falling apart. I love the story, and really need the comfort of a familiar friend at the moment. *Anne* fits the bill, with the added bonus that it's not a romance, which is actually kind of hard to find on my shelves. Normally I love romance novels, but reading about someone else's happily ever after while mine is in pieces is the last thing I want.

"So?"

I look up at Tara, still leaning against the counter with her arms folded. "So, what?"

She rolls her eyes at me. "Come on, Ames. I want to help."

"You are helping." I close the book and try to smile at her. "Thanks for switching your vacation time. It means a lot. Are you sure Jeremy doesn't mind you staying here with me?"

"He doesn't care—he knows you're practically family. Besides, you'd do the same for me. *And* you would handle all the dirty work so I wouldn't have to." She gives me a knowing look, coming to sit beside me on the couch. "Why won't you let me do the same?"

I pick at a spot on my shorts, searching for another excuse. "All right, fine. Can you cancel the manis and pedis you booked for us?"

"Done."

I stare at her as her grin widens. "Done? Like, you already did?"

"Yup." She's starting to look like the Cheshire Cat.

"Did you even remember to book them in the first place?" I tease, half expecting her to confess that she'd actually forgotten, and that's why they were already cancelled.

Tara feigns offense. "*Yes,* I *did.* Geez. I'm not that terrible, am I?"

I give her a look and she scoffs, hitting me with a pillow. I almost laugh, but my chest feels too tight. "All right, I'm sorry. Thanks for booking them. And thanks for canceling them too, I guess."

I look down, my nose pricking, and she rubs my arm. "You're welcome. I canceled the hairdresser, too."

"Thanks."

"What else can I do?"

"Can you take my dress over to your place?"

"Sure."

"And..." I swallow. "Can you post something online? Just... don't go into details."

"Of course. Where's your phone?"

I pull it out of my pocket and hand it to her. She starts tapping on the screen and I go back to my book, trying not to think about what she's doing. After several minutes she sets my phone down next to me.

"Done."

The word sends a stabbing pain into my chest, igniting my tear ducts. I nod, trying to lose myself in the story before I really start crying. But the words in front of me start swimming, and pretty soon I can't see the page at all.

"Ugh, I hate this!" I growl, getting up from the couch. I drop the book and grab some tissues, blowing my nose and letting the anger work through me. If I'm mad I don't cry as much, and I'm so sick of crying.

"Have you thought anymore about going home?" Tara asks.

I buy time by blowing my nose—again—and throwing all the Kleenex away. Then I wash my hands. Tara just sits on the couch, giving me the I-know-what-you're-doing-and-it's-not-going-to-work look that she wore through most of high school. Back then it was usually because I was trying to talk her out of something I knew she'd regret later, like shaving her eyebrows. This time, it's because she knows I'm avoiding the question. I guess that's what happens when you've been best friends for ten years—you know each other so well that you can't get away with anything.

I slump onto the couch, leaning my head back. "I've thought about it."

"And?"

"And what? I've thought about it."

"Come on, Ames. You should go. You know it would be good for you to get away."

I grimace. "Yeah, I know."

"What did your mom say when you told her about Derek?" she asks softly.

I toss her my phone with a sigh, reliving the conversation from yesterday while Tara reads along.

AMIE

Hey mom

MOM

Hey sweetie! We are so excited to see you next week! Did you pick up your dress?

AMIE

Yeah, but I won't be needing it – the wedding's off

That's when she called me. I ignored it. I ignored the next call, too. And the next. Finally she texted me back.

MOM
Call me

AMIE
Not ready to talk about it. Just wanted you to know so you can cancel your flight.

MOM
Is it really off?

AMIE
Yes

MOM
Ok

AMIE
Can you tell the family? Do you still have the list from the invitations?

MOM
Yes, I'll let them know. Sweetie I'm so sorry.

AMIE
Thanks mom. Love you

MOM
Love you too

I'm crying again, and Tara gets up to bring the tissue box over to the couch. I grab a handful.

"I just don't want to have to explain myself, you know? I don't want to talk about it," I say.

"So tell them that."

I shake my head. "I just... I don't know. Going home might be worse than staying here."

"How can it be worse? If you stay here, you're going to be

thinking about Derek all day long, because everything here will remind you of him. You'll cry everyday and have a headache for a month, and then you'll start thinking you have a brain tumor or something. But if you go home..." Her voice trails off, and she raises her perfectly shaded brows.

If I go home, nothing will remind me about Derek, because he's never been to Spokane. Even when I invited him to meet my parents, instead of going home with me for Thanksgiving, he arranged to fly them down for Christmas. It was so exciting, and fun, to show my parents all my favorite things in Vegas. And every year since, Derek's flown them down in January, to celebrate my birthday with me. He's never gone to Washington once.

Wait.

We'd been together three years, and Derek never once went home with me?

Huh. I'd never thought about it like that.

Tara is still scrolling on my phone. "Amie, your mom has been texting you and calling you, like, all day."

I groan. I put my phone on mute and turned off notifications when I went to bed last night for that very reason. "Now you can see why I don't know if I should go home," I grumble, wiping my nose again. Geez, how much snot can one person make?

"Well, you're going to have to, now."

I freeze. She's still on my phone. I reach for it, but she pulls it away.

"Tara!"

She tosses it on the couch with a smug look. "I told your mom you're coming home. You better book a flight."

"Ugh. I hate you," I say, pulling up whatever conversation she just had with my mother.

"You might now, but you'll thank me later."

"Is this just so *you* can go home, too?"

She rolls her eyes, getting up from the couch and walking into the kitchen. "I told you, Jeremy doesn't care that I'm here." She starts digging in the fridge and I put my phone down, watching her.

"But you miss him."

She knows it's not a question, but she nods anyway. "And my bed. That couch isn't very comfortable."

She smiles, and while I know she's teasing me, I also know she's right. I hate it when Tara is right. If she was still single, I could probably stay in Vegas. I could get through this, because we'd be in it together.

But we're not in it together. She's got Jeremy now. And I've got... no one.

She brings me a bottled water from the fridge and another blue pill. "Thanks," I say. "But I still hate you."

"I hate you, too," she says lightly, sitting down and turning on the tv.

I pick up my phone again and open the browser. The tab is already open to an airline travel page, with LAS and GEG plugged in to the arrival and destination fields. My lips stretch, trying to smile.

I guess she doesn't miss *everything*.

Chapter 3

Derek and I met at a party during my first semester at UNLV. I was nineteen and had no idea what I wanted to do with my life. He was several years older and had just graduated law school. We started dating shortly afterward, and the next semester I changed my major from undeclared to Political Science. Derek was, after all, a lawyer.

I don't know what it was that originally attracted me to Derek. He wasn't bad to look at, but not exactly what you'd call eye candy. I was just drawn to him, like a fly to one of those brightly lit bug zappers. He was charming. He was smart. He was ambitious. He was everything I ever thought I wanted. In fact, I often asked myself what *he* saw in *me*. I was average height, average size, with average brown hair and more than an average amount of freckles. But something must have appealed to him because we continued dating. On the third anniversary of the day we met, he proposed, and it felt like the most natural thing in the world to say yes.

Up until the day he dumped me, two weeks before the wedding.

Maybe I should have seen it coming. Isn't that what people say? *I should have seen it coming.* But I honestly don't know how I would have. He was so excited about our future together and so involved in the wedding plans—he picked my dress, secured the venue, he even ordered the flowers and booked the caterer, because his taste is better than mine. Nothing in his behavior had given me any warning. It was as if a trap door had opened up underneath the stage, and instead of my place in the spotlight as the glowing bride-to-be, I found myself plummeting into the black abyss below.

It totally sucked.

I hand the airline attendant my phone and he scans the boarding pass, handing it back to me. "Have a nice flight," he says

"Thanks," I mumble, stopping myself before I say *you too.* It's such a knee-jerk reaction, and I've been running on autopilot for days.

I pull my carry-on behind me as I walk down the jet bridge, anxious to be on the plane. The attendants are waiting to greet the passengers, and I fake a smile as I step up into the aircraft. I find my seat and stow my luggage overhead—handle out, like Derek taught me. Stashing my purse under the seat, I glance at the little old woman in the window seat beside mine. Glance, but then I stare. Her hair is bubblegum pink, and she's wearing far too much lipstick. "Hello," I stammer, taking my seat.

"Why hello! Where you headed, sugar?" the older woman asks, her voice like a Georgia summer.

"Spokane, Washington."

"And are you going or coming from home?"

"Both, I guess. I'm a student at UNLV so I live in Vegas now, but I'm from Spokane."

She pats my hand in a way that would be condescending if she didn't have pink hair. "Then you're *going* home, honey. Home is where your mama and her cooking is, you know."

I smile. "Yeah, I guess."

"I'm going home, too. I live with my daughter in Billings, Montana. You ever been there?"

"No."

"No, *ma'am*. Didn't your mama ever teach you to respect your elders?"

"No ma'am. I mean, yes ma'am." I smile, and it feels foreign. It's the first real smile I've worn all week.

"That's more like it. I'm Sylvia."

"I'm Amie."

My phone pings, and I pull up a text from my brother. He messaged me the day after I told my mom about the breakup, offering his sympathy. I hadn't responded. He'd tried calling, too, but I hadn't answered his calls, either.

> BRANDON
>
> Mom said you're going home for the summer. I'm glad. I'll be there the end of June for a visit so it will be nice to see you. We have a lot to catch up on.

Brandon's going home too? Ugh. I never should have let Tara talk me into this. The last thing I want is to spend a week hiding in the shadow of my perfect brother. I'd rather wallow in self-pity by myself.

The captain comes on the intercom to tell us we're about to take off. I buckle my seat belt and pull it tight, then switch my phone to airplane mode.

"I hate this part."

I look over at Sylvia and see her gripping the armrests, the veins in her hands bulging like overstuffed sausages. I pry one of her hands off and hold it in both of my own. She closes her eyes.

"That feels real nice. Thank you, darlin.'"

I hold her hand through the entire takeoff, until we're high in the sky and the captain comes on again to tell us we're free to move about the cabin. Sylvia sighs, and I'm surprised at how much air such a tiny person can keep inside.

"You would think with all the flying I've done in my life I'd be used to it by now," she says.

"Do you travel a lot?"

"Not much anymore. But when my husband was alive, we went all over: Italy, Egypt, China—anywhere Darryl got a hankerin' to visit."

"That sounds wonderful."

"It certainly was." Her eyes disappear in her wrinkles when she smiles. "Darryl and I were married sixty-three years before he died. That was four years ago now."

"Oh. I'm so sorry for your loss."

She pats my hand again. "Thank you, sugar, but don't feel sorry for me. We had a wonderful life here, and I'm anxious for the good Lord to take me home so we can continue it together on the other side." A glint of gold catches my eye when she smiles.

I smile back at her, and she looks down at our hands. "Are you married or engaged?" she asks, nudging my hand to indicate the ring I still wear.

"Oh." I feel the blood drain from my face. "Um, neither, actually. Not anymore."

I pull my hands back into my lap, wishing I could disappear. Tara has been trying to get me to take off the ring ever since the night Derek broke up with me, but I can't bring myself to do it. Not yet. I guess I'm just not ready to let go of him yet.

My tear ducts shift into overdrive as I think about Derek. I swallow, trying to dislodge the lump caught in my throat, but it doesn't budge.

"Oh, honey, I'm so sorry. Do you want to talk about it?"

I brush angrily at the hot tears now spilling down my cheeks. "No. It's nothing."

Sylvia's feather-soft eyebrows disappear in the cotton candy puff covering her brow. "Those tears don't look like nothing." She digs in her purse for a minute, then holds out a small package of tissues. "Here you go, honey. He must have been someone real special, to be cryin' like that."

That does it. What little success I've had in stemming the flow is completely obliterated. Suddenly I'm raining a tsunami-sized torrent of tears on her shoulder, blubbering about how wonderful Derek is and how much I love him and how I will never find another man as brilliant as him if I searched the whole world over.

People around us are staring, but Sylvia just pats my hand, letting me cry. It's not long before a flight attendant with dark hair and cheerful freckles hurries over.

"Are you okay?" she asks, crouching beside me. "Do you need anything?"

I try desperately to stop the flood, but I can't. Sylvia looks past me, addressing the stewardess.

"She could use a drink, honey."

"Of course." The attendant begins to stand, but Sylvia stops her.

"And I do mean *a drink*."

"No-o," I moan. "I d-don't drink."

Sylvia frowns, but the flight attendant hurries off, coming back with a small bottle of water. She crouches beside me, rubbing my other arm, and I imagine how ridiculous I look, bawling my eyes out on a jumbo jet at thirty-five thousand feet.

At last I manage to stop crying, and I dig in my purse for another painkiller. The stewardess hands me the bottled water and I wash it down, exhausted. I feel drained and empty, like a punctured beach ball. You know how pathetic those things look?

Yeah. Me too.

"Do you feel any better?" Sylvia asks.

I shrug. "I don't think I'll ever feel better."

She nods. "That sounds about right. The world has ended —how can you ever feel better after the world ends?"

My swollen eyes flicker to her face. She's smiling at me, with a look that says she understands. I look away again.

"Maybe the world has ended," she says, more softly this time. "Maybe this Derek really *was* the sun and moon and stars. But you know what, sugar? I can promise you that there's someone out there who thinks that *you're* the sun and moon and stars. And that's who you're really meant to be with. Not this man who's broken your heart."

I shake my head, wincing at the movement. She's wrong. Not about Derek breaking my heart, because he certainly has. But wrong about finding someone else. If Derek didn't love me when I was everything he'd ever wanted, when I'd done everything he ever asked of me, what are the chances there's someone out there who would love me just the way I am?

Chapter 4

M om wraps me in a hug the minute I see her. "Oh sweetie, I'm so sorry," she says, and I can hear the catch in her voice. I steel myself.

"It's good to see you too, Mom," I say dryly.

She laughs, pulling back to wipe her eyes. "Sorry. It's good to see you, sweetie."

"Hey punkin," my dad says, stepping forward.

"Hey Dad."

He gives me a brief hug and grabs my carry-on. "Did you check any bags?" he asks.

"Of course she did," Mom breaks in. "She's staying for the whole summer." She beams at me, and I force myself to smile.

Mom and Dad talk on the way home while I sit quietly in the back seat. Well, Mom talks, Dad listens. Or pretends to listen. She's complaining about all the construction going on downtown near the library, where she works. I'm not really paying attention, just letting their words wash over me like the lights flashing past the window. Mom looks back occasionally, but doesn't say anything.

I'm glad. Silence is easier.

It's late—almost eleven—when we finally pull into the driveway of my childhood home. A single light illuminates the small porch, my memory filling in what I can't see in the dark: the hydrangea bushes under the front window, the weathered roof my dad keeps saying he'll replace. The cool night air is soft on my cheek as I climb out of the car, my ears filling with the sound of crickets. I take a deep breath and catch a hint of the last lilac blooms, one of my favorite scents in the whole world.

I've missed it here.

Most of the homes on South Hill are big, sprawling things, with too many windows and more rooms than most hotels. But the neighborhood surrounding the northwest corner of Manito park, where I grew up, is filled with quaint little homes built in the 1920s and 30s. What they lack in size they make up for in character, with steeply pitched roofs, beautiful brick chimneys, and dormers and gables to satisfy even the most romantic of architects.

Dad pulls my suitcases out of the trunk while I follow Mom into the house. A familiar black cat greets me at the door, rubbing against my leg to beg some attention. I crouch down and scratch behind his ears—just enough to start him purring but not enough to get him drooling.

"Hey Ebenezer," I croon. "It's good to see you."

He meows back at me, rubbing his head against my hand. I give him one last scratch and then stand.

"Are you hungry?" Mom asks. "You look thin."

"I'm fine, Mom. Just tired."

"All right. Get some rest. I'll see you in the morning."

"Thanks Mom."

Another hug, and then I head up the stairs to the tiny front bedroom overlooking the park. Dad is there already, putting my bags down by the far wall.

"Welcome home," he says with a smile.

I force my lips to curve. "Thanks, Dad."

"It's good to have you here. Just wish it was for a different reason."

I nod, feeling the familiar chokehold starting. He gives me a brief hug, kisses my forehead, and moves past me into the hall, shutting the door behind him.

I stand by the door, looking around. The walls are still painted sage green, the old hardwood floor covered with the same braided rug, the white ceiling still pitched like the roof of the house. My old dresser sits in the corner between the two windows, and the faded yellow bedspread I got when I turned fourteen still covers the twin-size mattress. Everything looks the same, with the exception of my bookshelf across the room. The dozens of books that used to fill it are back in my apartment in Vegas, though a few odds and ends still grace its shelves. I walk over to it, picking up a framed picture of my family. It was taken several years ago on one of the rollercoasters at Silverwood Amusement Park. Brandon and my dad have joyous smiles on their faces, Mom looks sick, and I look... terrified.

I hate rollercoasters.

I set it down and look at the rest of the items on the shelves. A chipped mug that I made in ceramics class, my high school yearbooks, and a battered black ball are the only things left. A wave of nostalgia washes over me when I see the old toy. Jason got me the Magic 8 Ball for my sixteenth birthday. He meant it as a joke, knowing that I sometimes had a hard time making decisions about things.

Jason. I haven't thought about him in a while. I wonder what he's up to these days?

I pull one of the yearbooks off the shelf, the one from my junior year. Jason was a year older than Tara and me so he didn't graduate with us, but the three years we were all together in high school were the best years ever. We were practically inseparable, the three of us. Except on those nights when Tara had a date—then it was just me and Jason.

I flip through the yearbook until I get to the senior section. Past all the professional portraits and cheesy personal quotes is the "Voted Most" section. Jason's picture is there, his single dimple smiling up at me under a heading that reads "Most Likely To Be Mistaken For Someone Famous." We had a good laugh about that at the time, trying to figure out which celebrity he might be mistaken for. I suggested Chris Evans. Tara suggested Quasimodo.

I pick up the black ball, feeling the familiar weight in my hand as I turn it over. *Signs point to yes* floats to the top. Too bad I didn't ask it something important, like *Will I wake up tomorrow and find this is all a dream?*

I put the toy down and sit on the bed, kicking off my shoes. Aside from the nearly-empty bookshelf, the room looks exactly like it did when I graduated from high school. The walls, the floor, even the cracked outlet cover on the far wall. It's like the last four years never happened.

Like Derek never happened.

I pull at the ring on my finger, shifting and wiggling it to get it passed my knuckle. The simple band is completely eclipsed by the 2-carat diamond mounted on it. I turn it over in my hands, feeling the weight of the stone dragging the entire ring downward.

Pinching the ring between my fingers, I glare at it. The diamond flashes in the light, blinding me with its brilliance, just like Derek. He's all I saw. He's all anyone ever saw. No one ever saw me. Not even Derek.

I clench the ring in my fist, anger washing away my pain like undiluted bleach. Not anymore. I'm going to forget Derek ever existed, forget I ever cared about him. I'm going to spend the summer erasing every trace of Derek from my life until he's nothing but a scar on my heart.

I open my hand. There's a rectangular indentation in my palm from the diamond, and though I can't feel them, I know there are thousands of similar marks all over my skin, all over my life—marks left by Derek.

The bed creaks when I stand up, but my steps are sure as I cross the room to my old dresser. Yanking open the top drawer, I drop the ring inside and shove it closed.

I take a deep breath and look at my palm. The mark left by the ring is already starting to fade.

Tomorrow I'll start erasing the rest of them.

———

Soft light filters through the curtains on the window when I open my eyes, unable to feign sleep any longer. I've been awake for an hour—I forgot how much earlier it gets light up here.

I roll over and glance at the clock on the bedside table. 6:25. I groan, wishing I could go back to sleep, but knowing I won't be able to. Sitting up, I catch a glimpse of the aspen trees outside my window. It's strange to see something so green right in the middle of town. I've gotten used to the sparseness of Vegas.

Ebenezer is curled up at the foot of my bed, a fluffy ball of inky black fur. I reach over to pet him and he trills a purr, stretching.

"Hey, you," I say, stroking his head. His motor starts thrumming and I smile, seeing the first drop of drool pooling on his jowls.

My bedspread will be soaked through if I keep petting him, so I withdraw my hand, reaching up to comb my fingers through my tangled hair. For the first time in months my hand doesn't catch. I glance at my bare ring finger, then flip my hand over to check my palm.

The mark is completely gone.

I take a breath and let it out with a big huff, puffing out my cheeks like a squirrel. A month ago, I'd be texting Derek right now to let him know I was on my way. We always met up for CrossFit on Mondays.

But not anymore. I start making a mental list of things to change or get rid of in order to purge my life of Derek's influence. No more Derek means no more CrossFit. Period.

Climbing out of bed, I stretch my arms wide, arching my back like a cat. The sun glints off the pond across the street, inviting me to take a stroll. I pause, considering, then move to get dressed.

In ten minutes' time I'm downstairs in the only workout clothes I brought: hot pink leggings with a matching top and black Nikes, all compliments of Derek. I make a mental note to ditch the clothes and buy myself something a little less... well, Derek.

"Hey sweetie, you're up early. Do you want some breakfast?"

Mom is sitting at the kitchen table with her iPad and a cup

of coffee, but I shake my head. "Thanks, but not yet. I'm going for a walk in the park." I open the fridge and glance around. "Do you have any water I can take?"

"Bottled water? Sorry sweetie, we don't."

"That's ok. Be back soon."

The handle is warm as I pull the front door shut behind me, facing directly into the sun. I squint, jogging across the street to get under the trees growing just inside Manito Park. It's still early enough that there's a big change in temperature between sun and shade. I shiver, reveling in the feeling.

The gravel crunches under my feet like popcorn, and I hurry my steps to keep warm. Halfway around the pond I break from the path to climb up the hill. The grass is slick with dew, and I slip a couple times before breaking into the sunlight at the top.

I keep walking. On and on and on—the grass and trees and shrubs never seem to end. Sometimes I follow the paths that wind between the towering pines; other times I trek across the lawns to reach another part of the park. It's huge— bigger than I remember—and the longer I walk, the steadier I feel. There is nothing about Derek in this beautiful place. Only grass and green, trees and leaves, sun and shade and wind and sky.

After a while, I sit down on a bench and pull out my phone to text Tara.

AMIE

Made it home

I anticipate a quick reply because Tara always has her phone with her. Unless, of course, she's lost it. Again. I look around as I wait for her response. A couple people are jogging

29

and a few others are walking their dogs. It's still too early for any kids or teens to make an appearance.

My phone buzzes and I swipe to open her response.

TARA

Good! How are your parents?

AMIE

They're fine. Mom is already trying to fatten me up.

TARA

The way your mom cooks, that could be really dangerous. But also delicious.

I smile, because she's right. Mom really is an amazing cook.

TARA

How are you doing? Feeling any better yet?

AMIE

A little. I took off the ring.

TARA

Good. I hope you chucked it out of the plane

I think about where I left the ring, rattling in my old dresser drawer.

AMIE

Not quite. But it feels good to get it off. I'm ready to let go of him.

TARA

Glad to hear it

I get to my feet, stowing my phone in the mesh side pocket of my leggings. It's getting warmer now, and I've been gone an hour. Mom is probably wondering where I am.

I wander back across the park a different way, taking new trails and passing new flowerbeds. I stop to snap some pictures, adding them to the hundreds of others on my phone that I never do anything with. Just as I put my phone back in my pocket, it chirps.

PETALS AND PROMISES

Hello! We're excited to see you at your [10:00AM] appointment today. Please arrive ten minutes early to ensure you have enough time with our floral designer.

Text YES to confirm

Text STOP if you no longer wish to receive these notifications

I groan. I'd forgotten about our final meeting with the florist. I should have let Tara handle the cancelations when I had the chance, because apparently Derek didn't. I locate the number for the florist in my contacts and hit the call button.

It rings, and rings, and rings. Finally I get a voice message stating their business hours, with the option to leave a message.

"Hi, this is Amie Cunningham," I say after the beep. "Um, I won't be able to make it to my appointment today, and we won't be needing the flowers this week. The wedding has been called off, so please cancel our order. If you have any questions, call Derek Carter—he should be listed as the alternate contact. Thanks."

I hang up, shaking. Ugh. How do people do this? I know I'm not the world's first jilted bride—how do other women handle dealing with the aftermath of a broken engagement? I mean, besides eating their weight in Rocky Road ice cream. I've got that part covered.

I know the florist isn't the only thing that was supposed to happen today. As I open my calendar to see what else was scheduled, my phone alarms again.

(Personal reminder) Call the caterer to finalize the drinks menu

I choke on the lump forming in my throat, shoving my phone back in my pocket. Forget it. If Derek didn't have the courtesy to cancel the arrangements, I'm not going to put myself through the agony of doing it for him.

My vision starts to blur, and I brush roughly against my eyes, stumbling as I catch my toe on the edge of the sidewalk. Looking around, I realize I've come to the edge of the park. I turn left, following the sidewalk as it wraps around the grass, breathing deeply in an attempt to regain control.

"Amie?"

I pause and look around when I hear my name, but when I don't see anyone nearby I keep walking. Taking another deep breath, I pull out my phone to text Tara again.

"Hey, Amie!"

The voice is louder this time, coming from off to my right. I glance at the houses across the street, which are around the corner from my own, and see Jason standing in a familiar driveway next to a small red pickup, grinning at me. My body reacts before my brain has a chance to catch up, and in a moment I'm walking across the street, grinning back at him. He meets me at the end of the driveway, opening his arms for a hug. I step into his embrace without even thinking.

"I wasn't sure if it was you at first—I didn't know you were back in town!" he says, stepping back.

"Yeah, I just got in last night," I say. "How've you been?"

He shrugs and smiles, the dimple in his cheek more pronounced than I remember. "Pretty good. You?"

"Uh..." The smile on my face wavers. How am I supposed to answer that? If he was a grocery clerk or a bank teller I'd fake a smile and say "fine." But he's not a clerk, or a teller. He's Jason. I've never had to fake anything around him.

I clear my throat. "I've been better."

"Oh." His smile disappears. "Are your parents all right? I haven't seen them in a while."

"Yeah, they're fine."

"Oh, good." Even through his relief, I can tell he wants to ask *Then why did you come home?* but he doesn't. Because that's not Jason.

"How are your parents?" I jerk my chin at the house, twisting my face into a smile. "You still living at home?"

He laughs, the sound bringing a tidal wave of memories crashing into my brain. I *know* that laugh. It's the sound of a can of warm soda being opened in the garage behind his house. The sound of text alerts at eleven PM. The sound of summer nights lying on the hood of his car, counting satellites and lamenting the coming school year. The sound is *home*, and I've missed it.

Jason's voice breaks into my thoughts, and I scramble to recall what we're talking about.

"No, my parents built a house across town a couple years ago, so this is my place now."

I glance quickly at his left hand, but he's got his thumbs hooked into the back pockets of his jeans and I can't tell if there's a ring or not. He notices my look and smirks.

"I'm not married, Amie. I've got a girlfriend, though."

I blush, and he raises his eyebrows at me. "Are you?

33

Married? I haven't been online in ages, but I thought I heard something a while back about you being engaged."

My thumb rubs against my bare ring finger. "Not married, but you're right. I was engaged."

"Was?"

"Yeah. He broke up with me last week." I wrap my arms around myself, taking a deep breath in through my nose. I scrunch it up when it starts to prickle.

"Oh man. I'm sorry, Ames."

Ames. Jason and Tara are the only friends who've ever called me that. It's warm and comfortable, like my favorite orange hoodie.

"Thanks," I say, feeling awkward. Which is weird, because I've never felt awkward around Jason in my life. Well, unless you count that one time, after the homecoming game my junior year, when he *didn't* almost kiss me. That was awkward.

"Well anyways, it was good to see you, Jason," I say, taking a step back toward the sidewalk.

"Hey, we should hang out while you're here," he says, pulling out his phone. "Catch up and all. How long are you in town?"

"All summer."

He smiles, flashing his dimple again. "Great. What's your number?"

I tell him, and he punches it into his phone. After a moment he looks up, just as my phone buzzes. "Sent you a text," he says. "I've got some errands to run this morning and then I have to work, but are you free tonight?"

I laugh weakly. "I'm free all summer, Jason."

"Good." He smiles and goes around to the other side of the truck. "See ya later, then."

He climbs inside as I wave, walking back up the street. I hear him start the truck and drive away, and as soon as I'm around the corner I pull out my phone.

JASON
If he's dumb enough to dump you, it's a good thing you didn't marry the guy.

I stare at Jason's text, a strange bubble growing in my chest. Though we didn't really stay in touch after high school, he's known me even longer than I've known Tara. We grew apart the way day-old balloons drift away—slowly, gently, bobbing in the breeze of life as we went our separate ways, our interactions limited to likes and the occasional comment on Facebook or Instagram. But somehow, with that one text, it's like we haven't missed a beat.

I smile, saving his number in my contacts.

Chapter 5

By the time I get home, Mom has a ten-course meal waiting for me. Bacon, eggs, homemade biscuits, sausage gravy, pancakes, buttermilk syrup—it's like the Sunday morning buffet at Golden Corral, minus the geriatric customers dissolving Citrucel in their orange juice.

"Uh, Mom?" I call, standing in the entrance to the kitchen.

"There you are! I was starting to wonder if I should send out a search party." She emerges from the pantry holding a container of flour.

"Are you having company for breakfast?"

"Just my favorite girl," she sings, setting the flour down and wiping her hands on her apron.

"There's no way all this food is just for you and me," I say, picking up the pitcher of orange juice and taking it to the table.

"Well, you were taking so long, so I just kept cooking. Now I won't have to fix breakfast the rest of the week."

She smiles, but she's lying. She'll be cooking breakfast again tomorrow. Because that's my mom.

I haven't had much of an appetite lately, but I surprise

myself by eating everything on my plate. I can practically hear my mom purring as I help myself to more eggs and bacon.

"When is Brandon coming to town?" I ask.

"He'll be here the middle of June, and plans on staying for a couple weeks."

"Is his girlfriend coming with him?"

"No. She was going to come with him for the wedding so we could all meet her, but now..." She gives me a look that makes me instantly feel guilty, though I'm not sure how any of this is my fault. "Brandon is coming by himself," she finishes.

I nod, stabbing a fried egg with a little more force than necessary. The runny yolk bleeds all over my hash browns, congealing on my plate in a visceral pool of gold.

"So, what do you want to do today?"

I freeze, a forkful of dripping eggs inches from my open mouth. "Don't you have to go to work?"

"No, I decided to keep my vacation time, since you were coming home. I wasn't about to just leave you here alone."

I force myself to swallow the eggs, then take a long drink while I do some quick thinking. I love my mom, but I do *not* want to be trapped with her alone in this house the rest of the week. Mom's a talker, who thinks every problem can be solved by hashing things out. And since her only daughter getting dumped by the man formerly known as Mr. Right is a BIG problem, she'll definitely want to talk about it. Me? Not so much.

"That's great, Mom," I say, guarding my look. "But you don't need to take time off. I'll be fine."

"Sweetie, you hardly ever come home anymore, and this will give us a chance to talk."

What'd I tell you. I take a deep breath and try to channel

Derek's lawyer look. "I appreciate the thought, but I really don't want to talk about it, Mom."

She starts clearing the table. "Talking about it will help you process your emotions. I read this book once, and it said—"

"Mom! I *really* don't want to talk about it. Not now. Maybe not ever. I need you to be okay with that."

"But sweetie—"

"No, Mom."

She frowns, but doesn't say any more—for now, at least. I take my dishes to the sink, trying to think of a way to occupy my mom today with something other than how disappointed she is with me.

"Since you have the day off," I finally say, "I could really use some new clothes. Can we go shopping later?"

She lights up again, as I knew she would. "Of course! Do you want to go into the Valley or up to North Town?"

"I'm fine with wherever."

"I think the Valley Mall would be best. I've been wanting to stop at the Nordstrom Rack for some time now."

Leaving my mom to finish cleaning up, I run upstairs to take a quick shower. I pull my hair into a ponytail out of habit, wondering if I should cut it, since it's getting so long. I haven't cut it since Derek mentioned he liked long hair when we were first dating. I scowl at the memory. Definitely getting it cut.

By the time I'm ready Mom is finished in the kitchen, so we head out for a day of spending way more money than we should. Shopping is one of my mom's favorite things to do—it's right up there with reading tragic biographies and cross-stitching cat samplers.

After several hours of dodging gray-haired power-walkers

and stroller-wielding moms, I find myself in possession of a new summer wardrobe. My shopping bags are full to bursting with artfully distressed shorts, tanks, and tees, all of which are decidedly NOT Derek's style. He usually dressed me in tailored capris and button-ups, which meant that my closet looked like an advertisement for Ann Taylor. Now it looks like I won a shopping spree from Old Navy.

"Do you mind if we swing by the library real quick?" Moms asks as we're driving home, already heading for downtown. "I forgot to tell Jen about the special order coming in this week."

"Sure. I'll pick up some books while you take care of things."

Downtown Spokane is a maze of old brick buildings and one-way streets that visitors always complain about. But I like it. It feels homey and close, but I suppose that's partly because I grew up here. The downtown library is right near the river, with a huge wall of glass overlooking the falls. We park under the building and head for the elevator.

"They just finished the renovations," Mom says.

The silver doors slide open, and instead of the decades-old stench of dirt and body odor I was expecting, the smell of new carpet fills my nose. "Nice," I say, stepping inside the cab.

The doors slide open again two stories later, and the new carpet smell mingles with that of fresh paint and old books. I look around with interest as we step through the security sensors. Paintings and sculptures from local artists are scattered around the library, lending an eclectic yet sophisticated feel to the space. Everything has been rearranged, so nothing is where I expect it to be.

I wander through the rows, pulling books off the shelf at

random to check the covers and read the backs. Whoever said not to judge a book by its cover was probably talking to me, because that's literally all I do. I'm a total cover snob—if it's pretty, I'll read the back. If it's not, I won't even bother. The only exception to my rule is if a book comes recommended from a friend, but even then, the cover determines where it goes in my to-be-read pile. I still haven't made it to the ratty secondhand copy of *The Great Gatsby* a friend gave me in high school because the cover makes my eyeballs bleed.

After twenty minutes of browsing I have a nice big stack of books and a not-so-nice kink in my neck from reading spines. I take my treasures and go in search of my mom, finally locating her standing outside an office talking to Jen, the Assistant Librarian. Mom waves when she notices me.

I walk over to them, balancing my books carefully so as not to drop any. Dropping a book is a cardinal sin in the library, second only in severity to turning down the corner of a page instead of using a bookmark. Ask me how I know this.

"Jen, you remember my daughter Amie?" Mom says. "She's home from school for a while."

"Amie, good to see you again," Jen says, the light of recognition in her voice.

"Thanks, you too."

"So she's out for the rest of the summer?" Mom asks, returning to their conversation.

Jen shrugs. "That's what she said."

"Oh dear. What did Kenneth say?"

"I talked to him about hiring another part-timer, but you know the process takes awhile. We'll be halfway through July before we can get somebody trained and ready to step in. And by then, what's the point?"

Mom looks over at me. "Our children's librarian is in Mexico for a month, and her assistant was just put on bedrest, apparently. She's expecting."

"Oh wow. So you're a little understaffed?" I ask, carefully shifting the books in my arms.

Jen shakes her head. "If we were only understaffed, we could manage. But the Summer Reading Program is about to start, and there are all sorts of activities and events that go along with it. Cassandra has been in charge for years, but Melissa was taking over this summer since Cassie has had her vacation planned for months. But now Melissa is out, and I don't know what we're going to do. We might have to cancel a lot of the activities."

My arms are about ready to fall off, so I set the pile of books carefully on the floor next to me. Shaking out my wrists I ask, "Anything I can do to help?"

"Sweetie, you're home so you can relax. You shouldn't be working," Mom says.

"I'm not an invalid, Mom. I'll be bored out of my mind if I don't have something to do for three months."

"Are you here all summer?" Jen asks.

"Yes, I'll be here through August."

"It would take too long to train you in the library computer system," Jen says. "But you could help with some of the events. Are you any good with kids?"

I shrug. "I haven't had much experience with them. But I like kids."

"Perfect. Can you be here at ten tomorrow to help with storytime? I'll talk to Kenneth and see what he thinks about bringing you on part-time to help with events for the summer."

"Sure." I bend to pick up my books, handing half the stack to my mom.

"Are you sure you want to help out?" she asks, after Jen walks away. "You don't have to. You can just hang out at home for the summer."

"I want to help," I say, heading for the circulation desk. "It will be good to get my mind off things and figure out where to go from here."

"Aren't you going to finish school?"

"Well, yeah, but I don't think I want to finish my studies in pre-law."

"Because of Derek? Sweetie, you can still be a lawyer. You don't have to give it up just because you're not with Derek anymore."

"I know." I plop my books on the counter, and Mom starts scanning them for me. "It's just, law school doesn't really appeal to me anymore. I really only majored in Political Science because Derek is a lawyer."

She doesn't say anything as she finishes checking out my books. Finally she looks up. "So what are you going to do instead?"

I sigh. "I have no idea. What did I want to be when I was a kid?"

"A librarian," she says, smiling as we turn to leave. "Like me."

We walk in silence to the elevator, but I know she's not going to let the matter drop. Because that's not my mom. We make it all the way to the car—a good two minutes longer than I anticipated—before she brings it up again.

"You're really not going to be a lawyer?"

"Nope."

"But you don't know what you want to do instead."

"Nope."

She sighs, giving me a look that says I-hope-you-know-what-you're-doing-but-I'm-not-so-sure-you-do.

I guess that makes two of us.

Chapter 6

I'm curled up in my room reading one of the new library books when my phone pings.

JASON

Want to grab something to eat?

I grin. I know Jason said he wanted to hang out, but I'm pleasantly surprised to get his text. After a day spent deflecting my mother's attempts at psycho-therapy, catching up with Jason sounds heavenly.

JASON

I'm meeting some friends for pizza – you should come

Hmm. That adds a whole other element to the question at hand. I'll have to pretend I'm fine in front of a bunch of strangers, but anything is better than continual harassment from my mother. Besides, I'll be with Jason.

AMIE

Sure. What time?

JASON

Come over whenever. We're meeting up at 6

It's 5:17, and since I have no idea where the pizza place is, I figure I should get ready sooner rather than later, especially since I'm still wearing one of the outfits I brought from Vegas: a button-up blouse with tan slacks. Totally Derek. Totally going in the trash.

I slip into a new pair of jean shorts and pull a T-shirt over my head. Shorts and a tee are okay for getting pizza with friends, right? I can't even remember the last time I had a casual night out with friends. I was always with Derek.

Mom is sitting in the living room working on a new cross-stitch when I come downstairs.

"Hey Mom. I'm heading over to Jason's house. Do you need anything from me before I go?"

She gives me a blank look. "Jason Henley? I didn't know you guys were still in touch."

I shrug. "I ran into him at the park this morning. He just texted me and invited me to get some pizza with him and his friends."

"Oh, that was nice of him. Did he ever get married?"

"I don't think so," I say, sensing danger. "But we're just friends, Mom. He has a girlfriend."

"I was only asking, Amie." She gives me a stern look before turning back to her stitching. "Have a nice time. Do you know when you'll be home?"

"Not sure, but I have my phone if you need me. See ya later —love you."

"Love you too, sweetie."

I glance at my phone as I head down the sidewalk. 5:32. Does that give us enough time to get to the pizza place? Or is it too much time? Will we be standing around feeling awkward while we wait to leave? I roll my eyes at myself. Chill, Amie, it's *Jason*. The guy's mom probably has photos of the two of you running around in diapers together.

Somehow the thought doesn't calm my nerves.

It's just because he's a guy, I tell myself. *The only guy you've been hanging out with for the last three years is Derek.* Unless I count Jeremy. But an awkward mathematician—especially one married to my best friend—most definitely does NOT count.

Within minutes I'm standing on Jason's front porch, memories floating through my mind like those tiny puffs of cotton that fill the air every spring. Riding bikes in the street the summer I turned seven. Sneaking cookies from the cooling rack while his mom switched the laundry. Learning to drive a stick shift in his old Honda Civic. Pretending to study AP History but really watching stupid cat videos on YouTube.

I raise my hand and knock, and in less time than it takes to overthink my outfit (again), Jason pulls open the door, his face splitting into a grin the minute he sees me.

"Amie! Glad you could make it."

He stands back and I step inside, the tang of citrus and seasonings filling my nostrils.

"Are you cooking something?" I ask.

"Yeah—come on in. I just need to put it away."

I follow him down the short hall to the little kitchen almost as familiar as my own. The same worn old table sits in front of the bay window, the same flowery curtains hang from either side of it. A smile tugs at the corner of my mouth. It doesn't look like much of a bachelor pad.

Jason pulls an empty jar from the cupboard and sets it on the counter. Grabbing a towel, he wraps it around the handle of a skillet and picks it up, reaching for a rubber scraper with the other hand. In one smooth motion, he pours the contents of the pan into the glass, scraping the sides to get every last, golden drop.

"What is it?" I ask, eyeing the thick yellow syrup now filling the jar. Tiny dark flecks float suspended in the gleaming liquid.

"Basil lemon sauce," he says, pulling a spoon out of the drawer. He dips it in the jar and offers it to me. I take it from him, popping it in my mouth.

"Wow, that's really good."

"You like it?" He grins, grabbing a spoon for himself. "Mm, yeah. That's good."

"What's it for?" I ask, setting the spoon in the sink as he screws a lid onto the jar.

"Just messing around. Trying to come up with something new to serve with pork tenderloin."

My eyebrows shoot up. "I didn't know you could cook."

He laughs. "Neither did I. At least, not until a few years ago. But I really enjoy it."

"So you're a chef, then?"

"You mean for work? Nah. My dad has me running the carwash now."

Ah yes, Henley's Car Wash. My brother Brandon and I both had summer jobs there, though not at the same time. A lot of our friends did, too. It was the perfect part-time gig for a bunch of rowdy teenagers.

"You're running the whole thing? That's great."

Jason makes a face. "Yeah, well, it pays the bills. It really bothers Veronica, though."

"Veronica—is that your girlfriend?"

"Yeah."

"How long have you been together?"

"This time around?" Jason runs his hand through his hair, smirking at me. "About six months, give or take."

I grin. "Think it will last?"

"Who knows. Want something to drink?" He pulls a couple sodas from the fridge and tosses one to me. I catch it by reflex.

"Thanks, but I don't drink Coke anymore." I set the plastic bottle on the counter, willing myself not to hear Derek's voice in my head.

"Don't tell me you've moved to the diet dark side," he says, twisting open the cap on his drink.

I smile. "No. I just... don't drink soda anymore. Do you have any water?"

He jerks his chin at the sink. "Glasses are in the cupboard over the dishwasher."

I almost laugh. "I keep forgetting I'm not in Vegas anymore."

Jason takes a swig from his bottle, giving me a funny look. "What does that have to do with where the glasses are kept?"

This time I do laugh. "It's not that. I just forget that you don't have to drink bottled water up here."

"Is that all they drink in Vegas?"

"Pretty much. Either bottled or filtered."

"Huh."

I pull a mismatched glass from the cupboard and fill it with water from the tap. I'm surprised—again—when the water is actually cold. Tap water never comes out cold in the middle of a Vegas summer.

"I've never been to Vegas," he says. "Is it as hot as they say?"

"Yeah. But I don't mind."

"You don't?"

"No. It's a dry heat. Besides, once it gets over a hundred it all feels the same."

He laughs. "That doesn't sound very pleasant."

I shrug. "It's all perspective, I guess. Five months of the year are hot as Hades, but the other seven? It's paradise. All you ever need is a light jacket. It's like fall blends right into spring and skips winter entirely. I love it."

"Hm, that does sound nice. I could do without shoveling snow for a change." He takes another drink. "What else do you love about it?"

I grin. "The shopping."

He rolls his eyes. "Why does that not surprise me."

"The food is good, too. It's so eclectic—you can find all sorts of different cuisines."

"I've heard of a few world-class restaurants down there," Jason says. "I can see the appeal in that regard."

"Oh, and the sunsets! There's so much more sky down there. The sunsets are breathtaking."

"Aren't there casinos everywhere, though?"

"Not everywhere. A lot of Vegas feels like any other normal town. Except for the slot machines—*those* things are everywhere."

"Really?"

"Yeah. It was strange when I first moved there, seeing them in all the grocery stores and gas stations. But now I don't really notice them."

Jason's phone chirps and he pulls it from his pocket. "Landon is on his way. He'll pick us up in five."

"We're not driving?"

"No, the place we're going to is downtown, and you know how parking is. We're trying to take as few cars as possible."

Jason excuses himself and leaves the kitchen. I finish my water and set the glass in the sink, wandering back into the hall as I wait. I look at the few photos hung haphazardly on the wall, obviously meant to fill the void where his mom took down all the family pictures when they moved. There's a photo of Jason and his parents at the carwash, a group shot with Jason and a bunch of other guys I don't recognize—maybe someone's bachelor party?—and a third, of Jason standing next to an olive-skinned woman with dark eyes and a plunging neckline. They're dressed in evening wear, and with the way she's hanging on him, I assume it must be Veronica.

"You ready?"

I turn when I hear Jason's voice behind me. "Yup."

"I hope you're hungry," he says, opening the door.

"Famished."

His dimple reappears. "Good."

Jason's friend Landon is one of those cool, laid back guys you just can't help feeling comfortable around. The ride downtown isn't long, and the others—all women—are waiting for us when we arrive.

"Finally," one of them says when we walk in the door. "What took you so long?"

"Landon couldn't find a parking spot. We had to hike in from Lincoln Street."

I half expect to see Veronica tonight, but the Latin beauty from the photograph isn't among the group, and her name isn't mentioned when Jason makes the introductions. I make a mental note to ask him about her later.

We wind our way through the restaurant to a large table in the back. The place is crowded and loud, and judging from the smell alone I can understand why. The tempting aromas of pesto and garlic mingle with the smoky, yeasty smell of wood-fired pizza dough, making my mouth water.

The friends chat as we take our seats at the table, and I hang back, feeling awkward. I've never really been what you'd consider shy, but after last week I'm feeling all sorts of vulnerable. I'd like to sit by Jason, but both seats beside him are already filled. I settle for the one across from him instead, tucking a strand of hair behind my ear as I sit down.

There are a few different conversations going at the table, and I sit quietly, listening. It's obvious that everyone knows each other well, and it sounds like they get together often. When the waitress comes to take our order, I'm the first person she looks to. I've been too busy watching and listening to the others to really look at the menu, so I glance at the page in front of me and ask for the first thing that comes to mind.

"Um, can I get a 9-inch with mushrooms and black olives?"

She nods and jots it down, turning to Jason, who's looking at me as if I just sprouted another head.

"Since when do you like mushrooms?" he asks.

His question catches me off guard, and not just because he remembers that I don't like mushrooms. Who remembers that kind of stuff?

"I don't know. I guess," I wrack my brain, trying to figure out how to explain that I always order mushrooms and black olives because it's Derek's favorite.

I freeze.

"Uh, never mind." I say quickly. "Can I change mine to a margherita pizza?"

The waitress scribbles on her pad. "Sure. And for you?"

Jason is still looking at me funny, so I pretend to study the drink menu. "I'll have a 12-inch Meatza Pizza," he finally says.

The others place their orders, and conversation breaks out across the table again.

"So, Jason said you and him go way back," the girl next to me says.

My eyes flick to Jason, who's chatting with Landon, before I focus on the girl speaking to me. Angela? I think that's her name.

"Yeah, we grew up on the same street and went to school together." I try to shift in my seat, but my bare legs stick to the vinyl chair like velcro. "And you? How do you know Jason?"

"Work. I help out at the carwash between my shifts at the hospital."

"I used to work at the carwash, years ago. Fun times." I smile. "What do you do at the hospital?"

"I'm a CNA, but I'm working on my prereqs for nursing school. What about you?"

"Oh." I guess I should have seen that coming, but since I didn't, I fumble for an answer. "I'm a student at UNLV." Dangit, now she's going to ask what my major is.

"Nice! I love Las Vegas. What are you studying?"

Called it. "Um, Political Science." The words come out more like a question than a statement. I blink, trying to head off the panic I can already feel building in my chest. Why did I agree to come tonight? I'm not ready for this kind of interaction. I don't know the answers yet. Not without Derek here to answer for me.

"Wow, that's a heavy major. Are you planning on law school?"

I take a sip of my water, trying to slow my racing pulse. "I'm not really sure," I say, offering a noncommittal shrug. I think she can sense my unease, because she offers me a polite smile and turns to join the conversation of her other friends. I blow out my breath and reach for my glass again.

"Political science, huh?"

I look up to see Jason watching me. His hands are below the table but he's leaning forward, interested. I didn't realize he was listening.

"Yeah." I take a sip and set the glass back down, looking at the condensation spilling down the side instead of meeting his gaze.

"I had no idea you were interested in pre-law."

"I wasn't. Not until I met Derek." I finally look at him, and his eyes narrow just a fraction. I remember that look. It's the look he used to get when working on cars, or a particularly troublesome math problem.

"Derek is the ex, right?"

"Right." My voice is hard and flat, my eyes flicking to the others around the table. I don't really want to talk about it, especially not here. He sits back, understanding.

"So what are your plans for the summer? I could use some part-timers at the carwash."

I smile, knowing he's not serious. "As tempting as that sounds, I actually have another job lined up."

"Already?"

"Yeah. The library is a little short-staffed for the summer, and since I'm available, they asked if I'd be willing to help with the summer reading program."

"Wow, that's great. When do you start?"

"Well, I'm going in tomorrow morning to help with storytime. I'm assuming I'll find out more then."

Our pizzas arrive, and after a few minor shuffles we all dig in. I haven't eaten much since the gastrointestinal Olympics at breakfast and I'm hungry. I listen with half an ear to the conversations around me as I savor each bite. I'd forgotten how much I love margherita pizza.

The rest of the evening passes uneventfully. I smile and nod with the others, grateful to be on the fringe. It's interesting to watch Jason interacting with his friends, not having seen him in four years. He hasn't changed much: he still gets loud when he's excited about something, he still tips his head back when he laughs. I watch how the others interact with him, too, trying to gauge where their friendships lie. It doesn't surprise me that there are more girls than guys tonight—it was usually that way with Jason.

By the time we climb back into Landon's car I'm feeling almost normal. I haven't thought about Derek in 7.2 seconds, and I think my smiles were more genuine than forced. I even manage to join in on the guys' conversation as we head toward South Hill, offering my opinion as to which Marvel movie really is the best. (Winter Soldier, of course.)

Landon pulls into the driveway and Jason and I hop out. "It was nice to meet you, Amie," he says. "I'm sure we'll be seeing you around."

"You too, Landon. Thanks."

Jason jerks his chin down the street as Landon drives away. "Come on, I'll walk you home."

The crickets are out in full force tonight, and I'm content to listen to their chorus as we walk to my parents' house. Silences have always been comfortable with Jason, and with everything that *has* changed in my life, it's nice to know that hasn't.

"Thanks for coming tonight, Ames," he says when we get to the door. "I hope you had a good time."

"It was great," I say, and I mean it. "I can't remember the last time I just hung out with normal people."

He cocks his head to one side. "You never hung out with friends in Vegas?"

I shrug. "I didn't really have friends. Except for Tara."

"And Derek."

I grimace.

"Did he have friends? Did you ever hang out with them?"

I inhale slowly, filling my lungs with the cool, sweet air. "Not really friends, no. But he had clients we'd go to dinner with occasionally. Derek is a lawyer."

"Ah." I see my comment from earlier clicking into place in his mind. Before I can read his reaction, he grins at me. "Well, you're welcome to share mine while you're in town." He takes a step back. "Have a good night."

"Goodnight."

I slip inside and lean against the door, imagining him walking back down the street and around the corner. It feels almost like high school again, in a good way. All those nights Jason and I spent hanging out at his house, all those walks home in the dark, laughing at ourselves. For a moment I let my thoughts wander to a simpler time, until the reality of my life— where I am and why I'm here in the first place—comes crashing back into my consciousness. I sigh, taking the stairs up to my room.

Chapter 7

"Most of the kids will already be enrolled, but if anyone asks, here's the signup sheet. And the packets are in the drawer."

I nod, adding her instructions to the mental list of things to remember. Jen hands me a calendar of events printed on neon yellow paper. "We've got several different storytimes, plus special guests and extra events each week. I'd like you to handle Preschool Storytime, as well as all the activities on Thursday afternoons. Think you can do that?"

"Sure." I glance over the calendar, noting that Preschool Storytime happens twice a week, and the events listed on Thursday afternoons vary. This week there's a guest speaker coming to talk about birds.

"Great." Jen points to the large, open area behind me. "Storytime takes place over there. In the closet here," she indicates a nearby door, "there are all sorts of things for the kids to play with. Beanbags, foam blocks, maracas, scarves—whatever works with the book you've chosen."

"Am I supposed to choose the book?"

"You can if you want to, but there are some suggestions in the closet if you need them."

I relax at her words. I'm still getting used to making decisions for myself again—the last thing I want is to start making decisions involving other people.

"When we have a special guest on Thursday afternoon, you just need to introduce them and assist with anything they need. And make sure they end on time."

"And what do I do for storytime?"

She shrugs. "As long as you read a book to the kids, you can do whatever else you want. The kids can be kind of wiggly, so give them something to do or they'll be climbing the walls."

A vision of child-sized squirrels dressed in jeans and T-shirts assaults my mind, the theme song from Alvin and the Chipmunks playing in the background. I blink. As if she can read my mind, Jen gives me a reassuring smile. "You'll be fine."

She's obviously never watched the show.

Jen walks me through the rest of the main floor, showing me where and how to clock in and out as well as the break room, where I can stash my stuff. She introduces me to a few other employees along the way, and soon we find ourselves back in the children's area.

"I'll take care of storytime today so you can get a feel for it. The kids should be arriving soon."

A few families have been wandering around for a while, but as it gets closer to ten o'clock they begin congregating on the large, colorful rug. I position myself in the back of the group so I can see everything going on. By the time we're ready to start, a dozen preschoolers are milling about like tiny Tasmanian devils. Maybe it's my imagination, but half the adults herding them seem to have the same wild-eyed look of someone who's been locked in confinement for years.

"Who's ready for storytime?" Jen claps her hands, walking to the front of the group. A chorus of voices answer her and she smiles. "I'm glad to hear it. I know that usually Miss Melissa is here to read with you all, but she won't be able to join us this summer. Instead, we have a brand new friend who will be doing storytime! Miss Amie will be helping us with the summer reading program this year, and she'll be in charge of storytime with all of you," she says, pointing to me.

Two dozen heads swivel in my direction, and my neck grows warm. I smile and offer a half-hearted wave to the crowd. After a moment everyone turns their attention back to Jen, who is now introducing the book for today.

Well, almost everyone.

A little girl with round, pink cheeks and pudgy elbows watches me. Her wispy blonde hair is pulled into two high ponytails and she wears a large pair of glasses, which magnify her eyes *a la* Professor Trelawney. I smile at her, and she blinks.

I look up at Jen, sitting on a stool at the front of the group, calmly turning pages while she reads aloud about a giraffe named Gerald who likes to dance. My eyes flicker to the little girl, still staring at me. I look down at myself, wondering if something is amiss. Is my shirt on backwards? Did I forget something important, like pants?

Nope, everything seems to be in order. I give the girl a double thumbs up and her face splits into a grin. She glances up at Jen, then looks back at me.

For the next ten minutes, Pigtails and I steal glances at each other. Every time our eyes lock, she grins, and I can't help but smile back. Finally, Jen finishes the book and puts it away.

"Amie, can you help me for a minute?"

I hold the closet door while she pulls out two large tubs of foam blocks. The children squeal in delight, clamoring for the chance to be first to grab the blue squares. She sets one tub down in front of the rug, and I take the other tub to the back, near where I was standing. Pigtails watches me, one little finger hooked in her lip.

The minute I set the tub down the squirrels—er, children—attack it. Two boys grab a foam block each and start hitting each other with imaginary swords. Pigtails shuffles away from them and I step forward to intervene.

"Hey guys, let's build something!" I try to infuse my voice with excitement. "Can you build a tower as tall as you are?"

Both boys immediately start stacking blocks on top of each other, their towers toppling before they get anywhere near their respective heights. Pigtails starts edging toward me and I crouch down, ready to greet her.

"What's your name?" I ask.

She glances behind her at a woman sitting on a chair, absorbed in her phone. She looks back at me.

"Evelyn."

"Hi Evelyn. I'm Amie. Do you want to build a tower with me?"

She nods, and I start gathering blocks. The two boys have had as much fun demolishing their towers as building them, leaving large foam rectangles scattered all around. Evelyn starts placing one block on top of another as I bring them to her.

Our tower topples a few times, and I make a big show of being surprised each time it happens. At first Evelyn just giggles. But after the third tumble she's full out belly laughing. Soon she starts knocking over the blocks on purpose, watching me for my silly reaction and then dissolving into peals of laughter when I give it to her. Each time she laughs, a little burst of joy blossoms in my chest, pushing out the depression and darkness that's been weighing me down for the last week. Soon I'm laughing right along with her. We take turns stacking a few blocks, knocking them over, and laughing our heads off.

I have no idea what's wrong with me.

By the time the half-hour allotted for storytime is up, my cheeks hurt from smiling so much and I've gotten my ab workout for the day. I help the children gather up the blocks and Jen and I put the tubs back in the closet. Most of the children leave with the adults who brought them, including Evelyn, who trails along after the woman and her phone. I watch her go, waving when she turns to look back at me.

I can see her smile from clear across the room.

"So, do you think you can handle that?" Jen asks, moving toward the main desk.

"No problem," I say, trying to recall everything Jen had done. I was too busy with Evelyn to really pay attention. What exactly did she do? A book, a song, some blocks... I think that was about it. And the kids seemed pretty well-behaved, so I guess it's really not that big of a deal.

"Great. I'll let you take storytime from here, then. Think you can manage Thursday afternoon on your own?"

"Introduce, help when needed, end on time, right?"

"Right."

"Sure, I can do that."

"Great, I'll see you Thursday."

Chapter 8

Mom let me use her car to go to the library this morning, but I know we can't share the car all summer. Part of me already feels like I've been transported back to high school, and not having my own ride will just exacerbate the feeling of being totally dependent on my parents.

On the drive home I wrack my brain for ideas of alternate transportation. The library is too far away to ride a bicycle, but I guess I could take the bus. I cringe at the thought. Public transportation is only slightly better than public toilets in my opinion. I'm not crazy about the idea, but it's better than asking my parents to borrow a car all the time.

I puff out my cheeks in an exaggerated sigh. I hadn't really needed a car in Vegas. I had one when I first got to school there —a beat up old Chrysler that only barely survived the trip south. But Tara and I lived close enough to campus to walk, and once Derek and I started dating, he drove me everywhere. The Chrysler just sat in the parking lot, collecting dirt and pigeon poop. He'd offered to buy me a new car once, but it was early enough in our relationship at the time that I'd declined. I was overwhelmed at his philanthropy, in awe of what a kind, generous man he was. I grind my teeth at the memory, knowing better now. It wasn't generosity. It was pride.

I chew on the thought, picturing Derek's disgust—concealed as polite surprise, of course—the first time I offered to drive us somewhere. He insisted that chivalry demanded *he* drive, and lovestruck as I was, I believed him. After sitting in the parking lot for over a year, I finally sold my car. I didn't miss it at the time, but I sure miss it now.

The thought of missing my beat-up old Chrysler with the mismatched bumper makes me smile, and that settles it. I'll buy myself a car—the kind of car Derek wouldn't be caught dead in. I'll buy myself a car and get leopard print seat covers and hang fuzzy dice from the rearview mirror and I'll never wax it. Ever.

The idea makes me laugh out loud.

Mom is taking a nap when I get home, so I climb the stairs to my little room and perch on the bed, still thinking. A car would certainly be nice, but I haven't really got the funds. The cash from my student loans is tied up in tuition and dues, with only a little bit left in my account to get me through the summer. And without the income from my internship this year, I'll be feeling the pinch by July. I frown. How else can I get cash for a car?

The answer hits me like a rock between the eyes. A 1.95-carat, Tiffany-cut rock, to be precise.

My eyes zero in on the top drawer of my dresser, my heart thudding in my chest like an off-balance washing machine.

Dare I do it?

Derek would be furious, of course. And appalled. The thought carries me across the room, pulling open the drawer to retrieve the ring. I pick it up, noticing again how heavy—and cold—it is in my hand.

Clenching my fist, I turn on my heel and head out the door before I lose my nerve.

———

"Hey, Dad."

Dad looks up from his desk with a surprised smile when I come through his office door. "Amie! What are you doing here?"

"I need some advice."

He chuckles. "I can't remember the last time you came to me for advice. Hang on, I'll be right there."

He turns back to his work and I glance around. His office looks very much the same as I remember it, except that his model car collection has grown. The two-room suite is divided by beautiful french doors that always stand open. In the smaller, front room, a few plush chairs are arranged around a low table, and a bookshelf filled with die cast metal cars sits against the far wall. Through the french doors, my dad's massive mahogany desk dominates the space, surrounded by floor-to-ceiling bookshelves filled with even more cars. He must have at least three hundred now.

After a moment my dad emerges from behind the double computer screens. I sit down in one of the leather chairs and he sits in the other, an expectant look on his face.

I take a deep breath. "Do you know any reputable jewelers in town?"

I can see that my question surprises him, but unlike my mother, who would have immediately peppered me with questions of her own, he doesn't respond right away. One eyebrow dips a bit lower than the other as he contemplates an answer. I wait, counting my breaths and hoping my courage won't give out.

"Jack Stapleton is the only jeweler I know, though I haven't seen him in years," he finally says.

"You know him personally?"

"I went to school with his son," Dad shrugs. "His business was just starting out back then, but I hear he's done really well for himself. They used to have a little store downtown, but they built a nice big place on the other side of the Valley a few years ago."

"Do you know if they buy used jewelry?"

"Most jewelers will accept rings and such for trade in, but it's usually only store credit, to put towards new jewelry."

"Oh."

"Are you considering selling your engagement ring?" he asks gently.

"Yeah."

"Have you thought about selling it online?"

I shake my head. "I'd rather not risk it. Besides, I need cash now."

He frowns. "Can I help? What do you need the cash for?"

"Thanks, Dad. But it's not just about the money."

"I see. Well, you can always stop by and see what he says."

"Yeah, I think I will. The other side of the Valley? Is it over by the mall?"

"Yup. Stapleton Jewelers, on Broadway."

"All right. Thanks Dad."

We both stand, and Dad puts his arms around me. He's not

an awkward hugger, my dad, and I can feel his love and concern with his arms tight around me.

"Your mom said you're not going to be a lawyer anymore," he says, stepping back.

"Nope."

"Any idea what you want to do instead?"

I sigh. "I'm not really sure what to even change my major to. I can't think of anything I'd really like to do." I cock my head to the side. "Do you remember what I wanted to be when I was little?"

"An architect," he says, his face expanding to accommodate the mammoth grin he gives me. "Just like me. You said you were going to design the world's tallest building someday. I'm still waiting on those plans." He winks at me, and I give him a half-hearted smile.

"I'll see what I can do. Love you, Dad," I say, turning to leave.

"Love you too, punkin."

———

I chew on my lip as I drive down the highway, thinking over what my dad said. I'd wanted to be an architect, like him? I vaguely recall building cities and towns out of blocks, and drawing pictures of skyscrapers and houses, but there's no conviction in the memories. Mom said I wanted to be a librarian like her, and I have an equal number of memories, maybe even more, of being curled up on my bed reading, or playing "bookstore" with my stuffed animals in my room. I dig deeper, trying to find the moment of resolve in any instance, when I determined what I wanted be when I grew up. Brandon knew by the time he was seven what he wanted to do. But my memories are fuzzy, and by the time I arrive at the jewelers I'm no closer to remembering my childhood ambitions than I am of remembering what I had for lunch yesterday.

I push open the glass door to Stapleton Jewelers and an electronic bell chimes overhead—the kind that sounds like a wind-up toy that got stepped on too many times. Around the perimeter of the room, display cases filled with rainbow jewels wink and flash in the light. In the very center of the store, a leather sofa and two matching chairs surround a low table. A young woman with sleek black hair and four-inch heels smiles at me from the far corner.

"Hello! Welcome to Stapleton Jewelers. How can I help you?" she asks, stalking toward me.

"Hi. I'd like to speak to Mr. Stapleton, if I could."

"Of course. May I tell him what it's about?"

"Well, I have a ring I'd like to see if I can sell."

"An engagement ring?"

I grip my purse more tightly. "Yes."

Her smile turns sympathetic. "Do you know if it was it purchased here?" she asks.

"Um, no, it wasn't."

"I see. Well, we don't usually sell used jewelry, and we will only accept jewelry purchased here for trade-in."

My stomach flip-flops, but I press on. "I understand. But Mr. Stapleton is a family friend," I say. "Could I please speak with him?"

She hesitates for only a moment before her polite professionalism kicks in. "Of course," she says. "Just a moment."

I sit in one of the leather chairs while she heads through a door in the back of the room. Setting my purse on my lap, I open the inner zipped pocket and make sure the ring is still there.

I've only rehearsed what I want to say two and a half times before the same woman reenters the room, followed by a tall, gangly man about my father's age. This must be the son—the one my dad went to school with. He has wavy, salt-and-pepper hair and a smile to melt the polar ice caps. I stand to greet him, willing my knees not to wobble.

"Hello!" he says, reaching for a handshake. "Mai said you wanted to speak with me?"

"Yes, Mr. Stapleton. My name is Amie Cunningham—I believe you know my father, Walter?"

I can feel Mai's pretty black eyes boring into me when Mr. Stapleton cocks his head in confusion. "You went to school together?" I prod, hoping they actually *did* go to school together and that tidbit of info wasn't one of my father's momentary lapses in memory.

Suddenly Mr. Stapleton snaps his fingers. "Wally Cunningham! He played baseball, didn't he?"

"Yes, he did." Relief drips into my voice.

"I remember him. How's he doing?"

"He's great, thanks."

Mr. Stapleton perches himself on the arm of the leather sofa across from me. "Glad to hear it. So, Miss Cunningham, what can I do for you?"

I can tell by the set of his mouth that Mai has already told him what I'm going to ask, and that he's already decided to say no. The nerves start churning in my gut again, but I take a breath and forge ahead. "I have a diamond engagement ring from Tiffany's that I'd like to sell."

Tiffany's must be the magic word because the answer he'd prepared doesn't roll off his tongue. In fact, nothing rolls off his tongue. I rush through the rest of my explanation before I lose my nerve. "It's a Tiffany-cut solitaire set in platinum," I say, sounding like a sales pitch. "One-point-nine-five carats."

I open my purse and retrieve the ring, holding it out to him. He takes it, brow furrowed, and studies it for a moment. "Mai?" he calls over his shoulder. "Can you bring me a lens, please?"

Mai's stilettos don't make a sound on the plush carpet as she brings him the small black instrument. She watches as he studies the ring through the magnifier. Finally he looks up, handing the ring back to me. My heart drops.

"It's a beautiful piece of jewelry," he says. After a brief pause he adds, "I'm sorry you no longer need it."

He says it gently, and I wonder if he has daughters of his own. I swallow, dislodging the lump that threatens to form before it has a chance to find purchase.

"Thank you."

He studies me for a minute, and I don't know whether to meet his eye or look at the ring in my hand. I settle for looking at the floor.

Finally he clears his throat. "Well Miss Cunningham, we don't normally accept trade-ins on jewelry we didn't sell. And I'm not too keen on the idea of selling used jewelry in general." He pauses. "Have you considered selling it online?"

"I have. But I would rather not."

"Any particular reason why not?"

I shrug. "I'd be nervous sending it in the mail. Or accepting such a large sum of money from a stranger."

He nods. "I see." Another pause. "Do you have the original documentation?"

"Yes," I say, reaching in my purse for the paperwork. Derek gave it to me the day after he proposed, so that I could get the ring inspected regularly.

I hold out the forms and Mr. Stapleton takes them from me, looking them over. After a minute he folds them back up and taps them against his knee.

"All right, here's what I propose."

The irony of his word choice isn't lost on me.

"I'll sell the ring on consignment. I'll list it at $31,000 and take thirty percent when it sells."

I measure my words carefully, not wanting to lose what may be my only opportunity. "I could really use the money now. What will you give me for it straight?"

A small cleft appears in his chin as he frowns, thinking it over. "Seven thousand."

Seven thousand could buy me a nice little car, but I shake my head again. That's almost a seventy-five percent commission in his favor and though I'm desperate, I'm not stupid.

"How about an advance?" I counter. "You pay me a portion of the amount I would get when it sells, and deduct it from the total when the time comes."

He shrugs. "Maybe. How much would you want up front?"

"Five thousand."

"No good. One thousand."

I narrow my eyes. "Three."

He laughs, admiration and exasperation fighting for dominance in his look. "Alright, Miss Cunningham, I'll give you a $2000 advance and take a commission of forty percent. Final offer."

I think it over, doing the math in my head. Two thousand

could probably get me a little car to last for the summer, but it would likely need some work. Jason could help me with that, I'm sure. And I'd still have a nice chunk coming to me whenever the ring sold, to get something better...

"Done," I say, getting to my feet and holding out my hand. He shakes it with a wry smile.

"Miss Cunningham, you certainly know how to drive a bargain. Have you ever thought of becoming a lawyer?"

I grimace. "I've thought about it."

He laughs, and motions for me to follow him into his office.

Chapter 9

Mom is fixing dinner by the time I get home, after depositing the check for two thousand dollars in the bank. "There you are," she says when I walk into the kitchen. "Did Jen ask you to stay longer? I thought you would have been home hours ago."

"Sorry. You were sleeping when I got home from the library, and I had some other errands to run so I just went."

"Oh, that's fine. Where did you go?"

"I stopped by Dad's office and then went down into the Valley." I shift from one foot to the other, anxious to escape. I know she's going to flip when she finds out about the ring, and I'd like to have a chance to practice my defense. Plus, I really want to see what kind of cars are available for two grand.

"Sorry I wasn't awake. I could have gone with you."

"That's ok. Do you need any help?" *Please say no, please say no.*

"No, all I have left to do is peel the potatoes. We'll eat when your dad gets home."

"Ok. I'll be in my room."

I take the stairs two at a time, my anticipation building with each step. I close the door and kick off my shoes, turning on my laptop. A quick internet search produces almost half a million results, and I groan. I manage to sift through a few of them before finally giving up and grabbing my phone to text Jason.

AMIE

Hey, any idea where I can find a cheap little car for the summer?

I barely have time to wonder how long it will take him to respond when my phone chimes.

JASON

How cheap?

AMIE

2k or less

He doesn't answer right away, so I put the phone down and start tidying up my room. I gather my old clothes into a pile and finish putting my new clothes away. When my phone pings, I practically dive across my bed to grab it.

JASON

I know a couple different dealers because of the car wash. I'm off on Friday and Saturday so I could take you over to see what they've got if you like.

AMIE

That would be great! Friday works for me

JASON

10ish?

"Amie! Dinner is ready!" Mom calls.

I send a quick text back to Jason to let him know that will

be fine. For the first time since before the breakup, I'm genuinely excited about something. It feels good.

Mom is standing at the bottom of the stairs in an apron when I come out of my room. She watches as I come down the steps with my arms full of Derek. "Need to do some laundry?" she asks.

"No—these are my old clothes. I'm going to donate them."

"Oh. Well, your dad is home and we're ready to eat."

"Be right there."

She walks back into the kitchen as I drop the clothes on the couch. Dad comes in just as I straighten up. "Hey sweetie," he says. "Did you stop by the jewelers? What did he say?"

I glance quickly into the kitchen, but Mom is standing at the stove with the fan on and can't hear us. Dad sees my look and chuckles.

"Haven't told her yet, huh?"

"Not yet."

"Well, she'll find out sooner or later. Best get it over with."

I groan, following him to the table.

My mom firmly believes that the most appropriate way to show love to anyone is by feeding them to death. If cooking were an Olympic sport, she'd be the gold medal champion in every event. Not only does she *like* to cook, but she's dang good at it, which is practically a lethal combination. It's a wonder that Brandon and I made it to adulthood without our girth surpassing our height.

For tonight's family dinner she made pork chops with gravy, apple dumplings, mashed potatoes, a layered salad, roasted green beans, and homemade rolls.

Like I said, she's lethal.

Dad keeps raising his eyebrows at me all during the meal,

though I purposely avoid his look. Finally he clears his throat. "So Amie, what did you do after you left my office this afternoon?"

I glare at him, but he's suddenly very occupied with his salad.

"I ran some errands," I say, and when Dad looks up I narrow my eyes at him.

"You said that earlier," Mom says. "Where did you go? What did you do?"

I sigh. There's no help for it now. "I went to a jeweler's in the valley," I say, resigned.

Mom frowns. "A jeweler's?"

"Yeah." I push the peas from the salad around my plate. "To see about selling my ring."

Mom nearly chokes on her mashed potatoes. "You did what?"

"I went to see about selling my ring."

"But you didn't sell it." Her voice makes it clear she's not asking a question.

I shrug noncommittally, and mom turns abruptly to my dad.

"You knew about this? You knew she was going to sell her ring?"

Dad keeps shovelling food in his mouth so he won't be forced to answer, but Mom wouldn't have listened to him anyway. Not when she's like this.

"That ring was a gift, Amelia," she says, her look as rigid as her tone. "A very *expensive* gift. What were you thinking!"

"I was thinking I needed a car more than I needed an engagement ring," I say calmly, still picking at my salad.

"But you're engaged, Amie!"

"No Mom, I'm not."

"Did Derek ask you for the ring back?"

I narrow my eyes. "No."

"Did he *say* he didn't want to marry you?"

"Not in those exact words, but—"

"Then you're still engaged," she says triumphantly. "And you had no business selling that ring."

"Now honey, the ring is hers," Dad says, finally coming to my defense. He better, after throwing me under the bus like that. "She has every right to sell it."

"Walter, how can you say that! Derek just needs some time. That ring is more than just an adornment, it's—"

"It's mine," I say, cutting her off. I set my fork down, sighing heavily. "Look, Mom, I know you're not happy about this. I'm not exactly thrilled that Derek broke off our engagement, either. But he did, and now it's over. We won't be getting back together. Derek is a jerk, and I don't want any trace of him left in my life anymore." I stand up and take my plate to the sink. "I'm going for a walk. I'll be back later."

———

Butting heads with my mother always leaves me feeling jittery, like I've had one too many cups of coffee. Even as an adult, I still feel like a kid getting caught doing something I shouldn't whenever we disagree about anything.

I cross the street to the park and make the circuit around the pond. The sun is going down, bathing the trees in a warm orange glow. Bits of dust float in the air, fading in and out of the light like tiny, allergenic sparkles. I sit on a bench and count the turtles that come up for air, trying to calm my mind and force my racing heart to slow down.

But now that the ring is out of my hands and I have time to overthink my actions, I wonder if my mom is right. Will I regret what I've done? Will I wish I had kept it? The only reason I can think of for wishing I still had the ring would be if Derek and I—

I stand abruptly, hoping to escape the thought before it reaches my tear ducts. There's no point in exploring that road and I refuse to consider the possibility—my heart can't handle the hope. I head back across the street, suddenly anxious for the refuge of my Derek-free bedroom.

I'm not ready to face my mother's critical glare and icy silence, so I slip around the side of the house, planning to enter through the back door. But as I pass the open dining room window, I hear angry voices.

My steps slow. Is that my *parents?* I can't remember the last time they had an argument. Usually they get along great. I inch closer to the window, wondering what triggered it.

"I can't believe you knew what she was planning and you didn't stop her."

"Honey, she's twenty-three years old. She can make her own choices."

I groan. Great. They're arguing about me.

"But selling her ring? Walter!"

"It was her choice."

"What if I had sold *my* ring?" Mom's voice is waspish, pelting my dad with the sting of her words. "Would you have bought me another?"

"Sweetheart, I know this is hard for you..."

"You don't know anything." Mom's voice cracks on the last word.

"Deanne, this is not about us," Dad says, his voice sharp. "This is about Amie."

"I *know* this is about Amie—why do you think I'm so upset? What will happen when they get back together?"

"I don't think they will."

"But *we* did, Walter. If I had sold my ring the minute we broke up, who knows what might have happened!"

I back away from the window, my mind reeling. My parents broke off their engagement? Their voices blend together, reliving painful memories I never knew existed. I fish my phone out of my pocket when I reach the sidewalk, shaking as I search for my brother's number.

It rings, and rings, and rings. I don't leave a voicemail, but swipe to text him instead.

AMIE

Did you know that mom and dad broke off their engagement before they got married?

How did I not know this? Why didn't my parents ever tell me? My mind races and my feet wander, waiting for Brandon to text me back.

My brother seems the most logical choice for someone to talk to about it, but as I turn the corner I see Jason's house, the light from the windows shining like a beacon. *Jason.* I could always talk to him. I turn up the sidewalk leading to his front door before I change my mind.

Jason answers my knock with a surprised smile. "Hey Ames, come on in."

"Thanks. I hope I'm not interrupting anything."

He gives me a funny look. "When have we ever considered our friendship an interruption?"

"You know what I mean." I follow him down the hall to the kitchen. "Dang, it smells good in here. Are you cooking again?"

"Yeah, I made dinner. Veronica is on her way over."

"Oh." I notice the dishes on the table and grimace. "Yeah, definitely interrupting. Sorry. I can go."

"Nah, it's fine. She won't be here for a while yet. Have a seat."

I sit down on one of the bar stools as Jason heads for the sink. "I sold my engagement ring today," I say without preamble.

His eyebrows shoot up. "You did?"

"Yeah."

"That's a big deal," he says, turning on the faucet and adding dish soap to the water. When I don't respond, he looks back at me. "Do you regret it?"

"No."

"Are you upset about something else, then?"

I nod. He waits, watching me.

"I overheard an argument between my parents."

"Ah." He shuts off the water. "What were they arguing about?"

"Me selling my ring. But then my dad said something about this not being about them, and my mom asked what he would have done if she had sold *her* ring when *they* broke up, and I heard enough to gather that my parents had a broken engagement themselves before they actually got married. And I never knew."

"Wow. Really?"

"Yeah."

"So now I'm all... I don't know. Worried? Upset? I mean, how come they never told me?"

He's silent for a minute, scrubbing dishes. "If you had known before now, would it have changed anything?"

"I don't know. Maybe?"

"Well, what would have been different?"

I hesitate, considering. "I probably would have been freaked out every time they fought, worried they would get a divorce. If I knew they broke it off once, I'd be afraid they'd break up again."

He nods. "Makes sense. Maybe that's why they never told you. They didn't want you and Brandon to worry."

I tug at my hair, wrapping it around my finger. "Maybe."

My phone pings just then, and I look at the screen. Brandon. I swipe to read his text.

BRANDON

No, I didn't. Did they tell you that?

I set the phone down. I'll call him later and explain.

"Would it have changed anything about you and Derek?" Jason asks, his back to me.

My thoughts shy away from the pain of thinking about *him*, but I force my mind to relive the events of the last ten days. Derek breaking up with me. Coming back to Washington. Selling the ring. I think of each event through the lens of the new information I've gained about my parents.

"I don't think so," I say slowly. "I don't know the reason why my parents broke it off. Maybe my dad got cold feet? But Derek didn't get cold feet. He was never unsure about anything."

"Is Derek the one who called it off?"

I wince. "Yeah."

Jason finishes the dishes and dries his hands on a towel. "If you knew about your parents before, would you still have sold the ring?"

"Probably. I need the money. So I can buy a car."

"All right. So even though the news that your parents broke off their engagement before finally getting married upset you, it doesn't actually change anything. Right?"

My natural reaction is to argue, because whenever Brandon used logic against me it was always to prove me wrong. I hated it when he did that and he was *always* doing that. But Jason isn't Brandon, and he's not trying to prove me wrong. He's trying to help me by talking things through—separating truth from emotional response. He was always good at talking things through. Asking questions, gathering information, looking at things from a different angle. That's why he's so good with cars.

I take a deep breath, filling my lungs with the spicy sweet smell hanging in the air. "Right."

He nods, sitting on the stool next to mine. "Anything else bothering you?"

"I don't think so." I smile half-heartedly. "Thanks for talking me down."

"Anytime."

The sound of the front door opening breaks into my thoughts, and Jason looks up. "Veronica?" he calls, standing. I look expectantly toward the hall, but there's no answer. Instead, the clipped staccato of high heels on the wood floor announces her approach.

"Oh. I didn't know you had company," she says, stopping in the doorway to the kitchen.

She's a curvy woman, with olive skin, long black hair, and

crimson lips that are *not* smiling. I stand as Jason walks up to greet her.

"This is my friend Amie—remember the one I told you about? From Vegas." Jason doesn't appear ruffled by her cool manner, but I feel myself shrinking from her curt nod.

"Hello."

"Hello," I echo.

Her eyes shift back to Jason, reducing me to the level of new furniture—novel enough to warrant noticing, but not enough to really care about.

"Smells good. What's for dinner?"

"Fettuccine Alfredo with seared scallops. And a spinach strawberry salad."

"Sounds delicious." She looks at the table, set for two, and then at me. "Will you be joining us, Amie?"

"No, I just stopped by for a minute."

"That's too bad. Have you tried Jason's cooking?" she asks, setting her briefcase—a sleek, black Kate Spade bag—on the counter. Her perfectly manicured nails snap it open.

"Um—"

"He's a brilliant chef. I keep telling him he needs to call Anton at The Italian Place but so far he hasn't." She gives him a look of exasperation, which makes him groan. "Have you even *considered* talking to your dad about how you feel?"

"Come on, Veronica, you know I can't do that."

"Do you want to be a chef?" I ask Jason.

"No," he says, at the same time that Veronica says "Yes."

Jason turns away, and I catch a look of annoyance on his face as he opens the oven. Veronica shakes her head, looking back at me.

"He could be making twice as much money as a chef, *and*

have a lot more prestige, but for whatever reason he doesn't want to tell his dad he wants out of the family business."

Jason pulls out their plates, shutting the oven rather harder than necessary. "Look, Veronica, we've been through this a hundred times. Would you please just drop it?"

"Look at this." She slaps a neon yellow paper which she's pulled from her bag onto the counter. "This is what you should be doing. You would eat them up alive."

Jason frowns. "What's that?"

I lean over the counter, reading the flyer. "It's a cooking competition."

"What?"

"A cooking competition," Veronica repeats, "put on by *Trois Fourchettes*."

Jason grabs the plates, heading toward the table. "I don't have time for that."

"Well, you'd better make time, because I signed you up."

Jason turns so suddenly he knocks over a glass. It hits the floor, shattering at his feet. "You what?"

"I signed you up. I knew you wouldn't do it yourself." Her voice is smug and confident, like she's done him a great favor. Judging from the look on Jason's face, he doesn't agree.

"You had no right to do that, Veronica," he says, his voice low. No one moves to clean up the pieces of glass. They rest on the floor, a million tiny daggers reflecting the light.

It's clear that I no longer belong in this conversation, but neither Jason nor Veronica seem to remember I'm still here. I inch toward the door, hoping to escape undetected.

"Jason, you're wasting your life at that place!"

"But it's *my* life, Veronica. Not yours."

"I'm only thinking about your future."

"What right do you have to make decisions about my future?"

My foot hits a stray piece of glass, which shoots across the floor and knocks against the wall. Both of their heads snap in my direction, their faces identical masks of fury.

"Um, I think I better go," I say, clearing my throat. "Jason, thanks for the advice."

My voice breaks the building tension, but it doesn't dissolve. It hovers in the air, a dark cloud of conflict I can almost taste. Jason sets the plates down and grabs the broom.

Veronica folds her arms across her chest. "Nice to meet you, Amie." Her words are polite but her look is anything but.

"You too."

I hear the shards of glass clattering into the trash can as I walk down the hall. By the time I get to the front door, Jason is coming up behind me. "Thanks, Ames," he says, quietly enough that Veronica can't hear. "Sorry about that."

"No problem. I, uh, hope you have a nice dinner," I say, and he rolls his eyes.

"No chance of that now."

I give him a commiserating smile and open the front door.

"Hey, Amie?"

"Yeah?" I pause, looking up at him.

"I only meant to help with what I said earlier. I wasn't trying to trick you into calming down or whatever. I really am sorry about your parents, and that they never told you." He rubs the back of his neck.

Warmth rushes through me, pulling my lips into a smile. "Thanks. I know what you meant."

"Good. So Friday?"

"Friday," I say, shutting the door behind me.

Chapter 10

I avoid my mom for the rest of the night and all the next day. It's amazing how such a small woman—barely five feet tall —can exude such a huge amount of displeasure. She crackles with annoyance, ready to pounce on the first hapless victim to run across her path. I hide out in my room like a scared mouse, reading books and playing on my phone until the storm blows over.

By Thursday morning things are almost back to normal, and when I come home for lunch after storytime, Mom's made chicken paninis and a Caesar salad for us to eat together. Delicious food is about as close to a peace offering as you can get from my mom, and I decide to accept.

"Looks good," I say, taking a seat at the table. She smiles at me.

"Well, I've been a bit of a grump lately. I'm sorry about that." She takes a bite of her sandwich while I dish myself some salad. I nod noncommittally, still walking on eggshells.

"You know," she says after a minute, "I was thinking today about when you and Brandon were teenagers."

I groan inwardly. So much for the peace offering. Any sentence containing the words "you and Brandon" is sure to compare my less-than-stellar efforts with my walking-on-water older brother's. I'll let you guess who wins at those comparisons.

"This isn't the first time you've changed your mind about something. You used to do it in high school, too. You'd jump from club to club, activity to activity, always searching for the right fit."

I blink.

"But Brandon always knew what he wanted to do. He always had a plan, always had a purpose."

"I'm not the one who decided I didn't want to get married, Mom."

"Well, no," she allows. "But you've changed your mind about law school."

I take a bite of my sandwich, trying to think of what to say. How can I argue with that? If I tell her I was only studying political science because Derek was a lawyer and I wanted to be able to have an intelligent conversation with him, it will only prove her point that I have no direction of my own. And if I agree with her? Well. There are few things more insufferable than my mother being told she's right.

After eating in silence for several minutes, I get up from the table. "Thanks for lunch. I have to head back to the library now."

She frowns. "Is that really all you have to say?"

"What do you expect me to say, Mom? You still want me to be a lawyer?"

"I didn't say that. I just don't understand why you can't ever seem to make up your mind about anything."

"Yeah, well, I don't understand either." I set my plate on the counter harder than necessary and head for the door. "I'll see you later."

Jason is walking up the street when I go out to the car. "Hey Ames," he calls. "You going somewhere?"

"Back to the library for my second shift. What's up?" The words come out clipped, as if they'd been cut with a razor.

He cocks his head, stopping in front of me. "Whoa. What's wrong?"

I sigh, rubbing a hand across my eyes. "Sorry. My mom is still on the warpath. Lunch was... less than pleasant."

"She still upset about the ring?"

"Yeah, but that's not what got my hackles up. She was comparing me to Brandon."

"Ahh."

I take a deep breath. "It's fine. I'll just have to lay low for a few more days." I try to smile. "How was your dinner with Veronica?"

He snorts. "We didn't even get to dinner. Just fought until we broke up again and she stormed out."

"Oh. Wow. I'm sorry."

He shrugs. "Don't be. Veronica's always been a little controlling, and it's always bugged me. But she crossed the line last night. We're through for good this time."

I give him a commiserating smile. "For what it's worth, she didn't really seem your type."

"Oh yeah?" He cocks his head, a sneaky grin pulling up one corner of his mouth. "So what exactly is my type, then?"

I laugh, even as my neck grows warm. "You need a jeans-and-T-shirt girl. Not a miniskirt-and-stilletos one."

He smirks. "I'll keep that in mind."

I unlock the car and open the door. "Sorry for biting your head off a minute ago. Was there something you wanted to talk to me about?" I ask.

"Oh. No, not really. Just wanted to check on how you're feeling today. About your parents and all that."

I'm not surprised at his sincerity—he's always been that way. It feels good to know he cares. "I'm all right. I called Brandon last night, but he wasn't much help. Just shrugged it off as not really important. But I'm ok. Thanks for checking on me."

"Sure—that's what friends do." He gives me a genuine smile, and my face responds in kind. "So, I'll see you tomorrow?"

"Yup. Unless you plan to stop by the library to learn about birds of prey this afternoon," I joke.

"Wait, Rosemary and her birds are coming today?"

"You know her?"

"If it's the same lady I'm thinking of. Rosemary... something or other. She came every summer when we were kids. I loved that event."

"I don't think I ever went. We usually went to the branch on Perry, not the one downtown."

He grins at me. "You'll like it. They're fun."

"I'm actually a little nervous. This is the first event I'll be in charge of."

"Want some moral support?" he offers. "I got off early today—I could come with you."

"You wouldn't mind hanging out with a bunch of kids and families at the library?"

"And you. Don't forget it means I get to hang out with you, too." He winks, walking around to the passenger door.

We climb inside and I start the car. "So, what was the deal with the cooking competition?" I ask, pulling out into the street.

"What do you mean?"

I shrug. "With as much as you like to cook, it surprised me that you weren't even interested."

"I don't have time for stuff like that."

His voice is flat, but when I peek at his face, I can see the gears turning.

"Hm. I thought I saw something about Sacred Heart on the flyer..." I say casually.

For a moment, he doesn't move, just keeps staring straight ahead. Finally he sighs, looking over at me. "It's a fundraiser for the children's hospital."

I try to hide my grin. If he knows that much, he must have at least read the information, which means that despite his protests, some part of him is interested.

I keep my voice casual. "Really? How does that work?"

He rolls his eyes, but pulls out his phone anyway. After a brief search he says, "Looks like *Trois Fourchettes* is sponsoring the competition and providing the grand prize."

"Which is?"

"Admission into the school and first semester's tuition."

I whistle. "That's a pretty sweet prize." I see him shrug out of the corner of my eye. "So how does it work with the hospital?"

"All registration fees, as well as the cover charge and auction proceeds, benefit the hospital," he reads.

"Cover charge?"

"For the public." He's quiet for a minute. "Huh. Interesting."

"What?"

"It's a three part competition, based on the school's name. *Trois Fourchettes* means three forks in French: one fork for salad, one fork for dinner, one fork for dessert. Contestants make one of each course. The competition and judging take place the middle of August—it's a charity lunch and cake auction. Contestants have to create a salad to feed a crowd, make and decorate a cake to be auctioned off, and create an original entrée for the judges. Each course will receive six individual scores, one from each of the judges, and the contestant with the highest cumulative score wins the competition."

"Wow. That sounds... intense."

"Sounds like fun," he murmurs.

I glance over at him. "I thought you didn't want to do it?"

He sighs and puts his phone down. "I didn't, because Veronica tried to force me into doing it. I didn't know it was a charity event, though." His voice drifts off. After a minute he picks up his phone again. I watch the road, waiting for him to speak.

"I wouldn't do it to win," he says abruptly, almost defensively. "I'm not going to cooking school, so the grand prize doesn't tempt me."

"Not even a little bit?"

"Nope." He pops the *P*, as if underlining the word.

"But you want to do it."

It's not a question, and he doesn't respond. We finish the drive to the library in silence.

We take the elevator upstairs, the smell of Jason's cologne filling my nostrils in the small space. Jason heads off to get some books, promising to meet me in the children's area in ten minutes.

"Hey, Amie. Good job with storytime this morning," Jen says, coming around the desk to walk with me. "You're a natural with the kids. They loved it."

My mind pulls up the mental picture of flying foam blocks and screams of *ACHOOO!* before I grin at her. "Thanks. It was a lot of fun."

She laughs. "It was a lot of fun to watch, too. I had no idea you could do voices. Have you ever considered a career in voice acting?"

"No—do you think I should?"

"You definitely should," she says, handing me a piece of paper. "You ready for this?"

I scan the page, nodding absently. "Sure. How hard can it be?"

Jen shakes her head, grinning at me. "You have no idea. Go on, she's setting things up."

Jen is still chuckling as I head toward the children's area and my first special guest. The morning's storytime really was amazing. I read the kids a classic picture book called *The True Story of the Three Little Pigs*. My second grade teacher read it to my class when I was a child and I loved it, so I figured it would be a good book for my first official day. I did all the voices, and as Jen said, my vocal antics were a huge hit with the kids. After the story we pulled out the foam blocks so the kids could build "houses" and practice sneezing so loudly they blew them over. There was a lot of huffing and puffing and blowing and spitting and laughing and yelling and can-we-do-it-again-Miss-Amie-ing and it was the best. thing. ever.

I went home for lunch in high spirits, but thanks to my mom's less-than-subtle hints that I should try to be more like my perfect older brother, my confidence isn't running high. Jen's words rekindle a bit of the excitement I felt earlier, and I attempt to shake off the melancholy, determined to make the afternoon as successful as the morning. I'm glad Jason came along for moral support.

The schedule of events indicates that Rosemary Hutchinson will be today's special guest. She'll be giving a live demonstration about birds of prey, and the kids might even have a chance to hold or pet them. I've never seen a bird of prey up close, so I'm pretty excited.

I'm not sure what exactly I was expecting "the bird lady" to be like, but it certainly wasn't what I found. Rosemary tells me (loudly, because she's going deaf) that she's eighty-one years old, has eleven (twelve, if you count the stuffed one in her dining room) different birds, and has been raising and showing raptors and owls for thirty years (legally, at least).

"I understand you've been to this library before." I say.

"Yes, yes, I come every year. The kids love it. I brought my owls today."

"That's great! Do you have a presentation ready, then? What can I do to help?"

"What was that?"

"What can I do to help?" I shout, and several library patrons turn in my direction. I feel my neck grow warm.

"Oh nothing, nothing. I'll take care of everything."

Jen told me that my biggest responsibility was to introduce each guest, make sure they end on time, and be available if they need my help. Rosemary *said* she didn't need any help, but she certainly looks like she could use it—and probably not just the help that I can give. Her wispy gray hair is sticking out in every direction from a messy braid that looks as if it has been slept on for a week. She mumbles to herself as she shuffles the boxes and cages she's brought, crooning to the animals inside like a mother to her babies.

"Rosemary?" I remember to use my outside voice.

"Hmm?"

"We'll be starting in fifteen minutes, ok? I'll introduce you to the children, and then you'll have until three o'clock." She nods absently, and I move around her to stand nearer the library entrance, so I can greet the kids as they join us.

I've never really spent a lot of time around children, but in the two days I've been helping at the library I've felt more useful and needed than I have in a long time—certainly since before I met Derek. It feels strange, but good. Like getting a mud facial.

As it gets nearer to two o'clock, more people start to show up. The Thursday afternoon events aren't just limited to preschool-aged children, so whole families are milling around, peeking into the cages and talking excitedly as they find seats. As with storytime, the kids plop down on a section of carpet, while the adults take the chairs set up around the edges. I recognize several familiar faces from storytime earlier, including Evelyn and her friend McKenzie. I walk over to greet them.

"Hi Miss Amie!" Evelyn jumps up to give me a hug.

"Hi Evelyn, hi McKenzie. Are you excited to see the birds?"

"I am!" McKenzie says. "My daddy took me birdwatching last year on a camping trip and we saw a mountain bluebird."

"That sounds like fun. What about you, Evelyn?"

"I like seeing the birds. The little ones are so cute!"

"I think they're cute, too."

I wave goodbye to them and look around at the gathered crowd. It's a good turnout—probably twice as many as we had for storytime. Jason is there in the back, smiling at me, and seeing him there gives me both a boost of confidence and an extra dose of nerves. I check to see that Rosemary is ready and then I step to the front of the group.

"All right everyone, welcome to the library!" A few stragglers hurry to find their seats. "We're so excited to have you joining us today. My name is Amie, and with us today are Rosemary Hutchinson and her owls."

Scattered applause greets my words, and I step back as Rosemary walks forward. For the next twenty minutes, she talks about the characteristics of owls and why they're so special. Her words are punctuated with random musings and anecdotes from her life—like the time she found a freshly dead squirrel on the side of the road and stopped to pick it up. "For dinner," she cackles. Whether she means *her* dinner or that of her birds is not clear. I suspect the former.

"All right now, enough of my gabbing," she says. "Who wants to see an owl?"

Dozens of hands shoot up, and an excited buzz fills the air. She pulls a small cage forward and removes a tiny ball of fluff. "This is a Burrowing Owl. They're one of the smallest species in North America." She explains a bit about their habits and what makes them unique, and then lets a few kids come forward to pet it.

"I need an adult volunteer for this next one," she says after putting the little owl back in its cage. "You there." She points to Jason, who's leaning casually against one of the low bookshelves.

He looks surprised at being addressed, and I shrug when he glances in my direction. Obediently he walks over to Rosemary, who hands him a large leather glove and tells him to wait for her on the other side of the rug.

"Now, since owls are nocturnal, they have special adaptations to help them hunt at night," she tells the group. "For one thing, they can see in the dark. What else do you think would be important for hunting at night?"

A few kids offer answers before one finally gets it right. "They have to be quiet," he says.

"Right you are. Owls are called silent hunters because they can fly in complete silence. Special feathers on their wings mute the sound of air so they can sneak up on their prey. Now, we have to be very, very quiet so I can show you how silently they fly."

From a large dog carrier she pulls out a beautiful Great Horned Owl. She shushes the murmurs that start until it's quiet once more. "All right, hold your arm up high," she says, nodding at Jason.

He holds his arm out and up, and suddenly the giant bird swoops across the space and lands on his gloved hand. Cries of delight and excitement erupt from the children, and Rosemary walks over to retrieve the bird.

"Did you remember to listen? Did you hear anything? Let's try again. Remember, you have to be completely quiet."

This time the silence is deeper as we collectively hold our breath. We watch, fascinated, as the bird once again launches itself silently across the room, lands on Jason's outstretched arm... and promptly poops all over his shirt.

Laughter fills the air as I jump forward, mortified. "Oh, Jason!"

Rosemary chuckles as she takes the owl from his arm. "Lucky you! Usually it lands on me."

Jason looks both amused and embarrassed, and I rush off to grab some paper towels. When I return, Rosemary is talking to the children again and I can't see Jason anywhere. Thinking I may have missed him on the way to the bathroom, I turn around and plow right into him.

"Oh! Jason. I'm so sorry." I step back, heat creeping into my cheeks. I thrust the paper towels forward, offering them to him.

"Thanks," he says with a wry smile. "That was pretty fowl stuff."

"I had no idea that would happen. I didn't even—" I stop, his words sinking in. "Did... did you just make a bird joke?"

He grins. "I was wondering if you'd catch that."

I roll my eyes. "Only you would make a joke like that at a time like this."

"Better to laugh than to cry, eh?"

"As if you would cry about getting pooped on by a bird."

"Have *you* ever been pooped on by a bird?"

"No, but I wouldn't cry about it if I did."

"But you would cry about getting muffin mix in your hair."

"Muffin mix in my—" Laughter bubbles out of me as the memory fills my mind. "Oh geez, I'd forgotten about that."

"Really? I didn't think you'd ever forget that. I know I haven't—it was the first time you were ever really angry with me."

"I think I was more embarrassed than angry." I smile,

remembering. Jason and I decided one Saturday afternoon to make muffins. His mom had a big box of powdered mix from Costco, and we were goofing off in the kitchen while mixing them up. We must have been ten or eleven at the time. Jason shut the box and pretended to shake it over my head, but the weight of the mix was too heavy for the flimsy cardboard flaps, and the entire package dumped out on top of me. The muffin mix got *everywhere*—in my hair, in my eyes, down the back of my shirt, and all over my clothes and the floor of his kitchen. For two seconds it was completely silent, and then Jason burst out laughing, thinking I would laugh, too. But I didn't. I cried.

"I still feel bad about that," he says.

"Well, consider us even now," I say, indicating the large wet spot on his shirt. He'd obviously cleaned himself up while I was panicking over what to do.

He looks down at his shirt, then back at me. "Are you saying you bribed that bird to poop on me?"

"Maybe." I grin, then hitch a thumb over my shoulder. "I should make sure Rosemary is doing ok. You coming?"

"As long as I'm not called on to volunteer anymore."

We walk back to the group, where Rosemary is now answering questions. A glance at my phone tells me she has only a few minutes left, so I step beside her and lean in.

"You have five minutes left," I say.

She turns. "What was that?" she says, interrupting a child's question. I flush.

"Five minutes," I say, more loudly. A few giggles from the children follow my shout.

"Oh, that's fine." She turns back to the others. "Last question."

Jason heads to the back of the group again, and when he notices me looking at him he smiles. I smile back.

The group begins to applause, and I realize Rosemary has finished. I clap along with everyone else for a moment before stepping forward. "Rosemary, thank you so much for joining us today. And thank you everyone for coming. Be sure to check out some books before you leave!"

The hum of conversation fills the space as I move to help Rosemary gather her things. Jason makes his way over to us. "Need any help?" he asks.

"I'll take all the help I can get," Rosemary says. She gestures to the largest crate, containing the Great Horned Owl. "You already know Winston. Why don't you take that one out for me?"

Jason squints into the cage. "Ah, yes. Winston and I know each other quite well." He picks up the cage. "I've got a bone to pick with him."

Rosemary blinks at him. "Winston is a girl," she says, as if it's the most obvious thing in the world.

I choke back a laugh at the look Jason gives me as he follows her to the exit.

Chapter 11

J   ason knocks on the door a few minutes before ten the next
    morning. He's wearing distressed jeans and a Captain
    America T-shirt. He looks good.

Not that I was checking him out. Just noticing his shirt.

"Hey Amie. You ready?"

"Yup, just need to grab my purse."

The morning is bright and warm, and I feel a thrum of excitement as we climb into Jason's truck. "So where are we going?" I ask.

"I thought we'd go down to First Class Auto to start, and if we don't find anything there, we can check out Benny's."

"Benny's?"

He chuckles. "It's been around for years. Trust me, it's a lot classier than it sounds."

First Class Auto is downtown, not far from the carwash. It's a small lot, and we see all the cars offered in less than half an hour. The only one that tempts me is an older Honda Civic, but they're asking $4700 and Jason assures me he won't be able to talk him down any less than thirty-five hundred.

"So, I've been thinking," Jason says as we climb back into the truck to head to Benny's.

"About the competition?"

He looks over at me. "How did you know?"

"Lucky guess."

He laughs, and the sound reaches all the way into my soul, pulling out a smile.

"Yeah, about the competition," he says. "I think I want to do it."

"I think that's a great idea."

"You do?"

"Of course. You love to cook, and you love to help people. This is a way you can do both. I mean, it was really awful for Veronica to just sign you up without even talking to you about it, but would you have known about it otherwise?"

"No. I don't really pay attention to that kind of stuff."

"Well, there you go." After a minute I ask, "So, what if you win?"

He shakes his head. "I'm not going to culinary school. I won't take the prize. I just want to cook, you know? Experiment with new flavors, come up with new recipes. And it would be great to get feedback from the judges—to see what real chefs think about my cooking."

"Who are the judges?"

"The three main judges are Chef Frank Laurent, the head of Three Forks, Chef Ivan Marić, and Olivia St. James, the manager of Williams-Sonoma."

"Ivan Marić from the cooking show?"

"Yup. The second place winner receives a set of professional cookware and cutlery from his private line, and the third place winner gets a gift certificate to Williams-Sonoma. I guess the sponsors get to be the judges, too. Well, half of the judges."

"There are more?"

His face lights up in the biggest grin I've seen in days. "Yeah—they're having three kid judges, too."

"Kids? Judging the competition?"

"That's what it sounds like. Since all the proceeds benefit the children's hospital, the theme is Kid-Friendly Food. So all the courses have to appeal to both kids and adults alike."

"Wow. That's an interesting twist."

"Yeah. It'll be a great challenge." he says. "I was thinking you could help me brainstorm some kid-friendly foods. Maybe we could even talk to the kids at the library sometime."

"That's a great idea. I can pick a book for storytime about food—oh, like *Cloudy With a Chance of Meatballs!*—and we can talk about their favorite foods."

"Perfect."

He doesn't say anything else, but I can feel his excitement. It vibrates in the air, like when the bass is turned up too loud in the car parked next to you.

My own enthusiasm about finding a car today is waning, but as we turn the corner onto Second Street, I gasp.

"Jason!"

"What?" He whips his head around. "What is it?"

"That car!" I point to a creamy gray Volkswagen Beetle, up on a lift in the corner of Benny's Auto lot.

"Uh, yeah, I don't think that will be in your price range, Ames."

"It's perfect," I say, as Jason pulls into the lot. "I've always wanted a Bug. Let's check it out."

A salesman approaches us as we get out of the truck. "Hello! Welcome to Benny's. What brings you out today?"

"Is Roberto here?" Jason asks, shaking the man's outstretched hand. I crane my neck, trying to get a better look at the Volkswagen

"Sure. Can I tell him who's asking?"

"Jason Henley."

The man nods and retreats back into the office as I grab Jason's arm, pulling him to the far corner of the lot. "Come on! We can look it over while we're waiting for your friend."

"I told you, it's way out of your price range."

"I don't care, it's pretty."

Jason chuckles, but allows me to drag him over to the curvy little car. The lift has it up so that the wheels are about shoulder height and I can't see inside, but I walk around it anyways, admiring the smooth curves and shiny rims. I can see up through the windows that it has a sunroof. I wish I knew what the interior looked like.

"I never thought I'd see Jason Henley looking at *that* car."

Jason and I both turn at the sound of the man's voice. Jason's face splits into a grin and he steps forward.

"Berto! How are you doing? How's business?"

"Good, good, everything's good. How are things at the carwash?"

"Just fine. We have a new summer crew, and that always makes things interesting." The men share a laugh, and I look back up at the car.

"Would you like me to bring it down so you can take a closer look?" Roberto asks me. His voice is friendly, with only the faintest hint of an accent. I sigh, shaking my head.

"No thanks. I love it, but it's way out of my price range."

"Well, don't be so sure. We always have strings we can pull and deals we can make." He's using his salesman voice, I can tell—just like Derek used to switch to his lawyer voice when he wanted to manipulate someone into seeing things his way. It grates on my nerves.

"Not a chance, Berto," Jason says. "We've got less than 3k to spend."

He whistles. "Yeah, I can't swindle a deal that good. Not even for you."

Jason grins. "Didn't think so."

"So, we're looking for a car for your girlfriend?" Roberto asks as we move away from the Volkswagen. I nearly fall over when I hear the g-word.

"Oh!" I squeak. "No, it's not like that—"

Jason's face is bright red. "She's not my girlfriend—"

"He's just helping me out since he knows cars—"

"We're only friends—"

Roberto watches with an amused smile as we trip all over ourselves, laughing nervously as we interrupt one another in our haste to explain. "Ah, forgive me," Roberto says, when he can get a word in. "I should not have assumed. I hope you're not offended."

"Not at all!" My voice is higher than normal, and I clear my throat. Jason looks like he's choking on a laugh.

"What kind of car are you looking for?" Roberto asks me.

"Nothing fancy—just something to get me around town for the summer." I avoid looking at Jason, since I can still feel the heat on my neck.

"Well, we have several available cars that fit that description. Let's take a look."

For the next hour, Jason and I walk around the lot, climbing in and out of cars, looking under hoods, and taking a few test drives. I finally narrow it down to two cars: a dark blue Hyundai Elantra and a silver Dodge Neon.

"Which do you think is the better car?" I ask Jason.

"They're both decent. Do you only need it to last for the summer?"

"Hopefully. I'm planning to trade in whichever car I get for something nicer, once my ring sells."

Jason shrugs. "In that case, I'd say pick the one you like best, since longevity isn't really a concern."

"I like *that* one best," I say, pointing at the Volkswagen in the corner. He rolls his eyes.

"Do you know how notorious those things are for engine trouble?"

"I don't care. It's cute. And fun." *And Derek wouldn't be caught dead in it.*

"And too expensive."

I sigh. "I know." Gesturing to the blue Hyundai, I say, "I'll take this one. I like the blue."

"You sound so excited."

I smile half-heartedly. "I *am* excited about getting a car. And I do like this one. It's just... I've wanted a Bug ever since I was a kid."

"Just like that one?"

"No, not exactly. I want a powder blue convertible Beetle, with cream leather interior and eyelashes on the headlights."

He laughs—that glorious, hearty laugh of his I love to hear. "Eyelashes, huh?"

"Yup." I look longingly at the Volkswagen one last time, then sigh and turn away. "Come on," I say. "Let's go talk to Roberto."

Chapter 12

Today is the day I was supposed to get married.

I wake up with the sun and lie in my bed, staring at the ceiling as I try not to think about Derek. I try not to think about my dress, now tucked in the back of Tara's closet. I try not to think about walking down the aisle on my dad's arm, listening to a double string quartet playing Pachelbel's *Canon in D*. I try not to think about the beautiful bouquet I had picked out—hydrangeas and roses and sweet peas—and the crystal chandelier I won't be dancing under tonight. I try not to think about any of it.

And I try not to cry.

As I lie there feeling sorry for myself, my phone buzzes on the table beside me.

> TARA
>
> Get out of bed and make today all about YOU

I smile reading her text. She knows me so well.

AMIE

What if I want to sleep in?

TARA

Too late for that. Get up. Go to the spa. Buy
yourself new shoes. Eat some cheesecake.
And send me pictures, or I'll be calling and
bugging you all day

I sigh, dropping my phone onto the bed and rubbing my
eyes. If Tara was here, she'd force me to do all those things.
She'd drag me around town to make sure I had the best worst
day of my life. Because that's Tara.

But that's not really me.

I'd rather spend a quiet day at home by myself, curled up
with a good book and a cup of tea and not talk to another living
soul. Except maybe Ebenezer, because he wouldn't talk back
and tell me all the reasons why my life is better without Derek.
But the chances of having a quiet day to myself under the same
roof as my mother are about as good as my chances were of
getting that Volkswagen yesterday.

I stretch, thinking about my options. I guess I could go to
the spa. Today would be a good day to get the haircut I've been
wanting, so I decide to start there. Even if it ends up being the
worst day of my life, it can only last twenty-four hours. I glance
at the clock as I climb out of bed. 8:02am

Eight hours down, sixteen to go.

———

"Hi, welcome to Arabella Salon. Do you have an
appointment?"

"No, I don't, sorry. Do you have any openings?"

"We might. What would you like to have done?"

"A cut and color. And maybe a pedicure?"

The receptionist checks on the computer, frowning. "Hmm. I can fit you in for a pedicure in ten minutes, but I don't have any hair appointments available today."

"That's ok. I'll take the pedicure."

I give her my name and she puts me on the schedule, inviting me to have a seat until they call me back. The salon is really nice, one of those posh places that smells like a mixture of peppermint and dirt. I sit in one of the low, modern armchairs and pick up a magazine, skimming past the ads of double zero models with pouty lips and too much hairspray.

"Amie?"

I'm knee deep in an article about pet yoga when my name is called. "That's me."

The nail technician is about my age, with purple-tipped hair and a diamond stud on her nose. She smiles as I stand up. "Hi, I'm Felicia. Are you ready for your pedicure?"

"Sure."

I drop the magazine on the table and follow her to another part of the salon. "How's your day going so far?" she asks.

"It's all right, I guess."

"Just all right?"

"Yeah. I was supposed to be getting married today, but my fiancé broke it off a couple weeks ago. So, you know."

"Wait, what?" She stops and stares at me. "Are you serious?"

I shrug.

"Wait right here," she says, turning back the way we came. "Pick out some nail polish!" she calls over her shoulder.

After a few minutes Felicia comes back with another

woman, closer in age to my mother than myself. "You must be Amie," she says, a mixture of welcome and sympathy in her voice. "My name is Thea Williams—I'm the owner of Arabella." She gestures to Felicia, who smiles at me. "Lecia told me about your plight, and I'd like to help. I understand you wanted a cut and color as well as the pedicure?"

"Yes, but I was told there weren't any appointments."

"Our stylists are fully booked today, but I'd like to give you a cut and color myself, with my compliments."

"Oh, wow. That's really nice of you. Are you sure? I don't mind paying for it."

"I insist. Your pedicure will be on the house as well, but I'd like to do your hair first, if that's all right?"

"Of course."

She flashes me a runway smile. "Perfect. Follow me."

She leads me back through the lobby and to the other side of the salon, where individual stations are set up for each stylist. Most of the chairs are occupied, but I follow her to an empty one on the far side of the room in front of a large, framed mirror and sit down.

"Do you know what you'd like?" Thea asks.

"Something short. And blonde."

She eyes me critically, one perfectly shaded brow raised in doubt. "Have you ever had short hair?"

"Yes."

"How short?"

I shrug. "About chin length."

"And blonde?"

I shake my head. "Never blonde. But I was temporarily red once."

She narrows her eyes, scrutinizing me, and I give her my

most reassuring smile. "My ex-fiancé loved my long, brown hair. I need something new."

The sleek black cape snaps like a whip before she fastens it around my neck. "I know just the thing."

———

I feel a hundred pounds lighter by the time I leave the salon— my short, choppy hair artfully styled in perfect disarray, now a dozen shades of sandy blonde. I almost didn't recognize myself in the mirror when Thea finished. When I arrived at Arabella I still looked like Derek's dress-up doll, despite my new clothes. Now I look like one of those twenty-something Instagrammers sporting flip-flops and shades online, without a care in the world.

It feels amazing.

My car is comfortably warm after the sub-zero temps of the air-conditioned building, and I snap a quick selfie to send to Tara before starting the car. I hum to myself as I drive home, thinking about her text this morning. My new 'do makes me feel daring and bold, so maybe I *should* take myself out on the town. I could streak the city in crimson shades, plastering myself in a rainbow of color to wash out the melancholy gray of the last few weeks.

I'm nearly home when a strange, acrid smell assaults my nostrils. It's sharp and smoky, like burning rubber. Or tar. I sniff, looking around for the source before I realize it's coming from my car.

My less-than-24-hours-old, new-to-me car. Great.

By the time I pull over, the smoke coming from under the hood is thick. I don't really know much about cars—should I turn off the engine? What if it won't start again? I reason to myself that smoke means something besides my dad's barbecue is burning, and that's not a good thing. If something is burning, I should turn off the car. So I do.

And then I call Jason.

Please pick up, please pick up, please pick up.

"Hey, Ames."

"Jason!" I practically shout his name, so glad to hear his voice. "I was driving home from the Valley and suddenly my car started smoking. What do I do!"

"Where are you?" His voice is calm, and it brings my panic down a notch.

I glance out the window, orienting myself. "I'm at Jacob's Java. On Ray Street."

"What part of the car was smoking?"

"The engine, I think? I smelled it first, and then I saw smoke coming out from under the hood."

"Is it still smoking now?"

"Yes."

"Ok, turn off the car and wait outside. I'll be right there."

I end the call and climb out of the car, going over to stand in the shade at the edge of the parking lot. The smoke drifting out from under the hood is almost gone now, and by the time I see Jason's little red pickup, it's stopped completely. I walk over to my car as he pulls into a parking space.

"Jason, you're a lifesaver."

He stops short when he sees me, his mouth dropping open. "Whoa, Ames, your hair!"

I smile self-consciously, one hand reaching up to touch my head. "Yeah, I needed a change. Does it look ok?"

"It looks amazing." The admiration in his voice washes over me, buzzing through my brain like a hyperactive bumblebee.

"Thanks."

"So, the engine started smoking?" He comes up beside me and we both walk to the front of the car.

"Yup. I smelled it first, though, while I was driving."

"Yeah, I can still smell it. Can you pop the hood, please?"

I reach inside the car and pull the lever so Jason can check out the engine. He pokes around for a bit, then looks over at me.

"What did the temperature gauge read when it started smoking?"

"Oh. Um... I don't know, actually. I didn't look," I say, feeling sheepish.

Jason nods, shutting the hood and crouching down to look under the car. "I think you overheated. There's not a drop of coolant in the tank, and it doesn't look like you're dripping. There must be a big leak somewhere."

"Is that bad?" I say *bad* but I mean expensive. Jason understands.

"Could be. But depending on the location of the leak, it shouldn't be too difficult for you to fix."

"Me?"

"Sure." He wipes his hands on his jeans, smirking at me. "You didn't think I would just do it for you, did you?" He winks, and a nervous laugh bubbles out of me.

"Actually, yeah, I guess I did."

He scoffs. "I thought you liked working on cars!"

"Jason, I don't know the first thing about fixing cars."

"Sure you do—you used to help me all the time in high school."

"I didn't help. I sat on the bench and talked to you while you did all the work."

One corner of his mouth turns up as if pulled by a string. "Then I'd say you're overdue for a lesson in mechanics. I've got some coolant in my truck—enough to get you home, at least," he says. "I'll follow you there just in case. When you get to my house, go ahead and pull into the driveway so we can take a look."

Chapter 13

B y the time I get to Jason's house my hands are stiff from gripping the wheel. I step out of the car as Jason pulls up along the curb.

"Yeah, you've definitely got a leak. Now we just need to figure out where."

"How do we do that?"

"We need to fill the radiator and let the engine heat up. Hop in, we can pick up some coolant at O'Reilly's."

My phone goes off just as I'm getting into his truck.

TARA

Wowza! 😜 You are smokin! 🔥

A breathy laugh escapes me, and Jason glances over. "It's a text from Tara," I explain. "I sent her a selfie after my haircut."

"What does she think?"

I grin. "She said I'm smokin' hot."

"Well there's a first—I actually agree with something Tara Bradford said."

My eyes dart to his face, but he's looking at the road.

"How is Tara these days?" he says after a minute.

"She's fine. Still Tara. She married a math genius a few years ago, so it's actually Tara McCullough now. They live in Vegas."

We soon arrive at the auto parts store, and with coolant in hand we head back to Jason's house.

"So where are you at with the competition?" I ask, buckling my seatbelt.

"I called to confirm that my registration was still valid. I wasn't sure if Veronica would cancel it after our fight. It wouldn't really be like her to do that, but I wanted to make sure."

"And?"

"It's still active."

"So, what's the next step?"

Jason's hands grip and ungrip the steering wheel. "I've got to come up with three original recipes. They have to be submitted by email to the judging committee by the first of August. And then I have to cook them for the competition."

"Do you know what you want to make?"

"I'm thinking about it. Whatever I do, I want to test it out on both kids and adults first, though."

"That's a good idea. Then you can make any adjustments before the competition."

"Exactly."

Suddenly my stomach growls—loudly. Jason raises his eyebrows.

"You hungry?"

I smile. "A bit."

He grins at me. "Good, 'cause I'm starving. I know this

great little Chinese place on the way home. We'll grab some takeout to eat while we're waiting for the engine to heat up."

———

When we get back to Jason's place, he fills my car with fluid while I take the food into the house. He comes in a few minutes later.

"All right, I've filled up the coolant and started the car. We'll let it get up to temperature and see if we can find the leak."

I nod, taking a mouthful of lo mein. "Wow. This is really good."

He grins. "Right? It's one of my favorite restaurants. Try the beef—it's amazing."

I spoon some more food on my plate while Jason heads to the fridge. He grabs a soda for himself and hands me a bottled water.

"Thanks," I say, twisting off the cap. The bottle is poised on my lips before I realize what it means. I take a sip and set it down.

"Since when do you drink bottled water?" I ask, taking another bite. Dang, the beef *is* amazing.

He shrugs. "You mentioned drinking nothing but bottled water in Vegas. I figured if you're here for the summer, I should keep some on hand."

Warmth spreads through my middle, and not just from the spicy noodles. I take another sip, the cool water sweet on my lips because Jason was thinking of me.

We finish eating and Jason stands up. "Let's see if we can

figure out where the leak is coming from." He heads outside and I follow.

It doesn't take long for Jason to diagnose the problem. "Looks like it's coming from the lower radiator hose."

"Can we fix it?"

"Yup—shouldn't be too hard. We'll replace the hose and you'll be good to go."

I head inside to clean up from lunch while Jason moves my car into the garage behind the house. The engine has to cool down again before we can do anything, so we hop into Jason's truck and head back to O'Reilly's. By the time we get back to his house with the part, my car is cool enough to start working on it.

"Unless you want to run home and change," Jason says, tossing me a pair of stained coveralls, "I'd suggest putting this on."

"Oo, sexy," I say, holding up the baggy blue fabric.

"You know it," he says, flashing me a dimpled smile.

I put the coveralls on over my clothes while Jason goes inside to change. When he returns, he quirks one eyebrow at me and grins. "Definitely sexy."

I roll my eyes. "Ha, ha. Come on, Henley, let's get to work."

When I was in high school, one of my favorite things to do was sit in the garage with Jason while he worked on his car. I'd sip a warm soda while Jason talked to me from underneath the vehicle, his voice muffled by the hoses and bolts and metal between us. Sometimes he'd ask me to reach in from the top of the engine while he did something from the bottom, working together to fix whatever it was that needed fixing. But mostly I just watched, and we'd talk. And laugh. We'd dream and plan and whine and groan about "growing up" and what we wanted to do after graduation. It was warm and safe and comfortable, those afternoons we spent together.

But this time I don't sit cross-legged on the workbench while Jason tinkers. Today I get my hands dirty. Jason talks me through the whole process, guiding me through the repair with the patience of a kindergarten teacher on the first day of school. We work side by side—Jason pointing things out to me as I carefully do as he instructs. I'm sure it takes twice as long and I make a way bigger mess than he would have on his own, but Jason doesn't seem to mind. It feels good, working together. Like old times.

A few hours and several mishaps later Jason declares the job done. "Now you know how to replace the lower radiator hose," he says, grinning at me.

"Forget law school—I should be a mechanic."

He wipes his hands on a rag. "It's still strange to me that you were studying law. It's so unlike you."

I shrug. "It was interesting. But I mostly did it because of Derek."

Derek. I've spent all day trying not to think about him, so the mention of his name leaves a bad taste in my mouth—like drinking orange juice after brushing your teeth. Jason shuts the hood of my car, puts away the tools we used and cleans up some of the mess.

"So do you think you'll go on to law school?" he asks.

"No. Definitely not."

"What will you do instead?"

I blow out my breath in a long sigh. "Still trying to figure that out. I'm planning to go back to school this fall, but I don't know what to change my major to."

"Does UNLV offer an Automotive Technology degree?"

I grin. "Maybe. Do you think I should apply for the program?"

"Absolutely not."

He laughs when I punch him in the shoulder. "You're the one who insisted I do the work!" I say.

"I know," he says, laughing. "And you did great. Even if it did take all day." He winks at me.

"I guess I did monopolize your time. Sorry about that."

He shrugs. "No problem. I didn't really have any plans today."

"Sure you didn't."

"No, really. I was going to try out a new macaron flavor, but that's it."

"For the competition?"

"No, the dessert has to be a cake. I just like making macarons."

"There's a French bakery near where I live in Vegas that has over a dozen flavors of macarons."

"You like macarons?"

"I love them," I say, pulling off the coveralls and tossing them in a heap on the bench. "And eclairs. And beignets. Pretty much all French pastries."

"I'll remember that."

We finish cleaning up the garage and Jason pulls my car back out into the driveway. He leaves it running for me as he steps out.

"Thanks for your help today," I say. "I was afraid it was going to be the worst day of my life, but it turned out all right."

"Why did you think it was going to be the worst day of your life? Because you had a little car trouble?"

I pause, not wanting his sympathy. I'm so tired of other

people's sympathy. "No, because today was supposed to be my wedding day."

He freezes. "You were supposed to get married today?" I nod, and he groans, rubbing the back of his neck. "Dang, Amie. I wish I'd known. I would have made you dinner. And we could have gone out and done something fun. I would have—"

"Now you sound like Tara," I say, forcing a laugh. Talking with Jason about my almost-wedding day makes me feel light and heavy and happy and sad all at once, like laughing and crying at the same time.

"Yeah, if Tara were here I'm sure she would've made it a day to remember," he says.

"Yeah. But it's fine. Really. Today was great, and I owe that to you. So thanks."

He shrugs. "Well, I still wish I would have known. I feel like... I don't know. Like it's a big deal."

"It is a big deal," I say, feeling the hollow ache in my gut expanding. "But you didn't know, so don't worry about it."

He shakes his head.

"Tell you what," I say. "Make me a batch of macarons and we'll call it good."

His eyes light up. "Done."

"Good." I climb into the car and shut the door, rolling the window down. "And don't wait too long—I haven't had a good macaron in months."

Chapter 14

After fixing my car, I treat myself to a pint of Phish Food and a late night watching all the classic chick flicks we own. By the time I finally fall into bed it's after two, so I let myself sleep in the next morning.

I spend the next day curled up on the sofa, reading a book and absently stroking Ebenezer's head. He hums like a Harley Davidson, and soon my lap is damp from the drool that dribbles down his chin. Good old Ebenezer.

Around 3pm my phone chimes from the table beside me.

JASON
Macarons at my place tonight?

My smile comes all the way up from my toes. I should have known he'd make them right away.

AMIE
I'm always up for macarons! What time?

JASON
7ish

AMIE

I'll be there

I turn back to my book, grateful for the hundredth time that I'm not stuck up here in Washington alone. I was so afraid that coming home was going to be painful and awkward, but hanging out with Jason has made the transition a lot easier. I still think about Derek on a daily basis, but the gut-punching pain isn't as raw, and I can go for longer stretches without mourning the loss of what almost was.

I knock on Jason's door a few minutes after seven, and the sweet smell of sugar and almond greets me as it opens. Jason stands there in a long white apron and a smile the size of Rhode Island.

"Hey Ames, come on in."

"Nice skirt," I tease.

"Thanks, my pink one's in the wash." He grins. "Have a seat—I'll be right there."

The front room is small, and I sit down on the faded blue sofa to wait. Pretty soon Jason comes back—sans apron—carrying a tray and two bottles of water.

"I wasn't sure what your favorite flavor was," he says, setting everything down on the coffee table in front of me, "so I made my favorites instead."

"They look delicious," I say, reaching for a soft pink macaron. He watches my face expectantly as I take a bite.

"Hm. Well, it's not bad," I say, trying to keep a straight face as I set it down and brush off my fingers. "Is this your first try?"

For a moment I think he actually believes me—I can see the shock flash across his face. But then he rolls his eyes.

"Ha ha, very funny. No, it's not, but it's certainly the last time I ever make them for you." He frowns, but I can see the pucker in his cheek from holding back a smile.

"Fair enough." I pop the rest of the macaron in my mouth, grinning at him. "Mm. This is good."

"You think so?" Jason grabs a cream-colored one and sits next to me.

"I know so. Where did you learn how to cook like this? Aren't they really hard to make?"

He shrugs. "It took a few tries. Getting the egg whites beaten to the right consistency took some practice. And making sure there weren't any lumps once I added in the flour and sugar."

"I'm going to pretend I know what you're talking about and nod my head."

He laughs. "It's not so bad. Just takes practice."

I try a periwinkle one next, which Jason tells me is blueberry. It's really good—and so is the peach.

"So how are things with your parents? Is your mom still upset?" he asks.

"Probably, but I think my hair shocked her anger into hiding."

"It shocked me, too. You've never done anything like that before." He takes another cookie. "What made you decide to change it?"

The familiar pain as I think about Derek pricks at my insides. "I wanted to try something different," I say.

"I thought you liked your long hair."

"I didn't really care about my hair, actually. My dad likes it long, so I kept it long growing up. And Derek liked it long, so..." I shrug.

"So you *really* wanted something different." He nods. "I get it. And what do you think?"

I grin. "I like it. A lot."

"Even the blonde?"

I run my fingers through my hair, looking at the strands. "Yeah, I like the blonde, but I probably won't keep it forever. Too much maintenance."

"Think Tara will try and talk you into keeping it?"

"Probably. She's always begging me to let her play around with my hair."

Jason chuckles. "That doesn't surprise me. She was always more fussy than you about stuff like that. And Brandon—man, I never saw a guy obsess about his hair the way your brother did."

I laugh. "I don't think he's quite as obsessed anymore, but he certainly keeps up appearances." I pause. "He'll be here in a couple weeks."

Jason stops with the water bottle poised on his lips. "Brandon's coming to visit?"

"Yeah. We were all going to meet up in Vegas for the wedding, but, you know." I shrug. "He still wanted to see Mom and Dad, so he switched his flight to come home instead."

"Wow. I haven't seen Brandon in years. Not since graduation."

"That's not much more than I've seen him, honestly."

"Really?"

"Yeah. Married to his job now."

"Where's he working?"

"Sacramento. He works for Raytheon."

Brandon is the only person I've ever known who decided as a child he wanted to be a rocket scientist, then grew up to be a rocket scientist. Crazy, right? But that's Brandon. He's never been wishy-washy like me. When he puts his mind to something, nothing can get in his way. Which is why he and Jason and I kind of drifted apart. The three of us spent a lot of time together when we were children, but once we hit the teen years, Brandon found me and Jason to be too much of a distraction. He was way more focused on his grades and future than either of us.

Jason finishes another macaron and sits back. "So how do you feel about that? Your brother coming for a visit?"

"I don't know. It will be good to see him. I'm just kind of dreading my mother for the duration of his visit, you know? Brandon's always been the favorite, and he's bound to come home with more stories of his success."

Which will make my failures all the more noticeable. I pick at the crumbs on my lap, the pain inside aching like a splinter I just can't dig out.

"So how come you don't want to go to culinary school?" I ask, changing the subject.

My question catches him off guard. "I don't know," he says. "There's not really a point in going to school if I'm not going to be a chef, right?"

"Well, why aren't you going to be a chef?" I persist, taking another macaron. "Because these are seriously amazing."

He rolls his eyes. "You sound like Veronica."

"She's right, you know."

He frowns. "About what?"

"About—well, not about wasting your life—but she's right about you being a really good cook. And I can tell you really enjoy it. So why aren't you cooking for a living?"

He's quiet for a time, but I'm not afraid that he won't answer me. Jason has always answered my questions, even if he had to think about them for a while. He would squint his eyes a bit, until two little dents appeared right between his eyebrows, and after a few minutes his face would smooth out and he'd turn to me with whatever answer he'd come up with.

I watch him now, seeing the same two dents between his brows, accompanied by a deeper line across his forehead. But it's not a line of concentration; it's one of worry. I want to reach over and smooth it out.

"All my life," he says at last, "my dad has talked about giving me the carwash. 'When you're running things around here,' he'd say, or else, 'Someday the carwash will be yours, you know.' It's always been assumed that I would take ownership of the business when he decided to retire, and I've gone along with it for years. I can't back out now. Not when I've been managing it since graduation. Not when he's been counting on me."

He looks at me, and I can see in his eyes the anguish he feels—torn between loyalty to his father and a burning desire to follow his own dreams. My heart aches for him, because I know which one he'll choose, which one he's already chosen. Because that's Jason.

"Have you told your dad you want to be a chef?"

"No. How can I?"

"You could make him a batch of these, for starters," I say, reaching for another bite of heaven. He smiles, but it doesn't reach his eyes.

"I wish it was that simple."

"Maybe..." I start to say, but then I shake my head. "Never mind. I'm not one to talk."

"What?"

"Well, maybe it is that simple. Maybe you just need to sit

down and say, 'Hey dad, I'd really like to pursue a career as a chef, but I don't want to leave you in a lurch with the carwash. Do you have a contingency plan in place if I decide not to take ownership?'"

Jason tips his head back, leaning it against the edge of the couch. "You make it sound so easy."

"Well, it's easy for me to say. Not as easy for me to do."

He lifts his head to look at me. "Is there something you've been wanting to say to someone but haven't?"

I brush at the crumbs in my lap, avoiding his gaze. "I don't know. I've never been able to nail down *what* I want, let alone get up the guts to tell Derek—or my parents, or whoever—what it is." I can feel his eyes on my face, but it's easier to speak if I'm not looking at him. "I don't even have the excuse that I forgot who I was or what I wanted when I was with Derek. I don't think I ever really knew myself in the first place."

A weight settles in my stomach, and I realize that the words I've said are the truth I've been ashamed to admit for weeks.

I don't know who I am.

"Well, I know you." Jason's voice interrupts my thoughts, and I look up at him. "I know your favorite color is turquoise and you love Mexican food. I know you chew on your hair when you get nervous—although that may be a little more difficult now," he says with a playful smile. "I know you love your brother Brandon, but feel like you've been living in his shadow all your life. You're quiet, but not shy. You love to read. You love to sing, too, but you don't think you have a very good voice."

I stare at him in disbelief.

"You love to play board games and you hate going to bed. Daisies are your favorite flower. When you were a kid, you were bitten by a dog and have been afraid of them ever since. Rainy days make you happy, and if you could go anywhere in the world it would be—"

"Italy," we say together.

Jason looks at me, and I can tell that he sees me—really sees me. Not just what I look like and what I do, but he sees who I am on the inside. After all those years with Derek, it feels good to be seen.

"Thanks," I say, my voice quiet.

"You're welcome."

"It's nice to know there's someone who knows who I am."

He laughs—soft and warm, like the air around us. "Yeah, well, if you ever need reminding again, just let me know. I'll always be here."

And I know he means it.

Chapter 15

Things settle into a routine over the next few weeks. Walks in the park, storytime at the library, dinner with my folks, and Jason. Sometimes he comes to the library with me. Sometimes I help him with new creations in the kitchen. Sometimes we just hang out and talk. It feels like old times, only now we're grown up with grown-up problems.

A thunderstorm rolls in a few weeks after I arrive home, bringing with it the sweet smell of damp earth and some blessed cooler temperatures. I spend the day curled up on the couch with Ebenezer and a cup of peppermint tea, lost between the pages of *The Nightingale*. The rain lasts all day, not letting up even when the sky darkens. I sleep with my window open, the sound of the rain lulling me into dreams filled with books and blocks and laughter and Jason.

Jason?

My half-conscious thoughts wonder why Jason is starring in my dreams, but I brush it off. We've been hanging out a lot lately. That's the only reason.

I dress in jeans and a T-shirt the next day, since it still looks pretty drizzly outside. I smile up at the concrete sky when I leave the house, laughing when a drop of water lands right in my eye.

It's going to be a fantastic day.

Jen has the day off, so there's not really anyone to greet me when I get to the library. But I know my way around now. I scan the list in the closet for a book idea, then pull a few off the shelves to see what catches my fancy. I decide on *If You Give A Mouse A Cookie* just before the kids start showing up at ten.

I try to remember their names as I greet them all. I don't see Evelyn anywhere, but McKenzie is there. I smile and wave, and she waves back.

Storytime is even more fun now that I know what I'm doing. The children are engaged and cooperative, and when we finish the book we play a silly if/then game.

"If you give me a pillow," I say, tucking my hands to my cheek as if I was going to sleep, "then I'll ask for a..."

"Marshmallow!"

"Blanket!"

"Teddy bear!"

The adults on the fringe chuckle at the answers the kids call out. "A blanket! And if you give me a blanket, I'll want to make a blanket fort. So then I'll ask for a..."

"Table!"

"A snack!"

"A light!"

We play a few more rounds, coming up with a ridiculous story that has everyone laughing. Just before time runs out, I pull out the giant parachute and the kids spread out in a circle to play. As we rush underneath the rainbow fabric, pulling it down behind us as we sit, I look at the faces around me. Tabitha sits beside me, her dark skin and black braids shaded blue and green from the fabric above her head. Across the circle, Jayden's white-blond hair is standing straight on end, tinted pink from the portion of canopy he sits underneath. I smile at him, and he sends a gap-toothed grin back at me. All around me I see smiling faces in rainbow hues, sharing the joy of living and working and laughing and playing together in the same space.

This is exactly where I want to be.

The feeling surprises me with its strength, but I can't deny how right it feels. I love working with children—a fact I never would have known if I hadn't taken this opportunity. Being in this position, without anyone to influence or direct my own opinion, has been a blessing I never knew I needed.

The parachute deflates, and the kids and I crawl out from under its billowy folds, laughing. They help me fold it up, and I thank them for joining me today. Cries of "Bye Miss Amie!" fill my ears, and I wave to them as they scurry off to their parents and caregivers. I put away the parachute and place the book on the reshelving cart. I write down the book title and the activities we did on the chart Jen showed me, and move the seats and beanbag chairs back into their usual positions. I wave to the librarians as I head out the door, smiling at the puddles and the slate gray sky.

My dad gets home at the same time I do, his car pulling into the driveway just as I'm getting out of my own.

"Hey Dad. You're home early."

"I'm waiting for several clients to get back to me, so I decided to take the afternoon off. We don't get to see you very often—I don't want to waste it all working."

"Did you want to do something together?"

"If that's all right."

"Sure. What did you have in mind?"

"A nap?" he says, sounding hopeful.

I laugh, and he puts an arm around my shoulder as we walk up to the house together.

We have chicken salad sandwiches for lunch, after which Dad and I sit down to a game of Rummikub. My dad loves board games, and I grew up playing everything from Go Fish to Risk with him and my brother. Mom's not really a fan of games —she stays in the kitchen while we go into the dining room to play.

"Are you any closer to knowing what you want to do when you go back to school in the fall?" Dad asks, setting a run of sevens on the table.

I smirk at him. "Did Mom tell you to ask me that?"

"I heard that," she calls.

"Your mother is just concerned that you don't seem to have a lot of direction at the moment," Dad says, his voice quiet so it won't carry.

"Yeah, well, if her fiancé of three years suddenly called off the wedding, she'd probably feel pretty lost, too," I mumble.

Mom walks in, carrying a gold-rimmed goblet and a dishtowel. "Maybe you should take a semester off and just stay home. I could talk to Ken—I'm sure we could find a place for you at the library."

"I'm not staying," I say firmly, rearranging the board to accommodate my new set. "I've got bills to pay and my apartment to take care of. My life is in Vegas."

Mom gives me a look, and I can almost hear the words she's thinking: *but what kind of life is it without Derek?* I try to ignore her.

"Honey, what are you doing with the goblets?" Dad asks.

Mom seems to recall what she was doing when she got distracted by our conversation and begins rubbing the glass with the towel. "I'm washing them all so they'll be clean for tomorrow."

Dad looks at her blankly. "What's tomorrow?"

She sighs in exasperation and returns to the kitchen. I wait for Dad to look at me before answering his question.

"Brandon's coming home."

"Oh." He takes a tile from the draw pile.

Oh. That's all he says because that's all the explanation needed. Brandon is, after all, the perfect child. He's got the perfect job and the perfect life and the perfect answer for every question ever posed. Of course my mom will be breaking out the fine china for her baby boy. Him coming home will make the summer *perfect.*

"So you still don't know what you want to study instead of political science?" Dad asks after a minute.

I shrug. "Not really. Although..." My mind drifts back to the moment this morning under the parachute. "I kinda like working with kids."

Dad's eyebrows shoot up. "Really?"

"Yeah. I mean, I know I haven't been doing it long. But something about it just feels right. It makes me feel good, you know?"

Dad plays his last two tiles and calls Rummikub. "I think that's great, punkin. So you want to work with children then?"

"Maybe. It's too soon to tell for sure. But I'm thinking about it."

"What time will Brandon be here?" I ask Mom at breakfast the next day.

"Sometime this afternoon," she says without looking up from her crossword. "He said he'll rent a car so we won't have to pick him up. You know how he is—so independent."

Oh, I know how he is. My gut twists nervously at the thought of seeing my brother again, though I know I shouldn't be worried. Brandon and I get along fine. Sure, we've had our tiffs and squabbles, but no more than any other pair of siblings, and probably far less than most. Though four years my senior, he never treated me like I was a nuisance, which probably fed my early adoration of him. I was certainly his first, though by no means his only, admirer.

But something about being with my brother always makes me shy away, like a dog afraid of an outstretched hand. Brandon has always been confident and charismatic, unlike me. Growing up in his shadow left scars on my soul that I'm only just beginning to realize are there, and the knowledge of their existence leaves me feeling vulnerable and raw. The last thing I want to do is expose myself to more injury in that state.

After breakfast I do laundry and help Mom clean up around the house. When everything is to her satisfaction, I hole up in my room to read while I wait for my brother's arrival. Ebenezer climbs onto my lap and I give him a few strokes—enough to settle him down but not enough to get the waterworks going.

Brandon shows up just after two. I look up from my book when I hear the front door open and his voice echoing up the stairs.

"Hey hey hey! We're here!"

We? I set my book down and nudge Ebenezer off my lap, suddenly anxious. Mom gets to the door before I do, her voice a delighted cry from the entry.

"Brandon! And this must be Claire!"

I freeze, halfway to the stairs. Oh. He brought his girlfriend. My steps are a little less enthusiastic at this news.

"We wanted to surprise you," Brandon says. "I met her family back in April and she's been dying to meet mine."

"Well, it's so nice to finally meet you, Claire," Mom says.

"Thanks Mrs. Cunningham."

"Please, call me Deanne."

Brandon turns as I step off the last stair. "Amie!" he cries, then stops short. "Whoa, you're blonde!" He grins, opening his arms for a hug.

"It's good to see you, Brandon."

"You too, sis." He gives me an extra squeeze. "I'm so sorry," he says in my ear, low enough that no one else hears him.

"Thanks," I whisper, pulling away. The blonde woman beside him is watching us with a gentle smile.

She looks exactly like the sort of woman I would expect my brother to date. Classy, pretty, and with an air of confidence about her that not many women possess. She has a bit more curve to her than some of his other girlfriends, but in a pleasant way.

"Amie, this is Claire," Brandon says.

She takes half a step forward. "Hi Amie, it's so nice to finally meet you."

"You too," I say, extending my hand.

"Is Dad here somewhere?" Brandon asks.

"Napping," Mom says. "Do you want to bring in your

things? Let me see, I wasn't planning on another guest and we haven't any more rooms..."

"Don't worry about it, Mom. We're staying at the Red Lion downtown."

"Oh." Mom looks taken aback, but smiles to hide her surprise. "Well then, I guess that's settled."

We move into the living room to chat more comfortably. Brandon is in the middle of telling us about his latest project at work when my dad shuffles in.

"Brandon!" he booms.

"Hey Dad," Brandon says, standing up to hug him.

"And who's this?"

"This is Claire." She stands as Brandon introduces her.

"Ah, the young lady you've been telling us about. Welcome Claire, we're happy to have you with us."

"Thanks, it's nice to be here."

We settle into our seats once more, but there's a buzz in the room now. I can feel the undercurrent of excitement emanating from my brother, like the buildup of static electricity before you accidentally shock yourself.

"Well, since we're all here," Brandon says, glancing at Claire. "There's something we'd like to tell you."

My stomach lurches, threatening to expel my lunch. I know that look.

Oh, no. No no no no no.

He takes Claire's hand and smiles, a look on his face I've never seen there before. I close my eyes, poised for the blow.

"Claire and I are engaged."

I don't really hear the way my mother shrieks in delight and jumps to her feet. I don't know what words of congratulation my dad extends, though I open my eyes and see his lips moving. All I can hear is the pounding of my heart in my ears and the rushing of blood to my head. I sit, frozen in place, until the feeling subsides and the consciousness of what's going on comes back into focus.

My family is too enraptured at my brother's news to take much notice of me, but soon enough Brandon's eyes find mine. I can't even offer him a smile.

"When did this happen? And where is your ring?" Mom asks.

"I asked her back in May," Brandon says. "But we didn't want to overshadow Amie's wedding," he glances in my direction, "so we decided to wait to announce anything."

Four pairs of eyes dart to my face. I could drown in the sea of pity that I see in them.

"I'm not used to wearing my ring yet," Claire says. "I can't wear jewelry at work, so I usually leave it at home."

I wonder if that's true, or if she's not wearing it out of kindness and respect for my situation. It seems like something she might do, this perfect woman planning to marry my perfect brother.

The rest of the day passes in a blur. Dad takes us all out to dinner to celebrate, and though I want to complain of a headache or a nosebleed or a gallbladder attack or *something* to keep from going with them, I know I can't do that. Brandon was kind enough to let me have my moment to shine, not knowing the spotlight would go black and I'd be left alone on an empty stage. The least I can do is let him have his moment, too.

But later that night, when I crawl into bed and stare up at the ceiling wondering what happened to the life I had imagined, I let the shock and fear and hurt and rejection work through me. The tears come heavy and hard, and as much as I want to chase after the same dream Brandon has caught for himself, I know it's not possible.

Because Brandon is perfect. And I'm not.

Chapter 16

"Brandon is engaged?" Tara asks, her voice as surprised as I expected.

"Yeah."

"Wow. When did that happen?"

"May, I guess. Brandon met her parents in April."

"But didn't they just get together?"

She's reading my thoughts, because I've had the same questions bouncing around my brain since my brother's announcement yesterday.

"They met at a party on New Year's. They've been together ever since."

I'm sitting on a bench at the park, having arisen early to escape my mother. She was already up and banging around the kitchen when I came downstairs, so I had to sneak around the back like a prisoner breaking parole.

"Huh. That doesn't seem like Brandon at all. He's never been one to rush into anything. And six months is hardly enough time to know you want to marry someone." She pauses. "Do you know when they're planning the wedding?"

I sigh, rubbing my eyes. "They've been throwing around some different dates. They're considering a destination wedding at the moment, and that takes a lot more time to put together."

"Wow."

She's silent, which is the Tara equivalent of a long-distance hug. I wish she was here. If she was sitting beside me, she'd wrap her arms around me while I'd lean my head on her shoulder and cry.

"So how are you feeling about everything?" she asks after a while, her voice quiet.

I take a deep breath and look around, trying to find the words to describe the ache of rejection and loneliness Brandon's announcement has produced. I'm not really paying attention to the other people in the park, but out of the corner of my eye I see a shirtless man jogging up the path, his tanned skin shimmering with sweat.

"I don't know. I guess I'm still in shock."

"Of course you are. The last person on earth you'd expect to get engaged in a rush is Brandon," she says.

The runner is coming towards me, and while I'm not necessarily oogling the man, there's something about a good-looking athletic guy that draws the eye almost automatically, you know?

I try to focus on the conversation with Tara instead of the hot guy heading my direction. "Yeah. And I know it sounds silly and doesn't make any sense, but I kinda feel betrayed, like —Jason!"

"Jason?" she says, confused.

"I'll call you back," I mumble, ending the call.

The runner, who I now realize is Jason, glances over as he nears my bench.

"Amie?" he says, slowing to a stop.

I force myself to look at his face and smile. "Hey, Jason."

"You're out early. Everything ok?" he asks, his breathing a bit heavier than usual.

Dang. How did I never realize how ripped Jason is? Not like in a gross, body-building way, but in a sleek, defined, toned-in-all-the-right-places kind of way. I blink, realizing that I'm staring at him, and that *he* sees me staring at him. My cheeks flame.

"Oh, yeah, I'm fine. Just talking with Tara." My voice is high and breathy, like a balloon.

"You're talking with Tara?" he says, confused.

"I was. And then I saw you. So I hung up."

I can feel my blush building in the awkward half-beat that follows. He doesn't look embarrassed though, which is amazing to me considering that he's running half-naked through a public park. He looks more thoughtful than anything. Concerned, even.

"Kinda early to be talking to Tara," he says, watching my face. "It's barely six-thirty."

I laugh—why am I laughing?—but it comes out more hysterical than humorous. "Well, I needed to talk. Brandon is home. And he brought his fiancée."

"Wait, Brandon is engaged?"

"Yup."

"Dang." He sits on the far side of the bench. "That's quite the homecoming surprise."

"Hail the conquering hero," I mumble, looking at the

ground so I'll stop staring at Jason's arms. And chest. And stomach.

"You ok?" he asks. "Sorry, that's a dumb question. Of course you're not ok."

His comment makes me smile, and I glance over at him. Jason is *way* more attractive than I ever gave him credit for, but looking at him keeps derailing my train of thought.

"It's unexpected, but I'm happy for him. She seems really nice."

"Yeah, but didn't you come home so you could get away from wedding stuff? That's bad form on Brandon's part. Couldn't he have waited?"

"For what?" My words come out more sharply than I intend. "It's not like I'll be getting engaged again anytime soon. Why should he have to postpone his own engagement on my account?"

Jason doesn't say anything, and I'm actually relieved. I'm tired of the consoling texts and sympathetic messages I keep getting from ex-wedding guests, assuring me that someday I'll find a nice young man and live happily ever after. My cheerful replies are as insincere as their condolences.

The silence lengthens between us and I close my eyes, tipping my head back so the sun washes over my face.

"Can I do anything to help?"

I open my eyes and turn to face him. "I could use a hug, but..." I gesture to his bare chest, slick with sweat, and he laughs.

"Are you saying you don't want a piece of this?" he crows.

"Tempting, but no."

"Ouch. There goes my ego."

I grin, and his face lights up. My pulse is thrumming like a hummingbird in my veins, the easy banter between us masking the growing embarrassment—and attraction—that I feel. At last I stand.

"Well, I should let you finish your run."

He shrugs. "I was headed home, so practically finished anyway. I've got breakfast calling my name. Want to join me?"

"Thanks, but I should get back. I need to get ready for storytime."

He nods. "I'm glad you have an escape plan."

"Couldn't survive without one," I quip.

"You'll let me know if you need anything, right?"

"Yeah, I'll let you know."

"You better." He flashes me another heartbreaking smile and jogs off.

———

"There you are! Where have you been?" Mom comes out from the kitchen as soon as I walk through the door. "Brandon and Claire are on their way over."

"I got up early and went for a walk."

"Well, they're coming to spend the day and we're having brunch in an hour. You should change."

"I have storytime at the library, remember?"

"No you don't," Mom calls, heading back into the kitchen. "I told Ken you wouldn't be available today. So we can spend time as a family."

I don't know what bothers me more—the fact that my mother made arrangements with *my* employer without my permission, or the fact that it doesn't surprise me.

I grind my teeth and turn away, my feet beating like war

drums on the stairs as I march up to my room. So much for an escape plan.

I take my time in the shower and spend a long time getting ready, hoping to avoid my mom for as long as possible. My leaden feet pay off, and I emerge from my room just as Brandon and Claire sit down in the living room with my parents.

"You mentioned last night that you're considering a destination wedding," my dad says. "Where are you thinking? Hawaii?"

"We're actually thinking about heading to Europe," Brandon says. "Greece, maybe. Or Vienna."

"But Fiji and New Zealand are on the table as well," Claire chimes in. "The thing we're trying to decide right now is whether or not we want a beach wedding. That will narrow things down."

Slivers of pain shoot through me. *Fiji.* Sandy beaches, crashing waves, crystal clear water full of coral and fish and memories I'll never make. I love my brother, but if they get married in Fiji I don't think I could bring myself to go. I take a shaky breath, forcing my mind to focus on the conversation the others are having.

"Well, let us know how we can help," Mom says. "We had money saved for Amie's wedding, but since Derek took care of everything there we're happy to help you instead."

An awkward silence meets her words, and my brother's eyes dart to my face. "Thanks Mom, we appreciate the thought. I think we'll be able to handle most of the expense, though. We're pretty well established."

"But a wedding is so expensive! Especially if you're traveling somewhere foreign."

I pull out my phone, my insides trembling. *Please get me out of here* I text to Jason.

I breathe slowly in through my nose, out through my mouth, silently counting to four. I let the rest of their conversation fade into the background as I repeat the exercise, praying for Jason to respond.

> JASON
>
> What's up? How can I help?

His text is a lifeline, pulling me to safety.

> AMIE
>
> I can't do this. We're sitting around discussing wedding plans and I feel like I'm going to scream and cry and vomit all at the same time 😖

> JASON
>
> What happened to storytime?

> AMIE
>
> My mom cancelled my shift without me knowing. So I'm stuck here.

> JASON
>
> I'm about to head into work. Want to come down to the carwash with me?

> AMIE
>
> Yes please

> JASON
>
> K. I'll be there in 10

I set my phone down, the tightness in my chest easing a little at his words. Just ten more minutes and I'll be free. My breathing slows and my mind drifts back to what the others are saying. Claire is explaining about her work at Raytheon, and the projects she's been involved in. The latest one had something to do with combustive elements used in rocket fuel.

"We met on a similar project last year," Brandon says.

"I thought you met at a New Years party?" Dad asks.

"The party is where we really got acquainted. But we met at work on the Anzel Project last year. She was so passionate about the process, and her attention to detail was amazing."

"And Brandon was so level-headed when things didn't go as planned," Claire dovetails, smiling up at him. "He kept everyone from freaking out and made sure the project continued on schedule."

The look they give each other makes me squirm, like I'm peeking into a private moment not meant for anyone else. Claire obviously adores him. And Brandon seems pretty smitten as well. Was it ever like that for me and Derek? Did he ever look at me with puppy-dog eyes, like I was the very air he breathed? I remember being pretty crazy about him, but I can't recall if it was the lovesick infatuation I can see in my brother right now. More than anything I remember feeling safe with Derek. Protected. Provided for. And feeling gratitude—so much awe and gratitude—for everything Derek did for me.

But gratitude isn't love. And merely taking care of someone isn't loving them.

Jason's knock comes right at a lull in the conversation. It startles me, and though my heart takes off at a gallop, I try not to give away that I know who it is and why he's here. I stay on the couch while my mom gets up to answer it, reminding myself to breathe.

"Oh, Jason! Come on in, it's good to see you."

"Good to see you too, Mrs. Cunningham. Is Amie here?"

"She is, and so is Brandon. He flew in with his fiancée

yesterday." It's impossible to miss the pride in her voice. "Come say hello."

They step into the room and Brandon stands up. "Jason Henley," he grins. "It's been a long time."

"Good to see you, Brandon," Jason says, shaking his hand. "And this is your fiancée?"

"Yes, Claire Johansen." Jason shakes Claire's hand as well. "Have a seat, Henley, we can catch up."

"Actually, I'm just here to pick up Amie," Jason says.

Four heads swivel in my direction, and I give Jason a grateful smile.

"Where are you going?" Mom asks, frowning. "You didn't tell me you had any plans."

What she *really* means is I-can't-believe-you're-taking-off-when-your-brother-is-here. I can hear the disapproval in her voice, but the pain in my heart trumps any guilt I might feel.

"Amie and I are going to lunch downtown," Jason says smoothly.

"Oh, well, why don't you stay and eat with us instead?" Mom says. "We were just about to sit down for brunch."

My breath catches, but Jason doesn't even miss a beat. He turns to my mom and says, "Your cooking is delicious, and any other time I'd be happy to stay, but Amie promised to help me brainstorm some new marketing techniques for the carwash. It's a business lunch, if you will."

I take the cue and get to my feet. "I'll get my things."

I run up to my room to grab my purse, then call out another goodbye as Jason opens the door. I catch a concerned look on Brandon's face before the door closes behind me.

I blow out my breath the minute we're outside. "Jason, you're a saint."

"That bad, huh?"

"Worse." I look at his truck parked behind my car at the curb. "Do you want me to drive myself? So you don't have to bring me back later?"

"Well, that depends. You want an excuse to be gone all day?"

I start walking. "Good point. We'll take your truck."

Chapter 17

"So, did you actually need help with marketing?" I ask when we get to the carwash.

Jason laughs. "No, I just said the first thing that popped into my head. I do have some work I need to take care of, though—think you can occupy yourself for a while? You're welcome to hang out in my office. I'll be in and out all day."

"Sure, no problem."

Jason's office is small and sparse, and after introducing me to the office assistant, he ducks out of the building. I pull one of the two chairs in the room into the far corner near the window so I won't be in the way, then pull out my phone. There's a text waiting from Brandon.

BRANDON

Everything ok? Seems like you left in a hurry.
I'm worried about you.

I sigh, trying to decide how to respond.

AMIE

I'm fine. Just hard to talk about wedding stuff, you know?

I start browsing through my Kindle app, looking for a book to read, when Brandon responds.

BRANDON

I get it. Sorry about that. You didn't have to leave though—we can keep the conversation on other stuff.

I snort. Like that would be possible. My mother will have nothing but wedding on the brain and coming out of her mouth until the blessed day arrives—and probably for years afterward. I mean, how often does your favorite child marry the perfect woman?

AMIE

It's fine. You and Claire deserve to be excited about your special day. I'll see you later.

Jason orders lunch for us at noon, and afterwards I settle back into reading my book. I get so wrapped up in the story I don't realize the afternoon is gone until Jason pokes his head in.

"Hey Ames, we're closing things up for the day. You about ready to go?"

"Sure."

"Great. I'll be back to lock up the office in ten minutes."

We grab some dinner on the way home, then head back to Jason's house to watch a show. By the time I get home, Brandon and Claire have already gone back to the hotel for the night. Part of me feels guilty for ditching my family for the day, but a bigger part of me is relieved. Mom is an angry porcupine when

I finally walk in the door—all bristles and spikes and stabs. But she doesn't say anything, and I slip quietly up to my room for the night.

I'm not as lucky the next day. Mom insists on "the girls" spending the day together to get better acquainted, and soon Miss Perfect and I are being dragged all over town, looking into and through every bridal shop this side of the Valley. Claire seems as reluctant as I am to be doing anything wedding related, saying that she's not ready to pick colors or shop for a dress just yet. But Mom insists. And when Mom insists, Mom wins. Part of me wants to assume that a portion of Claire's reluctance may have been for my benefit. She was probably trying to be sensitive, like perfect people usually are.

We stop for lunch at a little Italian bistro up by Northtown. I sigh inwardly, wishing for the hundredth time that Spokane had an In-N-Out. Italian food—no matter how delicious—just can't satisfy the craving for a good hamburger. My dad took me to his favorite burger place a couple weeks ago, but it just wasn't the same.

Mom seems to have talked herself into a comfortable silence at last, and I'm looking forward to a quiet meal alone with my thoughts.

Unfortunately, I'm not so lucky.

"Brandon tells me you like to read," Claire says with a smile.

"Yes," I say, looking over the menu. "I do like to read."

"I don't read much for pleasure. And research manuals are hardly exhilarating."

Since I have no response to her comment, I say nothing.

"So besides reading, what else do you like to do?" she persists.

Ugh. I really hate small talk. I should have found a way to get out of this, like tripping down the stairs and breaking my ankle. That would have been far less painful—and embarrassing—than this.

"Um, well..." I furrow my brow, trying to think of something. What *do* I like to do?

Thankfully our server arrives just then, buying me some time.

"Hello, I'm Nate and I'll be your server today," he says. "Can I get you started off with some drinks?"

"Water with cucumber for me, please," I say automatically.

"Coke with lemon for me," Mom says.

"I'll have a Diet Coke," Claire adds.

Nate nods. "Great, I'll be back with those in just a minute."

Claire raises her eyebrows as our server walks away. "Water with cucumber? I've never had that before. Is that a Vegas thing?"

She waits politely for an answer, but I don't have one ready. *Is* it a Vegas thing? I'm not sure. I know I *started* drinking it in Vegas...

I wrack my brain, trying to remember the first time I had it. Derek and I had just started dating. We were at a restaurant and I asked for water with lemon, but Derek stopped me. He said I should never order water with lemon because the lemons were usually disgusting and full of germs. Instead, he ordered us both water with cucumber. The cucumbers were washed before slicing, and they gave the water a refreshing taste. Since that time I've always ordered it, so now I'm trying to decide if I actually like it or if it's just a leftover Derek habit.

Dangit. As if this day wasn't already complicated enough.

I realize Claire's still waiting for an answer, but enough time has passed to make it awkward to respond now. I sigh.

"I'm sorry, Claire. Small talk has never been my strong suit —I tend to overthink everything."

She smiles politely. "That's ok, I understand."

Our server returns with Mom's and Claire's Cokes and a plain glass of ice water for me. He sets them on the table and turns away, but stops when Claire speaks up.

"Didn't you order cucumber in your water?" she asks me.

"Oh!" the server jumps to grab the water glass. "I'm so sorry, I forgot. I'll be right back."

"No that's ok!" I blurt out. Mom, Claire, and the server all stare at me. Nate's hand freezes on the glass. "Um, I actually don't want cucumber in my water. Plain water is fine."

"Really?" Claire asks.

"Are you sure?" Nate echoes.

I look from one face to another, my resolve melting. "I think so?" My hesitation only makes them more confused. Mom frowns at me, and I sigh, rubbing my eyes. "Yes. It's fine. No cucumber. Thank you, Nate."

I take the glass back and he turns away. Mom is looking at the menu again, but Claire has a funny look on her face.

"So, Claire," I say, trying to draw the attention away from myself. "What do *you* like to do in your spare time?"

I half expect her to tell me that she volunteers with the Red Cross, or runs a nonprofit dedicated to helping malnourished children, or some other such charitable hobby. That's what perfect people do, right?

"I like to go rock climbing," she says. "And hang gliding."

I blink. "Hang gliding?"

"Yes. Have you ever been?"

"No."

She grins. "I'll take you sometime. You'll love it."

Would I love it? I'm not sure. The thought of running off a cliff with an oversized kite strapped to my back doesn't quite sound like my idea of fun, but who knows?

Nate comes back to take our orders, which is the moment I've been dreading. I hate making decisions. Why did I have to come? Mom would have had just as much fun playing dress up with Claire without me along to make it awkward. I scan the menu, frantically trying to find something that A) isn't what Derek would order, and B) sounds like something I would actually enjoy.

"Amie? Do you know what you want?" Mom asks.

"Um... I'm not sure." I look up at our waiter, pencil poised over his notepad. "What would you suggest?"

"The house lasagna is really popular, as is the shrimp fettuccine. My personal favorite is the pesto ravioli though, if you want something a little different."

"That sounds good. I'll have that," I say, relieved to close the menu and hand it back to him.

"I'll take the lemon chicken linguini," Mom says, "but hold the capers, please."

"And I'll have the steak and mushroom fettuccine," Claire says.

Nate takes our menus, and Mom excuses herself to use the restroom. Now I'm left staring across the table at Claire's mammoth smile and wondering what the heck we should talk about.

"I understand you're studying pre-law," she offers.

"I was, yes."

"You're not anymore?"

"Nope."

She waits, but when I don't offer an explanation she persists. "What are you studying instead?"

I reach for a breadstick. "I'm not really sure at the moment."

She sighs, taking a sip of her Diet Coke. I think she's finally given up, for which I'm grateful.

Mom returns, and immediately peppers Claire with more questions about the wedding. My phone chimes, and I pull it out, checking my messages.

JASON

Think we can go to the library soon and get some ideas from the kids?

AMIE

Sure. Does Tuesday work for you? I have storytime in the morning.

JASON

I'll make it work. What time?

AMIE

10

JASON

Want me to pick you up?

AMIE

Sure

JASON

K, I'll be there at 9:30

I send him a smiley face emoji and put my phone down. I

know it was rude to be on my phone, but that brief interaction with Jason was like taking a deep breath before diving under the surface again. Mom keeps chatting with Claire, but throws me a we'll-talk-about-this-later look.

I have no doubt we will.

Chapter 18

"Today's book is called *Cloudy With a Chance of Meatballs*. Who here likes meatballs?"

The kids shout their answers at me, and I see Jason in the back, opening his notebook. He takes notes throughout storytime, and when we're finished with the book, I introduce him to the children.

"This is my friend Jason," I say, motioning for him to come up and join me. He stands and waves to the kids, and I tell them that he's a chef.

"Do you have your own restaurant?" one boy asks.

"No, but I might, someday," Jason replies.

"If you had your own restaurant," I ask the boy, "what kind of food would you serve?"

Some kids raise their hands while others shout out responses.

"Ice cream!"

"Chicken nuggets!"

"Bananas!"

"Pizza!"

"What if you owned a cupcake shop?" Jason asks. Their little faces turn from me to him. "Where you could make any flavor cupcake you wanted. What flavors would you want to sell?"

"Any flavor?" a little boy with black hair asks.

"Any flavor."

"Peanut butter!"

"Strawberry!"

"Candy cane!"

I raise my eyebrows at Jason and he nods, a grin stretching across his face. His question is a lot better than mine.

"What about frosting flavors? What would you put on a peanut butter cupcake?" he calls out.

The answers are, again, wild and varied, but at least they're headed in the right direction.

"Can my cupcake have sprinkles?" Evelyn asks.

"Of course!" Jason says. "You can have all sorts of sprinkles in your cupcake shop. What other toppings would you want to put on the cupcakes?"

By the time I dismiss the kids, they're all clamoring at their parents to buy them cupcakes. I smile sheepishly at the few adults who glance my way. Jason rubs his hands together.

"That was brilliant. I've got a bunch of ideas—now to try them out."

"What are you planning to do?"

"I've come up with a pretty good base cake recipe, so I'll start playing around with some flavors until I'm happy with the result. Then we'll test them out on some kids."

"I don't think they'll let you bring cupcakes into the library," I say, pushing the button for the elevator.

"Hm. I didn't think about that. Where else could we find a bunch of kids to try them out on?"

"What about the children's hospital?"

"That's a great idea. I'll call them up tomorrow and see if they'll let us bring in some cupcakes for the patients."

JASON

The hospital said yes! When are you free?

> AMIE
>
> That's great! ☺ I'm free a lot more often than you are—when would you like to go?

JASON

Friday or Monday if possible

> AMIE
>
> Let's do Friday

JASON

Great, I'll set it up with the hospital. We'll plan on taking them over after lunch

> AMIE
>
> Sounds good! See you then

Friday afternoon is hot, feeling more like Vegas than Spokane as I walk down the street to Jason's house. In high school, Jason and I had a "knock and walk" policy: you knock on the front door and walk inside. But it feels weird to do that now that we're adults and he lives by himself. The last thing I want is to accidentally walk in on Jason in nothing but a towel.

I knock on his front door, banishing the image that thought conjures in my mind.

The music coming from inside is pretty loud, so I'm not

sure if he hears me. I finally poke my head in and shout that it's me.

The volume drops. "Amie?"

"Yeah, it's me." I let myself in all the way.

"Come on in, I could use your help."

"Mmm, I can smell the cupcakes all the way from the street," I say, walking into the kitchen. The counters are laden with the fruits of his labor.

"Really? What do you smell?"

"Chocolate. Citrus. And something sweet—maybe cherry?"

"Close. Strawberry."

Jason's kitchen looks remarkably clean for the massive amount of cupcakes filling the space. He's piping pale yellow frosting onto pink-tinted cakes, ruffles of creamy sugar erupting from the tip of the bag like a magician pulling flowers from his sleeve. He jerks his chin at a bowl.

"Can you follow behind me and add the garnishes?"

"Sure. What do I do?"

He sets the piping bag down on the counter. "Sprinkle a bit of sugar over the top to give it some sparkle, and then place a candied lemon peel into the frosting, like this." He demonstrates with one of the cupcakes he just finished frosting. "It doesn't have to be perfect, so don't worry about messing it up." He picks up his piping bag and gets back to work.

"It's like you know me or something," I joke. I pick up one of the sugary twists. "Are these edible?"

"Of course they are. All garnishes should be edible."

"They're pretty."

He grins. "That's the point. People don't want to eat ugly food. If it looks pretty, they're far more likely to try it."

"So you're going to try that on the kids?" I ask, sprinkling sugar over the tops of several cupcakes.

"Yup. We'll see if it works."

We work in comfortable silence for a few minutes, the pile of finished cupcakes growing between us. At last Jason puts the frosting down and steps back.

"So they're lemon strawberry cupcakes?" I ask, placing a sugary twist on the last one.

"Strawberry Lemonade. I wasn't sure whether to make the cake strawberry and the frosting lemon, or vice versa. So I did one of each." He gestures to the far counter, where dozens of strawberry-topped cupcakes are already done. "They have different fillings, too. Some are just plain cake with frosting, but others have lemon curd or strawberries inside."

"And what about the chocolate ones?"

"Cookies and cream," he says. "Chocolate cupcake with a cream filling and Oreo buttercream frosting. We're doing those next."

I wash a few dishes while he turns up the music and whips together the buttercream. I lean against the counter, watching him work as he sings along to Imagine Dragons. I grin, soaking up his joy the way water seeps into the sand.

"Here, crush up the cookies while I pipe the frosting," he says.

I dump the Oreos into a bag and crush them with a rolling pin. The song *Lucky* by Colbie Caillat and Jason Mraz comes on, and I sing along softly.

Tara and I used to sing *Breakfast at Tiffany's* together in her room. No real reason for that particular song—one day it came up on a random Spotify station and we really liked it. We started listening to it all the time, until we had it memorized and could sing it together. We would harmonize on the verses and sing the chorus in unison, over and over again, until one of her sisters or maybe her mom would come in and ask us to *please* stop singing and turn the music down so they could concentrate.

Jason and I never had a particular song like that, but sometimes we'd sing along to the music in his car—old school favorites from *Good Charlotte, Green Day,* and *Bowling For Soup.* He hears me now, singing along to the peppy little melody and he grins, turning it up.

He joins in, piping the frosting onto the tops of the cupcakes while I follow behind with a sprinkle of cookie crumbs. Our voices blend together on the chorus and I glance up at him.

He's looking right at me.

My stomach jolts and I quickly look away, sprinkling the last of the crumbs onto the frosted cakes. Another song comes on that I don't recognize and Jason turns it down while I wash my hands.

"Thanks for the help, Ames."

"Anytime. Are there enough for me to try one?"

"Sure, which one do you want?"

"Hmm. I think I want to try the lemon cake with strawberry buttercream."

"With or without curd?"

"With, please."

"Right over there." He points to the platter of cupcakes nearest the fridge and I walk over. A perfect fan of sliced strawberry garnishes the tops, and I look them over, picking the one with the most frosting.

"Want a fork?" he asks, opening a drawer. He holds one out to me, but I scoff.

"Using a fork to eat a cupcake? What kind of heathen does that?" I open my mouth wide and take a huge bite.

A burst of flavor hits my tongue, dancing in brilliant citrus spirals around my taste buds. Creamy strawberry icing coats the roof of my mouth, and I hear Jason's laughter as I chew.

"This is amazing," I mumble. I swallow and take another bite.

"You've got a little something on your face," Jason says, trying not to laugh. I wipe my mouth with a napkin and move to throw it away.

"You missed a spot." He reaches out and brushes his thumb along the edge of my lip, gently cupping my face with his hand. My heart reacts in a ridiculous way, tripping all over itself in a race to jump out of my chest. His hand lingers for a moment, his eyes intent on mine before he pulls away. Blood rushes to fill the space where his hand was, and as he turns away I blink.

The way Jason looked at me pulls at something deep inside, something I can't quite put my finger on. It's strange and confusing and not altogether unpleasant, but it's *Jason*. We're friends. We've only *ever* been friends.

Jason starts loading the cupcakes onto trays and into the boxes. "Let's go see if the kids enjoy the cupcakes as much as you."

The elevator chimes softly, announcing our arrival on the second floor of Sacred Heart Children's Hospital. The floors and walls are decorated in bright, bold colors, with geometric prints and fun patterns all over everything. I follow Jason, carrying two covered trays of cupcakes in my arms, as he heads to the nurses' station to check in.

"Hi, I'm Jason Henley. We're here with cupcakes for the kids."

A plump nurse with dark hair greets us. "Oh, I heard you were coming! Do nurses get cupcakes, too?"

"Absolutely. You're doing all the work around here—you deserve to have a treat." Jason says.

She smiles. "The kids will be so excited. I'll make the rounds and let everyone know."

She strides off while another nurse in cheerful scrubs comes over. "So you're entering the competition?" she asks. "What kind of cupcakes did you make?"

"Strawberry Lemonade and Cookies and Cream."

"Mm, those both sound delicious." She points to the open waiting area behind us. "Go ahead and set yourselves up in there. We'll check with the patients who can't leave their rooms to see if they want any. Let us know when you're ready and we'll tell the families they can come out."

We set the trays down on a low sofa in the waiting room and take off the lids. "So how do you plan to do this?" I ask Jason.

He shrugs. "We'll just see which ones look more appealing to the kids, and listen to what they say and how they look after they try one."

We arrange a few of the small tables in a semi-circle and set the open trays on them. Jason brought a small backpack with paper plates and napkins in it, so I put those out while he runs back to the car. He returns carrying a case of mini water bottles, which he sets down by the closest table.

"I think we're ready," he says, sounding almost like a kid himself. His excitement is tangible, and I wish I could bottle it up and take it back with me to Vegas.

I let one of the nurses know we're ready, and she goes off to tell the patients and their families.

Soon a woman and two children emerge from one of the rooms and walk toward us. The eldest is a young teenage girl looking at her phone, while the other is a little blond boy with big brown eyes wearing a Thomas the Train t-shirt.

"Hi," Jason says as they walk up to us. "Would you like a cupcake?"

The woman smiles. "They look delicious," she says. "What flavors do you have?"

"Strawberry Lemonade and Cookies & Cream."

"Can I have a cookie one?" the little boy asks.

"Please," his mother prompts.

"Please."

"Sure thing buddy," Jason says. "Which one would you like?"

He deliberates for a moment—I can see the same hungry look in his eyes that I wore earlier, searching for the one with the most frosting. I point to an oversized cupcake in the corner, overflowing with buttercream and cookie crumbs. He grins and picks it up, then switches hands so he can lick the icing from his fingers.

The teenager stows her phone in a back pocket. She picks up one of the lemon cupcakes with strawberry buttercream and takes a bite. Her mother chooses one with candied lemon peel on top.

Another family approaches, and a girl about seven years old looks back and forth between all the trays.

"Do you have any cupcakes with sprinkles?" she asks.

"Sorry, no sprinkles today."

Her shoulders slump. "Ok. Can I have a pink one?"

"Here you go," I say, offering her one with a strawberry on top. She takes it meekly and walks away.

"Guess I should have done some with sprinkles," Jason murmurs.

"At least you had pink."

Several more families join us in the waiting room. Most of the kids choose the cookie cupcakes. I watch a few that chose the lemon ones take a bite, make a face, and put it down. I nudge Jason with my elbow.

"I don't think they like the lemon curd."

Jason shakes his head. "These kids have no taste for flavor," he says.

"But that's the point, right? To find out what the kids like?"

"Sprinkles and colors, apparently. I don't think they care about the flavor at all."

"As long as it's not lemon," I tease.

He rolls his eyes.

Chapter 19

J ason is anxious to get started on some salads, so he spends the next week putting together different flavors and ideas, while I spend time with The Perfect Couple™. The more time I spend with Claire, the more I realize (grudgingly) that she really is kind of great, and I don't think I'll mind having her for a sister-in-law. Eventually.

My family always has a barbecue for the Fourth of July, but it's usually a small, low-key thing with one or two neighbors, a few fireworks, and lots of good food and chatting. This year though, Mom decides to turn our cozy family bbq into a monstrous engagement party for the happy couple. She invites the whole neighborhood, plus family friends and some of her coworkers who know Brandon and want to wish him well.

I'm dreading it with every fiber of my being.

A few days before the barbecue, Jason and I go to Landon's place for dinner and a movie with friends. We eat and talk and laugh and tease, having a great time. It's fun to hang out with people—friends—my age.

"So are you coming on Saturday?" I ask Jason on our way home.

"Yup. My parents are coming too."

"Oh good! I was hoping they'd come. I haven't seen them in ages."

"My mom was asking about you the other day."

"She was?"

"Yeah. She knows I've been hanging out with you this summer. I talk about you a lot."

He throws me a smile before turning his attention back to the road. I blink. What am I supposed to make of a comment like that? I mean, we *have* been spending a lot of time together. And we've always been friends—of course he would talk about me. But something in the way he mentioned his mom, and that smile he gave me...

Stop overthinking things, Amie. It's *Jason*.

We pull up in front of my house, and while I expect him to just drop me off, he cuts the engine and climbs out of the truck as well. We walk up the sidewalk together, and when we get to the front door, I stop and look up at him. "Thanks for the ride. It was fun tonight."

"It was fun. I'm glad you came." He reaches out and tucks a strand of loose hair behind my ear. "Do you still like the blonde?" he asks.

My cheek feels hot where his hand brushed up against it. "Yeah. It's fun. And I like the cut—it's easy to do, and I can still pull it back in a messy ponytail if I need to." I cock my head at him. "Do *you* like the blonde?"

He reaches out again, fingering a lock of hair. He's so close I can smell the faint traces of his shaving cream. I force myself to breathe, inhaling the smell of him.

"I think you'd look amazing no matter what you did with your hair," he says.

Something about tonight feels different. Something about Jason feels different. The air is charged—if I looked down at my arm I'm sure I'd see the hairs standing on end.

But I don't look down, I look up. Right into Jason's eyes. My heart flips, tripping over my stomach and getting them both all tied up in knots.

"I guess I should say goodnight," he finally says, his voice low.

"Yeah, I... I guess I should go inside." I respond.

Neither of us move. I can see something in his eyes, something that I can't quite define but I can definitely feel. Stretching up on my toes, I give him a quick kiss on the cheek.

"Goodnight, Jason," I murmur, not meeting his eye. Then I open the door and escape into the darkness inside.

———

"Hi Sharon, welcome! Get some food, there's plenty of everything."

Mom greets another guest, directing them to the long tables laden with salads and chips and slices of watermelon. Dad is stationed at the grill, and The Lovebirds are standing amid a cluster of well-wishers, smiling and sharing affectionate glances with each other.

I'm hanging out by the lilac bush in the corner, trying to survive the sympathetic smiles and quiet condolences of my parents' closest friends. I'm sure they feel just as awkward as I do: here to celebrate the engagement of my older brother, just a month after they should have been celebrating my own wedding with me.

At least I know that Jason's coming.

As if summoned by my thoughts, Jason and his parents appear at the arched gate leading into the backyard. My face pulls into a grin, and the tightness in my chest eases up. I always feel better when Jason's around.

"Paula and Brian, so glad you could come!" my mom says, hugging our old neighbors.

"Thanks so much for inviting us. Oh Amie, it's so good to see you!"

"Hi Mrs. Henley," I say, coming to stand beside my mom. "It's good to see you too."

"Jason, you can put those on the table over there," Mom says.

I take a bowl from the stack in Jason's arms and head over to the food. "What did you make?" I ask, peeking under the lid.

"Confetti pasta salad, a fruit salad, and enchiladas."

"Enchiladas aren't a salad," I tease.

"I know, it's not for the competition. Just for the potluck."

"Sounds delicious."

We grab some food and nab a few chairs in the shade. Jason wants to keep an eye on the table to see (and hear) what people say about the salads. A handful of kids are running around, and he's most interested in their opinions. The pasta salad isn't a big hit, but the fruit salad disappears quickly.

"Guess you know which to make for the competition now," I say, licking my fork. "What's in the sauce?"

"You like that? It's an almond-lemon glaze I came up with."

"It's delicious. And cutting the fruit into stars and stuff is fun."

"Yeah, I think that's what sold it for the kids," he says.

Jason gets pulled into conversation with an old family friend, so I start gathering empty serving bowls to take inside to wash. Mom always said that was something a good hostess did —wash and dry the serving dishes so that guests could take them home clean. It's a way of saying thanks for coming and for bringing food to share.

I load up my arms and head inside, setting the dishes on the counter in the kitchen. I turn on the water and add some soap, grabbing a pair of gloves while the sink fills. Just as I start scrubbing, I hear the screen on the back door open and then slam. I wonder if Jason saw me leave and is coming in to help. That would be just like him.

I turn with an expectant smile, but it's not Jason—it's my brother. My eyebrows shoot up.

"Hey Brandon, what's up?"

"I saw you come inside and figured you could use some help."

"Oh. Thanks." I grab a bowl from the stack and plunge it into the soapy water. "I wash, you dry?"

"Sure."

We work in silence for a few minutes, until Brandon clears his throat.

"So, what happened?"

I rinse a large platter and hand it to him. "With what?"

"You know with what."

I shrug. "I'm sure Mom told you all about it."

"Yeah, but *I'm* sure you *didn't* tell Mom all about it."

I look up at him with a half-smile. "I told her most of it."

"Well, all she told me was that Derek called off the

wedding and you were coming home." He waits for me to say something, but I keep washing dishes in silence.

"So?"

"So what? She's right, that's what happened. Derek said he didn't want to marry me, and I came home. The end."

"Hardly," Brandon says, his voice brittle. "He must have given you *some* reason for calling it off. Was he cheating on you?"

"No, he wasn't cheating on me," I sigh, handing him the last dish. I pull off the gloves and hang them over the faucet to dry. "He just got tired of me, I guess."

"Not possible."

I turn around, leaning against the sink and folding my arms across my chest. "Of course it's possible—you got plenty sick of me, growing up," I say, trying to lighten the mood.

"That's different," he says, setting the final bowl on the stack of now-clean dishes. He blows out his breath in a big huff. "I just don't get it. You guys had been together for years. You were everything to him."

So much for lightening things up. The ache in my chest returns, and I draw a deep breath, trying to dislodge it. "That's what I thought, too," I say. "But I guess I wasn't."

Brandon walks over to the kitchen table and pulls out a chair, looking at me expectantly. I roll my eyes and sit down, while he takes the chair next to mine.

I tell him everything. About the phone call during my final dress fitting, what Derek said to me in the restaurant, and about Tara coming to my rescue when I fell apart that night. He listens intently, bringing over a box of tissues when my emotions start to get the best of me.

At last the tale is told, and I blow my nose for what seems

like the hundredth time. "It feels like it came out of nowhere," I say, looking down at my hands. "One day we were planning the honeymoon, and the next he was telling me it's over. I was so confused. I thought we were perfect for each other—I told Tara I didn't understand how he could break up with me, when I was everything he wanted me to be."

Brandon leans back in his chair. "It sounds like maybe the problem is that Derek didn't know what he wanted, and he certainly didn't know what he had."

I give him a grateful smile.

We lapse into silence as Brandon chews over what I've told him. I let my mind go blank—or at least, I try to. It's exhausting trying to think and feel all the time. Sometimes I wish I were a goldfish with only a ten-second memory.

"You know, I've always admired that about you," Brandon suddenly says.

I blink, confused. "Admired... what?"

"Well, you said you were everything Derek wanted, right?"

"Yeah."

"You were everything to him. Or at least, you tried to be. And that's what I admire—how adaptable you are. You can see what another person needs, and if it's someone you care about, you try to fill that need. You really have a gift."

"I don't know that I'd call it a gift. Or that I was being adaptable," I murmur. "More like I was being a doormat."

He frowns. "You are not a doormat."

"Not anymore, no. But I was. That's what I've always been."

"I don't think I'd go that far. You've just..." He searches for the right explanation. "You've just wanted to make other people happy, Amie. And there's nothing wrong with that."

"But what about when making other people happy comes at the cost of my own happiness?"

"Is that what happened with Derek? Were you unhappy with him?"

"No, I wouldn't say I was unhappy. Just... not myself."

"You can help make other people happy without losing yourself to them, Amie," he says gently.

"How?"

He shrugs. "You'll figure it out."

"Thanks," I say, rolling my eyes.

He laughs, standing up from the table. "I have full confidence in you," he says. "Just be yourself, Amie. That's enough to make anyone happy."

Chapter 20

Brandon and Claire were supposed to leave the morning after the barbecue, but decide to stay an extra week. I've already been forced to endure my mother's smiles and the lovebirds' PDAs on a near-constant basis, and the thought of seven more days of the same is almost more than I can handle. Jason is a saint and rescues me from my family as often as he can, but he has a life and a job of his own, plus prep for the competition, and sometimes I just have to grin and bear it.

Or frown and complain about it. Either works.

The night before Brandon and Claire leave, my family heads to a little ice cream shop in the Valley to share a Mount Everest: a mountain of ice cream topped with whipped cream, walnuts, sprinkles, and half a dozen maraschino cherries. At this point in the visit, the thought of spending an hour crammed in a little booth with Love Muffin and his sugar-mama Boo makes me want to vomit more than the thought of eating 29 scoops of melting ice cream does. So I convince Jason to come with us, and choose to ask forgiveness rather than permission of my mother.

"Any luck with your dad yet?" I say in a low voice to Jason, when everyone else is in conversation with each other. We're about halfway through the platter of ice cream and my stomach is starting to protest.

"No. I tried to talk with him last night but I couldn't."

"Why not? What happened?" I take another bite of ice cream. Ew, black licorice. No thanks.

"I invited my parents over for dinner so we could talk. I decided to make shrimp scampi and filet mignon to soften him up. I was so nervous I'd mess up the meal, but it turned out perfect. My parents really liked it, and when the meal was over my dad leaned back and said, 'Man, Jason, you really know how to cook. I might start taking my meals over here.'"

Jason stops talking and takes a bite of ice cream. I wait, but he doesn't say anything else.

"And?" I prod, but he shakes his head.

"And nothing." He leans back, frustration written all over his face. "It would have been the perfect time. I know what I *should* have said. But all I said was 'Thanks, Dad.'"

I swallow a spoonful of pralines and cream. Mmm, that's good. "Don't be too hard on yourself. You'll have another chance."

He mumbles incoherently right as my phone rings. I pull it out of my purse and glance at the name on the caller I.D.: Stapleton Jewelers.

"Hello?" I say, getting up from the table and taking a few steps toward the door. Mom frowns, as if I'd answered my phone in the middle of church.

"Hello, is this Amie Cunningham?"

"Yes, this is Amie."

"Hi Amie, this is Jack Stapleton. How are you?"

"I'm good, thanks."

"Glad to hear it. Listen, I've got some good news—your ring sold yesterday."

"That's fantastic!" I say. "How much did it sell for?"

"Thirty thousand. We just need to wait for payment to clear and the customer to pick up the ring, but if you'd like to stop by the store next week, I can give you a check."

"That's perfect. Thanks so much."

I hang up the phone, grinning like a kid on Christmas morning. I slide back into my seat next to Jason, but before I can tell him my good news, my mom asks who was on the phone.

"Jack Stapleton," I say reluctantly, hoping she won't recognize the name. For a moment her face is blank, but unfortunately my dad overhears.

"Was he calling about the ring?"

I sigh internally. "Yes."

The table goes silent, and all eyes turn to me.

"And?" my dad says.

I offer a cheesy, overexhuberant smile. "It sold!"

Jason grins and Mom glowers, but Claire looks incredulous.

"You sold your engagement ring?"

I nod, ignoring the prick of guilt in my gut. "Yup," I say, bracing myself for the judgment and sympathy I know is coming. For half a second she stares at me, and then she smiles.

"Good for you. I'd probably do the same thing."

I wish I could preserve the look on my mother's face at Claire's words. I'd put it in my pocket and pull it out whenever I needed a good, hearty laugh.

As conversation fills the table once more, Jason nudges my arm.

"So what's next?" he asks.

"He said I can pick up the check next week. And then you know what I'm going to do?"

He pretends to think about it. "Take a mechanics class?"

"I'm going to buy that Volkswagen."

He rolls his eyes. "Of course you are."

"Want to come with me?"

He gestures with the spoon to the mountain of ice cream still piled on the table in front of us. "If we ever make it through all of this, sure."

I pick up my spoon again and take another bite. "You know, ice cream is good and all, but I think I prefer cake."

"Really?"

"Yeah. Ice cream melts and gets all soupy, plus it's cold and numbs your tongue so you can't really taste it anyway. But cake is warm and soft and has such a great texture. It needs the right frosting, though. The wrong frosting can totally ruin a good cake."

He laughs. "You're starting to sound like me. Next time we should try a cupcake shop instead. There's one up north called The Cupcakery that I hear is pretty good."

"Anything would be good without Lovebird One and Lovebird Two making me feel sick after every bite," I grumble.

Jason hides his laugh in another spoonful of ice cream.

———

By the time Brandon and Claire head back to California, I'm ready to pack it up for Vegas myself. Because even after they leave, my mother won't stop talking about the wedding. I leave a full hour earlier than normal for the library the next day, desperate for a reprieve from her incessant rapturizing.

I arrive at the library in high spirits, anxious to see the children again. I've missed them, and I'm looking forward to storytime and this afternoon's guest. As I'm checking the schedule to find out who I'll be hosting later, a mother and her three kids walk by the children's circulation desk. "I don't care, Jaxon, just pick something. You need to get a book," I hear her say.

"But mom, they don't have anything I like!" the oldest boy replies.

He looks about ten or eleven years old, with messy brown hair and a spattering of freckles across his nose. His mother carries a baby on one hip and leads a little girl by the hand, a few years younger than the boy.

"If you don't pick something, I will," she says. "And you probably won't like it. So just pick something, please."

She heads toward the picture books, the little girl chattering as they go. The boy, Jaxon, stops and looks sullenly after them, then turns and ambles toward the junior fiction like a slow-moving raincloud. I take a few steps away from the desk, watching him. He stops in front of an aisle of books and stares at them, but doesn't pick any up. After a minute I walk over to him.

"Hey, do you need help finding a book?"

Startled, he looks up at me. "No, I'm fine." He looks back down at the row of books in front of him. I read a few of the spines.

"Do you like this author?" I say, picking up a book in a lengthy series.

He doesn't even look at the book. "No."

"Well, what authors do you like?"

He shrugs silently.

I think for a minute. What kind of books would a ten-year-old boy like to read? I flip the book over in my hand. It looks like an animal fantasy book about horses.

"Hmm... doesn't quite sound like your kind of book. Too boring."

His eyes flicker to the cover as I set it down. I pick up another book on the shelf, this one about a wolf.

"This one might be better," I say, reading the back, "but it still doesn't sound very adventurous."

"I like adventure," he says, looking at the book I hold. "And I like wolves." He takes it from me and reads the back, then sets it down.

"You know, one of my very favorite books is about a mouse with a sword who goes on a wonderful adventure."

"A mouse with a sword?" His voice and look are both skeptical.

"Yup. He travels across the forest to defeat an army of sea rats and weasels, with help from a badger and a mountain full of fighting hares."

"Hares?"

"Big rabbits. They're amazing warriors, you know. Deadly with a spear."

"Huh." He looks thoughtful. "What book is it?"

"Come here, I'll show you."

We head down a couple aisles until we find the authors that start with J. Two whole shelves are dedicated to books by Brian Jacques, and I spread my arms wide as we stop in front of them.

"Behold, the world of Redwall. Every single book is filled

with action and adventure, good guys and bad guys. Epic battles, magnificent feasts, terrifying monsters—they have it all."

He picks one up and flips through it. "They're old."

"Maybe, but that doesn't mean they aren't good. See how worn the pages are in that one? That's because it's been checked out hundreds of times. It's that good."

"Have you read this one?" he asks, showing me the book. It has a green cover with an otter on the front, wearing an eyepatch.

I grin. "I've read them all. I have the whole series at home."

"All of them?" He sounds impressed.

"All of them. This one is my favorite." I pull a book off the shelf with a mouse on the front, standing on the bow of a sailing ship. He takes it from me, flipping it over to read the back. "But I would probably start with this one—it's kind of the one that started them all." I hand him another book, this one thinner than most of the others. "It doesn't matter what order you read them in since they're stand alone stories, but they'll all be connected to Redwall Abbey and Martin the Warrior."

"Martin the Warrior—is that the mouse with the sword?"

I smile. "One of them."

A woman walks briskly past the aisle, then stops and turns back. "Jaxon, there you are! Come on, it's time to go."

"Ok, Mom. Look, I found some books!" He sounds excited, and that makes me happy.

"That's great. Grab a couple and let's go."

She walks off and Jaxon looks up at me. "How many can I check out?"

"As many as you want, I think. But don't take them all, or you won't have any to get next time."

He smiles, collecting an armful and heading to the checkout at the front of the library. I watch him go, feeling like a kid again myself. I loved reading those books.

Storytime passes in a blur. The kids are excited and engaged, and I have even more fun than I did with the parachute. Every day that I spend at the library I feel more and more sure that I want to work with children. I still don't know in what capacity, though. Do I want to be a children's librarian? A teacher? A speech pathologist? An internet search a few weeks ago made me realize there are hundreds of careers focused on children, and the list was more than a little daunting. But I don't have to figure all that out right now. It's enough to know I'm headed in the right direction.

As I walk to my car after storytime, my phone alarms in my pocket.

JASON
Got any plans on Saturday?

AMIE
I've got a date with my laundry but that's about it

JASON
Lucky laundry

I grin, unlocking my car. Sticking my phone back in my purse, I drop it in the backseat so I won't be tempted to check my messages while driving.

It only takes about ten minutes to get home from the library, but my phone rings like a slot machine the entire drive. Jason obviously has a lot to say. I pull up in front of my house and cut the engine, reaching for my purse so I can finally see what he's got up his sleeve for Saturday. Whatever it is, I know I'll be game.

> JASON
>
> If you're free Saturday, want to help me with some recipes for the competition?
>
> I figured we could try out a few different entrée ideas
>
> And make some sides
>
> And then go on a picnic with all the food

Hmm. A day spent cooking with Jason? Yes, please. I'm already planning to agree, but his next message seals the deal.

> JASON
>
> I can teach you how to make macarons...

Cheater. He knows my weakness.

> AMIE
>
> Alright, I'm in. What time?

> JASON
>
> Come over whenever, I'll be cooking all day

Chapter 21

"What are we making?" I ask, washing my hands. It's just after ten in the morning, and I've already gone for a run, taken a shower, and eaten enough breakfast to satisfy even the hungriest of Hobbits, thanks to my mom. Jason, on the other hand, hasn't shaved, hasn't showered, and looks like he rolled out of bed and threw on the first pair of clothes he could find. I mean, he still looks great—in a careless, scruffy-looking, hot-guy-next-door kind of way.

"I'm thinking of making some classic kid food but with a gourmet twist."

"Like what?"

"Mac'n cheese, chicken nuggets, corn dogs—you know, the kind of food kids like to eat. But I want to use artisan cheeses, balsamic marinated chicken—that kind of stuff."

"Huh. I never would have thought of doing that."

He starts pulling dishes out of the cupboard. "That's actually how I got started cooking."

"Really?"

"Yeah. I had all these favorite foods growing up, but they

lacked any adult sophistication." He grins. "Frozen fish sticks just aren't the same at twenty-two as they are at twelve."

I smile. "I would imagine not."

"So I started experimenting with different flavors and ingredients." He tosses me an apron. "Here, you'll probably need this. Though maybe not as much as you needed the coveralls."

He puts me to work shredding a bunch of different cheeses, most of whose names I can't pronounce.

"Tell me—what was the first thing you made more adult-ish?" I ask after a few minutes.

"Grilled cheese sandwiches."

"Grilled cheese sandwiches?"

"And tomato soup."

I shake my head. "Can't get more kid than that, I guess. How did you change it?"

He shrugs. "Just used more grown-up ingredients. Sourdough bread, Swiss cheese, bacon... I added avocado, too. It was really good."

"And the soup?"

"I made a tomato basil bisque."

"Wow. That sounds fancy."

He laughs. "Not really. The first time, I just found a recipe online. It called for canned tomatoes and dried basil. But it was better than Campbell's soup. Eventually I made my own version, using fresh tomatoes and herbs, and cream instead of milk. It's still one of my favorites."

"Sounds delicious. You'll have to make it for me sometime." I finish shredding the cheese and rub my hands on my apron. "All right, what's next?"

"Noodles."

"You're going to make your own noodles?"

He raises an eyebrow. "You don't think I'd use *box* pasta, did you?"

"Um... yes?"

I laugh when he throws a towel at me.

"Ok, Mr. Fancy Pants, let's make some pasta. How can I help?"

"Put some water on to boil and come over here. You can help roll the dough."

I fill a stock pot with water and set it on the stove while Jason gathers ingredients. Watching him work in the kitchen is like watching an artist mixing paints. He adds a bit of this to a bit of that and mixes it for a while, then checks the taste and texture before moving on to the next step. I'm fascinated, wondering what it would be like to love something as much as Jason obviously loves cooking.

He finishes the pasta dough and pulls off a handful. "All right, we need to roll the dough into half-inch ropes. Like this."

The process reminds me of rolling out play doh as a kid. Jason's ropes are smooth and uniform, while mine are... not. They look more like a snake about to die of a dozen different tumors.

"Need a hand?" Jason asks, trying not to laugh.

"Does it really matter if they're the same thickness all the way through?" I grumble.

"Actually, it does. If the noodles aren't uniform, they won't cook at the same rate." He makes a face. "There aren't many things worse than mushy pasta."

I sigh. "Well, it's a lot harder than you make it look."

He chuckles. "Here, let me show you."

I step to the side, expecting him to take my place, but he shakes his head. "Go ahead and grab another piece of dough."

I grab a handful and roll it into a ball in my hands, then place it on the flour-dusted counter. Jason reaches around me and starts rolling the dough into a long, thin rope. I freeze, wondering if he heard me suck in my breath. My back is pressed against his chest, and I can smell the flour and oil that clings to his clothes. I tell myself to breathe, and force myself to focus on his hands and his voice—telling me to start in the middle and press evenly with both hands as I roll. The stubble on his chin scratches my cheek, and I turn my head a fraction to the side, unconsciously leaning into him.

Oh, dear.

Jason's hands still, and his face turns toward me. My heart is pounding so loudly in my chest I'm sure he can hear it, if he can't already feel it. He's so close I can see the tiny flecks of blue in his eyes as I look up at him. His eyes meet mine, and he doesn't look away. I'm frozen, not knowing what I should do or when he will move or whether or not I like being in this predicament.

His breath tickles my ear, and an involuntary shiver runs down my back. "That's how you do it," he murmurs, pulling his arms away.

I blink, and he steps back. I miss the warmth from his body almost immediately.

"Think you can manage that?" he asks.

"Sure." My voice sounds an octave too high, and I clear my throat, pretending I'm not on fire.

He grins and turns away, leaving me stunned and breathless, wondering what the heck just happened.

———

I manage to get a few ropes of pasta mostly even, but when it comes time to cut and roll them into shells I give up. Jason is much more adept at the task, despite his larger hands, so I leave it to him.

While the pasta cooks, he whips up the sauce, and I set out some bowls for us. Jason says we'll make a potato salad for the picnic, but mac 'n cheese is best eaten fresh and hot, so we're having it for lunch.

"Alright Ames, the moment of truth," he says, holding his fork aloft. "Don't spare my feelings—it has to be amazing."

I roll my eyes, because he *knows* it's going to be amazing. The smell alone has my salivary glands working overtime, and I can hardly wait to find out if it tastes as good as it smells.

It doesn't. It tastes *better*.

The first bite is creamy and delicious, with a tangy burst of flavor I wasn't expecting. I burn my mouth trying to eat the rest of it too quickly.

"Slow down, Ames," Jason laughs. "This is a taste test, not a speed competition."

"Sorry," I mumble. "You're just too good a cook."

"Thanks." He takes another bite and chews it slowly, deliberately. He shakes his head, not smiling.

"What?" I ask.

"I think it's too tangy. Kids don't like sharp cheeses as much as adults. I'll have to try some milder cheeses next time."

I don't know what the kids will think, but that was the best bowl of mac 'n cheese I've ever had in my life. I all but lick the bowl when I'm finished.

After cleaning up, we make a basic potato salad. Well, basic by Jason's standards, but I've never seen a potato salad with purple potatoes in it. By three o'clock it's done and chilling in the fridge, and we're ready to start on the macarons.

"Do you mind if I take a shower and get myself cleaned up first?" Jason asks.

An image of Jason—shirtless, with a towel wrapped around his waist—bursts upon my mind, and my face instantly heats up. I blink. "Um, no, of course not." I hesitate. "Do you want me to come back later?"

He rolls his eyes, untying his apron. "You don't have to go anywhere, Ames. It's not like I'm showering here in the kitchen. Sit down and relax, you've been on your feet since you got here."

He tosses the apron on the counter and heads out of the room, while I try *not* to think about him getting undressed.

I need a distraction.

Moving toward the sink, I start gathering the dirty dishes and piling them on one side. *Don't think about Jason. Don't think about Jason.*

I turn on the sink, hoping the noise will drown out my thoughts.

I rinse the smaller dishes and place them in the dishwasher, then start scrubbing the pots and pans. The bubbles remind me of the carwash, and the carwash makes me think about Jason. And thinking about Jason...

GAH! I close my eyes and lean against the counter, trying to clear my mind. I take a few deep breaths, focusing on the sound the air makes as it moves in and out of my lungs. *Whooooosh, whooooosh. Whooooosh, baby I'm yours...*

Wait, what?

Is... is Jason *singing?*

I mean, I know Jason *can* sing. We were in choir together in junior high, and we used to belt out songs in the car all the time. Heck, we were singing in the kitchen together just the other day. But I didn't know he sang in the shower. I cock my head to the side, trying to make out the song.

It's Adele. Jason is singing to Adele.

I grin—the big, cheek-splitting kind—and sing along from the sink. By the time I finish the song I'm nearly done with the dishes. I can't hear Jason anymore, but I keep humming as I work, occasionally breaking out in the chorus of whatever song I've wandered into. Jason comes in as I'm wiping the counters.

"Nice pipes," he teases.

I turn around and cross my arms, leaning against the counter. "You too, Adele."

He blinks. "You could hear me?" He sounds surprised, rather than embarrassed.

I nod and he chuckles, tying the apron around his waist. "Well, glad I could entertain you while you did the dishes." He winks, walking toward me to retrieve the bowl I just finished drying. I catch the scent of citrus and patchouli, and the smell makes me pause—it's like comfort and desire and laughter and love all rolled into one delicious cologne. He smiles at me, and though his face is still unshaven, his damp hair is carefully swept to the side. I look away before my thoughts collide with trouble once more.

He grabs the bowl and a whisk and turns to face me. "Are you ready for this, Ames?" he asks, one eyebrow raised.

"Bring it on, Henley."

He barks a laugh and starts opening cupboards. "All right,

the first thing about making macarons is that you've got to whip the egg whites *just* right. Too much and they get really dense; not enough and you won't get the dome shape you want."

"Whip the egg whites. Got it."

I sift together the almond flour and sugar while he works on the eggs. When they're both ready, he starts folding them together, explaining the importance of working out the lumps as he gently mixes the ingredients. His face is so focused, his eyes so intense that I can't help but smile. In all the years I've known him, I never would have pictured Jason as a chef. But seeing him now, seeing how passionate he is and how happy it makes him, I can't picture him as anything else. He glances up at me and stops.

"What?"

"Nothing. Just watching the master at work."

He smiles—not the playful grin he's been throwing at me all day, but a real smile. The kind that touches not only his eyes and his devilish dimple, but the kind that starts in his heart and feels like a hug.

I love Jason's smile.

He places the dough in a pastry bag while I line a baking sheet with parchment paper. When the macarons are piped and ready to go, Jason taps the tray on the counter a few times.

"What's that for?"

"It helps get the bubbles out, so they'll cook evenly. Now they have to dry for a bit before we bake them."

We mix together the filling—raspberry, because it's my favorite—and pop the macarons in the oven. Jason pulls out some leftover fried chicken from the day before, and I wash and hull some strawberries to go along with our picnic. When the macarons are done and cool, we fill them and place them in a container. I look at Jason and grin.

"I can't wait to try them," I say.

"Me neither. Are you ready to get going?"

I nod.

"Great, I'm starving. Let's go."

Chapter 22

The late afternoon sun slants across the street as we walk across to the park, tiny golden flecks floating in the air like broken bits of summer. "Where do you want to go?" I ask.

"Anywhere. You choose."

I follow the path that winds up the hill and around an outcropping of massive trees. I've always loved Manito Park. It's huge and green and peaceful, with different gardens and trails and walkways where you can wander and get lost. Vegas has a few nice parks, but it's so hot for most of the year that the grass is parched and brown, despite the amount of watering they do. It's not like that here. Towering pine trees reach heavenward as we climb up the hill, skirting around the hedges and benches that dot the landscape. We follow a little trail that winds through the woods for a bit, until we reach a huge, rolling lawn overlooking the rose garden. I stop right in the middle of it.

"This looks good."

I spread out the blanket and Jason gets things unpacked. He holds out a bottled water, and I take it with a smile.

"So, should we start with dessert?" he asks, rubbing his hands together.

"Definitely."

He pulls out the container of macarons and pops off the lid, holding it out to me. "Ladies first," he says.

I pull one out and hold it up to my nose, breathing in the sweet scent. I nibble at it, then take a bite.

"Mmmm. Delicious."

Jason grins. "Not bad for your first try."

"You and I both know you did most of the work," I say, reaching for another one.

We fall into a comfortable silence, and I watch him while we eat. His cheeks and chin are scruffy, but not like he's growing a beard. More like he's been too lazy to shave for a couple days. He sees me looking at him and raises an eyebrow. "What?"

"You haven't shaved," I say, reaching for his face. "And you've got crumbs in your scruff." I brush my fingers against his jaw, just enough to feel the prickle and dislodge the crumbs before withdrawing my hand. Derek was always clean shaven.

"It's the weekend," he says. "I'm allowed to be lazy." He glances down at my bare legs. "And so are you, apparently. Ow!"

I smack him on the shoulder. "I shaved this morning, I'll have you know. Smart aleck." I shake my head, but I can't help the grin that pulls on my cheeks.

We eat everything backwards, starting with dessert. It's all delicious, but the chicken at the end of the meal has me licking my fingers.

"Dang, Jason. Your cooking is better than my mom's." I point a finger at him. "But don't tell her I said that."

He grins. "Thanks. But this was a team effort, you know. You're not so bad yourself. Definitely a better cook than a mechanic."

I toss my empty water bottle at him. He laughs, catching it and setting it down beside him. The tips of the clouds are starting to turn pink and I lean back on my elbows, looking up at the sky as it slowly catches fire. Jason leans back too, and we sit in silence together for a long time.

As the dusk settles around us, I glance over at Jason. He's looking off into the distance, smiling to himself. After a minute he turns his head and catches my eye.

"What are you grinning at?" I ask.

"I was just thinking about high school. All the stuff we did together."

"Like swiping Brandon's keys and moving his car in the middle of the night so he'd think someone stole it?"

Jason tips his head back, filling the warm night air with the sound of his laugh. "Oh man. I'd forgotten about that."

I smile at the memory. "He was so freaked out when he got up in the morning and saw it was gone. I'm surprised you didn't hear him yelling from your house. And then when I finally got him calmed down enough to tell him it was all a joke and his car was safely down McClellan street?"

"You were grounded for a month, weren't you?"

"Yeah." I lie back, looking up at the velvet sky. "But it was worth it. Brandon needed more excitement in his life."

Jason chuckles again, and I find myself thinking of ways to keep him laughing. "What was it you were thinking of?" I ask.

"Hm?"

"About high school."

"Oh." Suddenly his smile is gone. "Nothing, really."

Whatever it was, it certainly doesn't *sound* like nothing. I prop myself up on my elbows so I can see his face better. He's absently picking at the grass, drawing the blades through his long, calloused fingers. Without looking at me, he says, "Do you remember the homecoming game your junior year?"

Oh. *Oh.*

That's what he's thinking about?

I swallow. "Yeah, I remember."

One corner of his mouth pulls up in a half-grin, his dimple just barely a dent in his scruffy cheek. "You were so mad at me."

I sit all the way up, crossing my legs underneath me. "Can you blame me? I didn't know what got into you that night—at first I thought you were high or something. But then I found out you were doing it just for fun. That's what made me angry."

"I remember." He stops pulling at the grass and looks over at me. "Do you?"

There's a look in his eyes—one I've only ever seen once before, in all the years I've known him. It's the same look he wore six years ago, on the night of the homecoming game my junior year, the night we're talking about right now. Jason was a senior, and one of the most popular guys in school. All the girls were wild about him, especially because he was never really attached. He never had a steady girlfriend. Oh, he went out with plenty of girls, and he broke plenty of hearts, but it was never on purpose. Not until that night, anyways.

You see, Jason never kissed the girls he went out with. Crazy, right? He told me once that his first kiss was Emily Wheelwright in eighth grade, and it was so wet and awkward that he vowed not to kiss another girl until he graduated from high school. I laughed at him back then, but he was serious, and Jason was always true to his word. He had a lot of fun flirting and teasing, holding hands and taking girls out, but he never kissed a single one. I would have known about it if he did, even if he didn't tell me about it himself. All the girls at school knew that Jason Henley didn't kiss his dates, and they *all* wanted to crow to their classmates that *they* were the one to make him break his vow.

Well, all that changed the night of the homecoming game. I was there with Tara, of course, and Jason was there with some of his other friends. The bleachers were packed—it seemed like our entire school had come out to see us get creamed by North Central. By the middle of the third quarter we were losing by thirty points, and most of the students were looking for entertainment away from the field.

And boy, did they find it.

"Why were you so mad at me?"

Jason's voice jerks me back to the present. He's still looking at me the same way as before, searching for something in my face he can't seem to find.

I draw a slow breath and blow it out again, forcing myself not to relive the emotions of that night. "You were being a jerk." My voice comes out quiet, and I clear my throat to speak more loudly. "Kissing all those girls, knowing they all had crushes on you."

"Why did you care?" He starts picking at the grass again, avoiding my eyes.

"Why did *you* care is the better question. Why did you do it, Jason? And don't tell me it was to find out who the best kisser was—I still don't believe you actually cared about that."

He flashes me a grin, and my heart nearly stops. "Some of them really were good," he says.

I shove him playfully in the shoulder, and he laughs, leaning away from me but coming back to rest his shoulder against mine. My heart shifts into high gear at the casual touch.

"I told you why I did it, Ames," he says, looking sideways at me. "That night. Do you remember?"

"You did?"

"Yeah." It's too dark to tell for sure, but his neck and ears are looking awfully pink. "When you dragged me behind the stands and yelled at me for kissing all those girls, do you remember what I said?"

His face is so close, only a breath away from mine, that I can hardly keep my scattered thoughts on the conversation. "You said..."

"I said I figured it was the only way I'd ever get to kiss the girl I really cared about."

"But you didn't care about any of those girls."

"Not the ones I kissed, no."

"Not the ones...? Jason, you kissed every girl in school."

He smirks at me, and that maddening dimple of his reappears. "Not *every* girl."

Now I really can't breathe. And I can't think. All I know is that if I lean in just a bit, I can press my lips to his and find out what all those other girls did about the way Jason kisses.

And suddenly what he's saying—what he's *really* saying— crashes into my consciousness like a wrecking ball.

Jason had feelings for me in high school. Judging from our current conversation and the way he's looking at me, he *still* has feelings for me.

But what's even more crazy is the realization that the way I feel right now is the same I felt back then, too. I just didn't know what to call it. Racing heart. Sweaty palms. Shallow breathing. It can only mean one thing.

I'm in love with Jason Henley.

Chapter 23

My first kiss was Ernest Lockhart my sophomore year. I'd been waiting for him to kiss me for weeks, but he was so shy and nervous I finally realized he never would, so I kissed him. It was a simple, anticlimactic kiss, and I remember going home that night wondering what all the fuss was about.

But that's not what it's like kissing Jason.

Kissing Jason is like lighting a firework and swallowing it whole. It lights up my insides, burning through my fear and doubt and worry until all I can think about is the feel of his lips against mine.

I don't know who actually kissed who, but Jason is the first to pull away. He looks at me with such tenderness and wonder that I want to cry, until suddenly his eyes widen with a look that says oh-crap-what-just-happened.

I'm probably wearing the same look.

He sits back, bringing his knees up so he can rest his arms on them, then drops his head, blowing out his breath. I sit back, too, trying to stop the world—and my insides—from spinning. "That was... unexpected," I say in a shaky breath.

"You're telling me," he says, his voice muffled.

I wait, wondering if he's going to say something—anything —about what just happened. What did he think about kissing me? How did it feel? Did he like it? I close my eyes, growing more and more anxious as I wait for him to say something so I'll know how to react myself.

Wait.

My thoughts screech to a halt as I realize what I'm doing. I just shared the most amazing kiss with the most amazing guy ever, and I'm actually *waiting for him to tell me* how to feel or how to react to what just happened?

It's pathetic and ironic and wrong on so many levels, not to mention exactly what I've been trying to teach myself *not* to do.

"Amie, I—"

"Wait." I take a deep breath and turn to face him. "Whatever you're about to say, please don't say it." He frowns, and those two little dents appear between his eyebrows. "It's not that I don't want to hear what you have to say. Trust me, I do. But as I was sitting here, I realized that I was waiting for *you* to say something first, because then *I* could decide how to think or feel about it, too."

Understanding dawns on his face. "Oh man."

I rub a hand across my forehead, trying to focus. "This is all new to me, Jason. I've spent my whole life going along with whatever I was told to think or feel, taking cues from those around me so I'd know how I should react. But knowing that about myself, I'm trying to change. I *want* to change. I want to make up my own mind about things, and plan for my *own* future."

He nods. "That makes sense." He takes a deep breath and blows it out, running a hand up through his hair. "So, if you don't want me to say anything about what just happened," he says, looking at me anxiously, "do you mind telling me *your* thoughts?"

The left side of his mouth is quirked up just enough to make a tiny dent in his cheek, scattering my thoughts like a well-thrown bowling ball.

"Uh... yeah. I mean, no. No."

"No? Why not?"

My cheeks burn, remembering the fire that spread through my insides when he kissed me. "I guess... I'm still trying to make sense of it myself."

"Oh."

"I mean, you just broke up with Veronica, and my fiancé just broke up with me. Who's to say we're not just lonely, you know? On the rebound, or whatever."

His eyes narrow. "You really think that?"

My gut twists nervously at the accusation in his voice. I don't. Not really. But instead of shaking my head, I shrug.

He watches me for a minute, but I can't meet his eyes. Finally he looks away. The silence stretches between us as the air cools, both in temperature and tension. I shiver, wishing I'd brought my jacket.

Jason looks up at the sky, his face an unreadable mask. "I guess we should call it a night," he says. "Are you ready to go?"

"Sure."

Jason packs up the food and the dishes while I fold up the blanket. I tip my head back, looking up at the stars in the inky blue-black sky.

"We should head up Mt. Spokane sometime," Jason says, breaking into my thoughts. "It's so dark you can see the Milky Way from up there."

"Really?"

"Yeah."

I look skyward again. "I'd like that."

We trek back across the park, content to walk in silence as the crickets serenade us from the bushes. I wonder what he's thinking, and steal glances at him every so often. He seems deep in thought, but not angry or anxious. Is he thinking about the kiss, too?

Back at his house, I set the blanket on the counter. "Today was fun," I say, immediately feeling awkward. Ugh. I'm not used to feeling awkward around Jason.

He smiles. "Yeah, it was. Thanks for helping me with the food."

"Sure. Thanks for teaching me how to make macarons. I don't think I'll be trying it on my own anytime soon, but it was fun."

A pregnant pause follows my words. "Um, I guess I'll see you later then," I say, heading for the door.

"Amie, wait."

I freeze, my pulse shooting into the triple digits faster than a Las Vegas summer.

"I know you said you don't want to hear what I have to say about what happened tonight," he says slowly, "at least, not yet. And I completely respect that. But I do have a request."

I swallow. "Ok."

He rubs a hand across the back of his neck, squinting at me. "Can you promise me that you won't go back to Vegas until we've had a chance to talk about it?"

"Oh. Sure." I smile nervously at him, and he seems to relax. Classes don't start until the end of August, and I'm not heading back for another month. That gives me plenty of time to figure out how I feel about what happened.

Right?

Chapter 24

Things are awkward and tense between Jason and I for the next few days. For the most part, we both try to pretend like nothing happened. Which is kind of like pretending it's the middle of summer when you're up to your knees in snow.

When I'm *not* being weird and awkward with Jason, I'm thinking about him and the kiss we shared. I vacillate between blowing it off as a rebound-rendezvous and considering it a confession of undying love. Ugh. When did things with Jason get so complicated?

I send him a text when I get to the library for my shift on Tuesday.

AMIE

> Want to go pick up the Bug with me this afternoon? 😎

JASON

> Thanks, but I've got stuff I have to do after work. Bring it by later, though. I want to see.

AMIE

Will do

I'm distracted during storytime, wondering if he really does have things to do or if he's just avoiding me. I was afraid to talk about the kiss with Jason at the park, but now I wish I would have just let him say what he was going to say. Anything is better than all this wondering.

Despite my soap opera love-life, I enjoy my time with the kids. I read *Bruce's Big Storm* to the half dozen preschoolers that show up, and afterward we all take hands and stretch ourselves out, forming a human chain like the animals do in the book. The children giggle and shriek as we wiggle and weave around the rug. We have so much fun I hate to leave, but I'm anxious to pick up the check and finally get my dream car.

Jack Stapleton is bent over one of the jewelry cases when I go in, but he looks up when he hears the bell above the door.

"Ah, Miss Cunningham. Be right with you."

He locks up the jewelry case and heads to the back office, returning a few minutes later with an unsealed envelope. "There you are," he says, handing it to me with a smile.

I pull the check out of the envelope and look at it. $18,600 made out to Amelia Cunningham. More than enough to buy the Volkswagen *and* get it outfitted with a leopard print interior. I place the check back in the envelope and put it in my purse, smiling so big my face hurts.

"Thank you so much," I say, holding out my hand. He shakes it.

"My pleasure, Miss Cunningham. Say hi to your dad for me."

I deposit the check in the bank on the way downtown, my excitement growing exponentially the nearer I get to Benny's Auto Sales. All my life I've wanted a Volkswagen Beetle, and I can't believe I'm finally going to get one. It's not baby blue, and it only has a sunroof instead of a convertible top, but it's a *Bug*. My inner child is squealing in delight.

I turn the corner, and the first stab of disappointment hits me. It's not up on the lift anymore. But that's ok, they probably switch those cars out on a regular basis, right? I scan the lot as I pull in to park, hoping that it's somewhere out of sight.

Please be here, please be here.

Roberto comes out of the office just as I get out of my car. "Miss Cunningham," he says, walking over to shake my hand. "What brings you in? Are you having any trouble with the car?"

"No, not really." I look around, trying to spot the creamy gray fenders of the Beetle. "I'm actually here to see if the Volkswagen Beetle is still available."

"I'm sorry, no. We sold it last week."

Disappointment lands in my gut like an anvil. I hadn't considered that it wouldn't be available. "Darn. Well, ok. Do you have any others?"

"Beetles? No. But we have a couple Jettas if you have your heart set on a Volkswagen."

"Only if it's a Beetle."

"Sorry."

The sting of disappointment is sharp, like getting a C on a paper you thought you had aced. I climb back into my car completely deflated.

I feel like Eeyore all the way home, but instead of pulling

up at the curb, I go around the corner and park in front of Jason's house. He opens the door when I'm halfway up the walk—he must have seen me from the window.

"Roberto said the Beetle sold last week," I say glumly, stopping on the porch.

He steps back without a word, holding the door open for me. We sit down on his couch and I stare dejectedly at the wall.

"Do you want to see if there's another Beetle available somewhere else?" he asks.

"Only if it's a baby blue convertible."

He frowns. "That one wasn't baby blue, or a convertible."

I huff. "I know." He doesn't say anything else, and I lean back against the couch, resting my head on his shoulder.

"Want to watch a show?"

I shrug, which he obviously takes for a yes because he flips on the tv. A few clicks later and he lands on Food Network. Figures.

The show features several different hosts who sit around a kitchen and talk. They take turns making crazy complicated recipes that would never fly in a real house—I mean, who has time for that kind of stuff?—but Jason eats it up.

"You know, I would love to sit around with a bunch of chefs and talk food," he says.

"I would love to sit around with a bunch of chefs and *eat* food," I say, my mouth watering at the spicy apple dessert being showcased. Jason grins.

"I'll make you food anytime you want, Ames," he says, planting a kiss on the top of my head. My heart stutters, then pounds like a bass drum in my ears.

How can he do that? Does he know what that does to me?

Does it mean anything to him? Do I *want* it to mean anything to him? My thoughts turn once again to the kiss we shared in the park. Has Jason revisited it a thousand times, like I have? Has he wondered what it would be like to kiss me again, to wrap his arms around me and hold me tight enough that I'll never want him to let me go? I turn my head and raise my eyes to his face. He looks at me for a long moment, and my eyes dart to his lips. I tip my chin up, watching to see what he'll do.

He leans down, slowly, his eyes never leaving mine. The closer he gets the faster I breathe, still unsure whether I want this or not, whether it's real or not. But I can see that Jason wants it. I see it burning in his eyes as he reaches up and gently cups my cheek with his hand.

"Have you figured out how you feel about what happened last week?" he asks.

"I'm working on it," I say, my voice as soft as his. He looks at my mouth, gently tracing my lips with his thumb. I close my eyes.

His phone alarms half a second later, and I snap my eyes open. Jason sits up and reaches for his phone on the coffee table. I take a shaky breath, trying to gather my scattered thoughts.

"Five o'clock," he murmurs, glancing at the screen.

Was it an alarm? Does he have an appointment? Does he have a *date*? The thought makes my stomach clench.

I sit up, clearing my throat. "What's at five o'clock?" I say, my voice more steady than I feel.

"I'm making dinner for my folks. Trying out another entrée recipe for the competition."

"Oh, cool. So you're going to their house?"

He shakes his head. "No, they're coming here. That was my alarm to start working on dinner."

"Got it," I say, pulling myself up. I manage to smile semi-normally. "Well, thanks for commiserating with me."

"Sure." He reaches up, rubbing the back of his neck. The motion is one I'm starting to recognize as something he does when he's anxious or upset. "You want to stay?" he asks, his brow raised. "You can help me with the meal. And stay for dinner. My parents would love to see you again."

"Are you sure? I wouldn't be in the way?"

"You're never in the way, Ames. Come on," he says, grabbing my hand and pulling me out of the room.

For one wild, brief moment I picture him leading me into the kitchen, pressing me against the counter, and kissing me. The image sends shivers shooting through me, and I shake my head, dislodging the thought.

He releases my hand when we reach the kitchen, heading straight for the fridge. "We made mac'n cheese before, but I think we need to try something a little more universal—something I know everyone loves."

"And that is... ?"

He grins, placing ingredients on the counter. "We're making pizza."

"Oh, good call! But aren't you worried about the toppings? Kids can be really picky about what's on their pizza."

"Don't worry, I'm not putting any pineapple on it," he smirks. "Besides, as long as it's pizza, I figure the kids will at least give it a try, right?"

I nod. "So where do we start?"

"All good pizza starts with a good crust."

He starts mixing things together and talking me through

the process—letting the yeast foam up in the bowl while he blends together the flour and seasonings. Once the dough is formed, he covers it to let it rest.

"Are the tomatoes for the sauce?" I ask, picking up a Roma from the counter.

"No, but if we *were* making a red sauce they would be. Haven't we been through this before? *Everything* has to be from scratch, Ames. It's better that way."

"I'm surprised you didn't grind your own wheat for the flour, then."

He grins. "I thought about it. Here—" he sets a bowl of basil sprigs in front of me. "Start pulling off the leaves. If any of them are spotted or brown, toss them."

We make a classic margherita pizza and pop it in the oven, just as there's a knock on the front door. Jason is still mixing up the pesto, so I offer to answer it.

I open the door to find Paula and Brian standing on the porch. Their faces register surprise for only half a second.

"Amie! Are you joining us tonight?" Jason's mom asks, coming inside to hug me.

"If that's ok with you."

"Of course!" She smiles, the skin around her eyes wrinkling while a dent forms in her cheek. It's clear which parent Jason gets his dimple from.

"Nice to see you again, Amie," Mr. Henley says, his smile just as warm as his wife's.

"Thanks, you too."

The three of us walk into the kitchen together, and Jason looks up from his mixing bowl. "Hey Mom, hey Dad, glad you could make it."

"Smells delicious," Mrs. Henley says. "How can I help?"

"It's almost ready, but you and Amie can set the table if you'd like."

I spread out a table cloth while Jason's mom brings over the plates. "We didn't get a chance to chat at the barbecue," she says. "What are you doing these days? Are you in school?"

I smooth out the creases in the fabric, helping it to lay flat. "Yes, I'm studying at UNLV."

"Oh, that's right, Jason said you were living in Vegas now. Do you like it there?"

I smile. "I do."

"I hear it gets pretty hot," Mr. Henley pipes in.

"It does. But the winters are amazing. They make it worth the summers."

"Alright everyone," Jason calls, pulling the pizza from the oven. "Take your seats, we're ready to eat."

We gather around the table while Jason brings the pizza over. It smells heavenly.

"Where's the meat?" Mr. Henley asks, eyeing the pesto drizzle with suspicion.

"It's a margherita pizza, Dad," Jason says. "There is no meat."

Mr. Henley grunts, and Jason dishes everyone up. I take some salad and pass it to his mom.

"So, what are you studying in school?" she asks.

"I'm in the middle of switching majors, actually," I say. "I'm hoping to start classes in Early Childhood Education this fall."

"That's what I studied," she says fondly.

"You did?"

"Yes, ages ago. I just wanted to be a mom, really, but my parents felt an education was important, so I went to college. The way I saw it, if I ended up not getting married and having a family, being a kindergarten teacher might be the next best thing."

"What were you studying before?" Mr. Henley asks, his mouth full of pizza. Paula clucks her tongue at him.

"Political Science," I say, looking at my plate. "My ex-fiancé was a lawyer."

An awkward half-beat follows my words, and Paula lays a hand on my arm. "We were so sorry to hear about that, Amie," she says gently. "Are you doing all right?"

"Thanks. I'm ok. Glad I came home and ran into this guy," I say, pointing my fork at Jason. He smiles.

"That makes both of us," he says.

Dinner is delicious, and the company and conversation refreshing. Jason's parents banter and tease one another, and it reminds me of the way Jason banters with me. I keep stealing glances at him, trying to sort through the tangled web of thought and emotion inside me. But every time I catch his eye, he flashes me a smile and that dimple scatters my thoughts like a well-aimed grenade.

Jason walks me home after his parents leave. The night air is alive with the chorus of crickets and frogs, serenading us from the park across the street. It's a beautiful night, so instead of going straight home, we sit down on a bench by the pond and watch the reflection of the moon on the water. It shimmers in the dark, sliding across the ripples that dance on the surface.

"Do you miss Las Vegas?"

Jason's question comes out of the blue, but I don't really have to think about it. "Yes," I say, "I do."

"What do you miss about it?"

I turn to look at him in the dark, but it's only just light enough to make out the outline of the features on his face.

"Have you ever been to Vegas?" I ask.

"No."

I look out over the pond, imagining the fountains in front of the Bellagio. "The city is alive, at least at its center. There's always music and lights and stuff going on, whenever you want it. That's what most people love about Vegas."

"But not you."

It's not a question, and I smile in the darkness. "No. But I do love it. I love the huge expanse of it all, and the white-blue color of a hundred-degree sky. I love the spiky little bushes and the terra cotta rooftops. I love how varied and eclectic the shopping is—you can find anything you want in Vegas. I love the palm trees. I love the sunsets. And I love the monsoons."

"Almost makes me want to visit," he murmurs.

"You should," I say without thinking.

"Tempting. But if I come to visit, I might not want to leave."

His words sink in as my heart starts racing. I glance at his face, trying to make out his expression, but it's too dark.

"Why wouldn't you want to leave?" I murmur, knowing I might not be ready for his answer.

"Let's just say there's something in Vegas more appealing than anything I've got up here."

My pulse thrums in my ears, wondering if he's saying what I think he's saying. "What about the carwash? What about your dad?"

He looks right into my eyes. "If there was a reason for me to go to Vegas and stay, I'd talk to my dad tonight. I'd call him right now."

"You would?"

"I would. Of course," he says, and I can hear the smile in

his voice, "before I can talk to my dad, there's another conversation I need to have first." His tone turns thoughtful. "Are you ready to talk about the picnic yet?"

"I'm getting closer," I say, swallowing, "but not tonight."

He reaches up, brushing the hair away from my face. "Tomorrow?" he asks.

"Maybe."

"Then I'll see you tomorrow," he says, standing. "Goodnight, Ames."

He waves and heads off down the street, leaving me sitting alone on the bench, wishing I knew what to say to him.

———

The next two weeks are some of the happiest I can remember. Storytime at the library has become second nature, and I know all the kids and their families by name. I've always wanted to try yoga, so I sign up for a class a few mornings a week. My mom only talks about Brandon's wedding 95 percent of the time, and the rest of my days are filled with fun and laughter and food and Jason.

Jason.

I need to tell him how I feel.

Part of me panics. How do I tell him how I feel when I don't really even know myself? I've been avoiding telling Tara about the kiss for the same reason I wouldn't let Jason say anything that night—I don't want my feelings on the matter tainted by someone else's opinion. But the fact that I get butterflies every time I think about kissing Jason is enough for me to realize some of my feelings, at least. I guess I can start with that.

Just before I climb into bed one night, my phone rings. For a split second my heart soars, thinking it's Jason, but the number isn't one I recognize. I frown.

"Hello?"

"Hello, is this Amie Cunningham?"

"Yes, this is Amie."

"Hi Amie, it's Jen from the library."

I pace across the room, suddenly nervous. "Hey Jen, what's up?"

"I'm just calling to let you know that we won't be needing your help with storytime anymore."

The air whooshes out of me, like I've been punched in the gut. They don't need me anymore?

"Melissa has been taken off bedrest and is anxious to get her hours in before her maternity leave starts in the fall. I hope you don't mind, but since your position was only temporary anyway, we've given your shifts back to her."

She pauses, waiting for a response.

"Oh," I manage at last. "Ok."

"You didn't do anything wrong," she says quickly, "it was nothing like that. Kenneth wanted me to assure you that you've been great, and we'd be happy to have you back in the future, if a position opens up."

"Right. Yeah, of course. Ok. Thanks."

I hang up the phone, falling limply onto the bed. The library was my lifeline—the one thing that I had discovered about myself all on my own; the one thing that was keeping me going, pushing me forward into an unknown future.

My eyes are already pricking as I pick up my phone again and swipe to text Jason.

AMIE

You still up?

I curl up on the bed, holding my phone as I wait for him to reply. But he doesn't, and I fall asleep wondering if Sylvia with the pink hair from Montana was right, or if I really am destined to be alone, unwanted and unneeded, for the rest of my life.

Chapter 25

I wake up in the morning to a series of chimes from my phone, one after another.

JASON

Dang, my phone died

Everything ok?

Sorry I missed your text ☹

I was up though—I'm always up late. You should have just come over

Seriously, come over anytime

Call me

My lips pull into a halfhearted smile, imagining the look on Jason's face. He always was a worrier.

AMIE

Just woke up. Everything's fine, I just wanted to talk

His reply is waiting for me by the time I get back from brushing my teeth.

JASON

What about? I'm all ears

I groan. He probably thinks I wanted to talk about the picnic, since he brought it up again a few days ago. But I'm not ready to tell him how I feel. I need more time to figure out what to say to him, *and* what to do about it. Too bad time isn't something I have a lot of—I'm supposed to leave for Vegas in less than two weeks.

Vegas. It seems like a lifetime ago when I was there. As hesitant as I was to come home for the summer, I think I'm even more hesitant to leave. What will I find when I get back? So many of my memories in Vegas are tied up with Derek. Will it be painful? Will it be a relief? And what about Jason?

What about Jason?

I've been asking myself that question ever since the kiss. How do I feel about Jason? My initial reaction was to laugh off any idea of romantic attachment, because he's *Jason.* One of my best friends. He knows me better than anyone, except maybe Tara. He's seen me at my best, my worst, and everywhere in between. I've never thought of him romantically before, but I'd be lying if I said I wasn't thinking about Jason romantically *now.* Every time my mind recalls the warmth of his lips and the prickle of his cheek against mine, it's like being hit with a flamethrower. The sparks during the picnic ignited something deep inside me, something that burns in my very soul. It's not just attraction, or the headiness of newfound romance. It's something solid, something real, something I can't deny is there, even if I wanted to.

I sit on the bed and send Jason a reply.

AMIE

My temp job at the library ended abruptly and
I was feeling kind of down

JASON

What happened? Did someone else get
pooped on?

I laugh out loud. Leave it to Jason to lighten things up and make me laugh. He was always good at cheering me up.

JASON

Sorry about the library. I know how much you
enjoyed working with the kids

AMIE

Thanks

JASON

I'm going over to my parents house this
afternoon—want to come with me?

AMIE

Sure, what time?

JASON

I'll pick you up at 2

———

The Henley's home is warm and inviting, just like they are. Jason helps his dad with a few projects around the house, while Paula and I visit. We stay for a few hours, but they have plans with friends for dinner and soon it's time to go.

"I'm so glad you came home this summer," Paula says, hugging me goodbye.

"I'm glad I came home, too."

"It's been good for Jason," she says more quietly, glancing at her husband and son, talking about the carwash a few feet away. My insides flip.

"You think so?"

"I know so," she says with feeling. "He lights up whenever you're around. I haven't seen him so happy in a long time."

She gives me a warm smile as we head out the door. Her words echo in my mind as we climb into Jason's truck, confirming to me that I need to tell him how I feel, to open up my still-wounded heart and lay it bare in front of him.

"So, have you figured out which recipes you'll use for the competition?" I ask, before my traitorous heart runs away with my mouth.

"Yup. I sent them in this morning—there's no changing my mind now."

I smile. "I'm proud of you, Jason. You're going to do awesome."

"Thanks. I owe it all to you, you know. I wouldn't be doing this without your encouragement and support."

"Actually, I believe you owe it all to Veronica. She was the mastermind behind all this."

He rolls his eyes as I laugh, before settling into a comfortable silence.

I argue with myself about talking to Jason the whole drive home, and all too soon Jason pulls into his driveway and we both get out. For a minute I think he's going to invite me inside, but then he jerks his head down the street.

"Walk with me."

We head down the sidewalk toward my parents' house, and after a few steps Jason takes my hand. My heart skitters at his touch, my mind racing through all the reasons I wasn't going to tell him how I feel.

I can't recall a single one.

Jason's hand is warm, his fingers gently intertwining with mine. Our steps slow as we get closer to my house, until we stop altogether, and Jason turns toward me. His eyes study my face, his gaze finally landing on my lips. Desire bursts inside of me, and I lean forward, closing my eyes.

"Amie?"

My eyes fly open, startled. Jason drops my hand and we both turn to look across the street. A dark Mercedes is parked along the curb, and a familiar figure is climbing out of it.

"Wow, it is you. I didn't recognize you at first. I thought I had the wrong address."

I blink, convinced that I'm seeing things. "Derek?"

"Hey baby." He shuts the car door and walks across the street. His eyes travel up and down as he comes toward us, taking in my messy blonde locks and low sneakers—no doubt as surprised by my appearance as I am about his. He walks right up to me, places a hand on my elbow, and bends down to kiss my cheek. "It's good to see you."

Jason stiffens beside me, but I'm still frozen with shock.

Derek laughs at my expression—a careful, practiced laugh. "I know this is a surprise, but I had to see you again. I've missed you, baby."

Jason clears his throat, snapping me out of my daze. "Amie, you ok?"

Derek looks at him with polite surprise, as if he's just now seeing him. "She's fine," he says, before I even open my mouth. He turns to me with a dazzling smile. "Just a bit surprised."

Jason's eyes narrow and he takes half a step forward, shifting his gaze back to me. "Amie?" he asks again. "You ok?"

I blink, trying to focus on him. His eyes are trained on mine, his look one of genuine concern. I swallow, wanting to reassure him.

"I'm fine. I just..." I turn to look up at Derek. Dang—was he always so tall? Suddenly I feel about the size of an oyster. "What are you doing here?" I ask.

"I came to see you," he says, picking up my hand—the one Jason was just holding—and bringing it to his lips. "It's been a miserable summer without you, Amie. I came to take you home and make it right again." He's still holding my hand, and he rubs his thumb across the back of my ring finger, smiling at me. I gently pull my hand away, folding my arms across my chest.

"This *is* my home, Derek," I say, thinking of the pink-haired lady on the plane. "Home is where my momma and her cooking is."

Derek lifts his brow in polite surprise, but Jason grins. "Darn right it is," he says. Derek looks down at him with some annoyance.

"I'm sorry, I don't think we've been introduced," he says, using his lawyer voice. He thrusts his hand out, creating a barrier between Jason and me.

"Derek Carter, Amie's fiancé."

"Former," Jason and I say together. My eyes dart to his face, my mouth pulling into a half-smile at the same moment as his. Derek looks between us, his eyes calculating.

"Yes, former," he says, pausing thoughtfully. "Because I was stupid enough to let her go," he adds after a moment. He looks at me—really looks at me—and my heart trips.

I've never seen that look on his face before. He's sorry. He's *actually* sorry.

"Yeah, that shows some pretty poor judgment on your part," Jason says, his jaw tight. "Since she's the most amazing woman you'll ever meet in your life."

I draw in a breath, watching Derek's face as he turns toward Jason. His eyes are guarded, but I know that lift and tilt to his chin. He's considering, calculating, wondering how best to proceed to get the outcome he wants. My gut twists nervously.

Suddenly his expression smooths out. "You're right. She is the most amazing woman I'll ever meet. Which is why I'm here, to beg her to take me back."

The idea of Derek begging for anything is so ridiculous I almost laugh, but his smile is more sincere than I've ever seen it before, and I don't want to hurt his feelings. I glance at Jason, who's looking anything but amused.

Derek smiles benignly at him. "I never did catch your name, but if you wouldn't mind, I'd like to speak with Amie alone." His look grows serious. "I have a lot to say, and much to apologize for."

Jason looks at me, and I nod. "It's all right, Jason. I'll be fine."

Derek flashes me a brilliant smile, and I let him take my hand. He kisses it again. Jason shoves his hands into his pockets, frowning.

"I guess I'll be going, then." He gives me a meaningful look. "Text me later?"

I nod, and he heads down the sidewalk, back to his house. Derek watches me watching Jason.

"I didn't know you had such good friends up here," he says, his words more a statement than a question.

"Jason was one of my best friends growing up," I say, lifting my chin defensively. "I haven't seen much of him since graduation, but we ran into each other when I first got home. We've been hanging out a lot."

"I see." Suddenly he smiles at me. "Come on. Let's get some dinner—we have a lot to talk about."

An uneasy feeling worms its way into my gut. "I don't know, Derek," I say. "Why don't we just talk here? My parents won't bother us. Or we can take a walk in the park." I gesture across the street.

He looks over at the pond and nods, as if he's considering it. But I know that look, and he's definitely not. "It looks like a nice park, but there's so much to tell you I think we'd be better off sitting down somewhere more private. Let me take you out—we'll go to the finest restaurant Spokane has to offer and I can tell you how sorry I am. I was wrong, Amie, so wrong. But I'm going to fix everything."

I want to believe he's sincere, but so much has happened, so much has *changed*. I've changed. And I don't know that I want Derek to "fix" that.

I look out across the park, watching as the breeze forces the leaves to dance in the trees. "You never called. You never texted me. If you have so much to tell me, why haven't you contacted me before now?"

"I didn't know what to say."

I turn back to look at him, laughing humorlessly. "You? Not know what to say?"

"I wanted to talk to you in person," he amends. "I was afraid you wouldn't answer the phone if I tried to call."

I can tell that he's waiting for me to assure him that yes, I would have answered the phone. But I don't. I don't know that I would have.

"Come on, baby, let's get something to eat. I'm starving."

I sigh. "Fine. But it doesn't mean anything. We're just going to talk."

"I know, baby, I know." But he smiles at me in triumph, and all I can think is how little he really *does* know.

Chapter 26

True to his form, Derek manages to find a five-star restaurant in a three-star town. "I didn't even know this place existed," I say as we walk through the front doors. Derek smiles—that arrogant, know-it-all smile I used to swoon over.

But I know better now.

Derek has a reservation, of course, and the maître d' shows us to a secluded table in an adjoining room. It's a posh little bistro that looks like it belongs on the west side, not here in Spokane. I feel strange and out of place—not only because I'm wearing jean shorts and a T-shirt when the place is clearly meant for suits and stilettos, but like I'm in a whole other world. A world where I don't belong. Derek—with his cufflinks and Mercedes and smooth-talking smile—belongs in this world, but not me. Why did I ever think I did? Why did I ever *want* to?

The waiter comes up with a bottle of wine to introduce himself. "May I interest you in this Cabarnet? It's a particularly robust vintage from France, and pairs well with most anything."

"No thanks—we'll have water with cucumber. And hold the ice."

I stare at Derek as the waiter bows and turns away, a strange feeling rising up inside me, something I've never really felt before. It's not anger. Or sadness. Not confidence, either. It's kind of a strange combination of all three, with a little rage thrown in for good measure.

The minute our waiter comes back with two glasses of cucumbered water, I sit up straight. "I'd like a Cherry Coke, please. With cream."

The waiter looks only mildly surprised, but Derek frowns. "Amie, you don't want that."

"Actually, I do." I look up at the waiter. "With *lots* of ice."

He nods and hurries away, and I look back at Derek. He's not frowning anymore, but he's not smiling, either.

"You're feeling a little rebellious, I see. The hair, the clothes. But it's all right. I understand."

Rebellious. Is that what he thinks this is? I smile, wondering what Jason would call it.

"What did you want to say to me, Derek?" I ask, flexing my confidence like new-found wings.

"I told you before—I'm sorry. I want to make things right."

"Yes, you said that. But what does that mean, exactly? How do you plan to make things right? You dumped me *two weeks* before our wedding, Derek. Do you have any idea how that crushed me? How humiliating that was?"

He twines his fingers together, leaning forward on the table. "I know. I'm sorry, baby."

I rub a hand across my forehead, closing my eyes. "Please stop calling me that."

He doesn't respond, and when I open my eyes he's watching me. His look is guarded, cautious. I've made him uneasy, and that's a first.

"You've changed," he says.

I lift my chin. "Glad you've noticed."

His lips turn up, but I wouldn't call it a smile. "And you've found yourself a nice little playboy too, it seems."

I blanch. "Jason is my friend."

"With benefits, right?" He takes a sip of water. "Don't worry. I'm not upset. There's no competition there."

Anger flares up inside me, stealing my breath. *Darn right there's no competition.*

Our waiter returns and we both sit back, the tension growing between us like an out-of-control tumor. "Are you ready to order?" he asks.

Derek clears his throat. "Yes, she'll have the mushroom ravioli with marsala sauce, and I'll have—"

"No, I won't."

The waiter pauses, looking from Derek to me.

"I hate mushrooms. I'd rather have a steak, actually."

The waiter starts to ask me a question, but Derek holds up his hand. "Would you excuse us for a minute, please?"

The waiter hurries away, and Derek glares at me. But I'm not afraid of his displeasure. Not anymore.

"That's twice now you've contradicted me, Amelia. Twice you've embarrassed me. I won't allow you to do it again."

I stare at him in wonder. "Wow. I can't believe I actually agreed to marry you once."

"What's that supposed to mean?"

"It means you're a jerk, Derek. An egotistical, controlling, manipulative jerk."

Oh my gosh, did I just say that? I TOTALLY JUST SAID THAT! Tara would be so proud.

He sits back, his face hard. "You're still angry. I get that. I might even deserve it."

The heady feeling of telling Derek exactly what I think of him lingers, giving me confidence. "You definitely deserve it, but it's not anger. Not anymore, anyway. I'm just calling it like I see it."

He smiles at me in that condescending way of his, and I have to clench my fists to keep myself from reaching over and slapping him. Instead, I take a deep breath. "Whether or not I'm angry, or whether or not you really are an egotistical jerk is not the point," I say. "The point is that it's over, Derek. For good. I'm sorry you had to come all the way up here for nothing, but there is no way we're getting back together, and no way I'm ever going to marry you. So thanks for calling it off in the first place and stopping me from making the biggest mistake of my life."

I stand up, and for the first time ever he stays sitting. I've never looked down on him before—he never gave me the chance. He was always the one looking down at me.

"Goodbye, Derek."

"Where's the ring?" he throws at me.

I sling my purse over my shoulder and give him a hard smile. "I'm driving it."

And I walk away.

———

"Hey, Mom."

She looks up from the book she's reading. "Oh! I thought you were out with Derek."

"I was, but I called an Uber and left early."

"You did? What happened?"

I pick up a cushion from the couch and sit down. "I saw him for who he really is: an overbearing, manipulative jerk. And I called him out on it."

"Derek? Amie! Did you really tell him that?"

"I did."

She frowns. "That doesn't sound like Derek at all. I hope he didn't take you seriously."

"Well I hope he does. It's about time someone told him off." I shouldn't be surprised that my mom is defending him, but it still makes me prickle.

"After he came all this way to apologize? You're not even going to give him a chance?"

"Derek knows exactly what he's been doing, Mom, and he knows I'm right. The only reason he got away with it for so long is because I let him."

Her lips press together in a thin, straight line, and she looks at me for a long time. "You've certainly changed a lot this summer," she says. "I just hope you know what you're doing."

I don't respond, and after a minute she turns back to her book. The quiet stretches between us, broken only by Ebenezer, who jumps onto the couch and mews for attention. I stroke his inky black fur as he settles into my lap, the throaty hum of his purr filling the quiet room.

"Do you remember when I was little and we would go to the fair every summer?" I ask, breaking the silence.

Mom looks up. "Yes."

I stroke Ebenezer's head, avoiding her eyes. "What do you remember about it?"

She considers for a minute before answering. "I remember how excited you and Brandon always were for the carnival rides. You loved the flying swings. And the ferris wheel." She smiles at the memory.

I shift in my seat. "Actually, I hated the ferris wheel. I don't like heights—I've always been afraid I'll fall."

She blinks. "No, I remember. You loved it."

Maybe I should consider a career in acting, since I've obviously done a good job convincing people that I think and feel in a way completely inconsistent with what I actually do. I think carefully about how to respond.

"I know I said that. And I know I pretended to be excited. But I wasn't."

Mom looks skeptical. "Really?"

"Yeah. I only went on the rides because Brandon was so excited about them."

"But you loved the rides!"

I sigh, tired of the conversation already. "No, I didn't. I just loved seeing Brandon so happy. And you and Dad. I never liked the fair at all—there were always so many people and so much noise and it was hugely overwhelming for me. But I knew how much Brandon looked forward to it. It was tradition that we went every summer, and I didn't want to disappoint any of you by telling you how much I hated it."

"I had no idea," Mom murmurs.

I shrug. "I had a lot of practice pretending. It's what I've always done. I don't like to disappoint people, so I usually just go along with whatever someone else wants."

"That's a dangerous way to live."

"I know." I pause. "I'm just glad I figured it out before it was too late."

"Too late?"

"Too late to stand up for myself. Too late to change my mind." I shudder. "I'm so glad Derek called off the wedding."

"Are you sure this isn't about Jason?" Mom says abruptly. Defensively.

I blink. "Jason? What do you mean?"

She gives me *the look*—the one every child knows. The look that says don't-play-dumb-you-know-exactly-what-I'm-talking-about.

"I'll admit, Jason has been a big part of the solution," I say. "But this isn't about choosing Jason over Derek. I'd choose *anyone* over Derek at this point."

"*Are* you choosing Jason, then?" she asks.

I shake my head. "No. I'm not choosing Jason. I'm choosing me." I smile at her, but she doesn't smile back.

"Well, I hope you'll be happy with your choice, then."

She picks up her book again, and for a moment I consider letting her read. But there's something else I need to know.

"Hey, Mom?"

"Hm?"

"There's something I've been meaning to ask you."

She puts the book down again and looks at me. "Sure, sweetie."

I look at Ebenezer, now dozing in a puddle of drool on my lap. "It's about you and Dad."

"Your dad and I? What about us?"

"I overheard you arguing back in June, the night I agreed to sell my engagement ring. You asked Dad what would have happened if you'd have sold your engagement ring when you broke up." I take a deep breath. "And I was just wondering why you never told me that you and Dad had a broken engagement."

She doesn't move. She doesn't say anything. The longer I wait for her response, the more anxious I become, until at last she responds.

"I didn't know you heard that," she murmurs.

I shrug, waiting. Finally she clears her throat.

"Your father and I hadn't known each other very long when we got engaged," she says, reaching over to scratch Ebenezer behind the ears. "Only about four months. We were crazy for each other, of course, but that can only take you so far in a relationship. About a month into our engagement, we had an argument."

"What about?"

She shakes her head. "I don't even remember. Neither does your father. But whatever it was, at the time it seemed insurmountable. So I called off the wedding."

I blink. "*You* called off the wedding?" Wow. I wasn't expecting *that*.

She looks out the window, absently stroking the cat in my lap. "It was a big fight. I was really angry, and hurt. But once things settled down and life went back to normal, I realized how much I missed him. How badly I wanted to patch things up."

"So did you call him?"

She shakes her head. "No. I was too proud. But I put the ring back on, because it reminded me of him.

"We were both at a party a few weeks later. I hadn't heard anything from Walter in several weeks and I was pretty miserable. Still too proud to admit it, though," she says, shaking her head again. "Anyway, he saw the ring on my finger at the party, and came to see me the very next day. He told me how sorry he was and how much he loved me, and how much he wished we could start over with a clean slate."

I picture my dad—funny, kind, stubborn to a fault—and try to imagine what he must have felt. After a minute my mom continues.

. "He told me later that seeing the ring on my finger was the turning point for him. You know how your dad is—more stubborn than a burr, most of the time. He'd made up his mind not to talk to me again unless I approached him first. And of course, my pride was hurt and I was too embarrassed to apologize, so I wasn't about to talk with him, either. But I put the ring back on my finger, and that made all the difference."

I think about my parents and their marriage. It hasn't been perfect, of course, but they have a strong, loving relationship. I never worried they would get a divorce or that one of them didn't love the other. I never would have imagined they got off to such a rocky start.

"I guess I understand now why you were so upset I was selling my ring," I say.

She nods. "I was afraid you would regret it. I was afraid you and Derek would get back together and then you wouldn't have it."

Her words are like needles—stabbing me with tiny, maddening pricks.

"Mom," I say slowly, watching for her reaction, "why did you like Derek so much? Why did you want us to get back together?"

"You know, once upon a time you liked Derek, too."

"I did, but for all the wrong reasons. And now I want to know your reasons."

She huffs. "Who wouldn't want their daughter to marry a

man like Derek? He's handsome, and smart, he's charming and wealthy and charismatic. He's just—"

"Like Brandon?" I say, feeling a hole open up in my stomach.

She lights up. "Yes, like Brandon. Derek is a lot like Brandon. He would have been the perfect son-in-law."

And there it is. Whether she's meant to or not, my mother has always placed Brandon on a pedestal—one I've been trying to climb all my life. But if she's put Derek on the same pedestal, it's not one I want anything else to do with.

I squeeze her hand and offer a small smile. "Well, it's not going to be Derek. But hopefully someday the man I marry will still be the perfect son-in-law."

"And if he isn't?"

I give Ebenezer another scratch under the chin. He yowls in protest as I unfold myself, depositing him on the couch as I stand. "Then I guess you'll have a son-in-law *and* a daughter that disappoint you."

I leave the room, not caring to see her reaction.

Chapter 27

Back in June, the summer seemed to stretch before me like an endless wasteland—nothing but misery and pain as far as I could see. Now I can hardly believe it's over. In a little over a week, I'll be heading back to Vegas and my life there.

I consider leaving the car with my parents and flying back to town, but since I'll need a car when I get back anyways, I figure I may as well take it. Tara has agreed to fly up for the weekend and travel back with me, which will make the sixteen-hour drive a lot more bearable.

Things have been a bit tense between me and my mom since our little talk. She hasn't said anything to me about it, and I'm not in a hurry to bring it up. I've had enough life-altering conversations for one summer—I'm content to finish that one another time.

And then there's Jason.

He knows what happened with Derek—I called him that night and told him all about it. But something is different. I think having Derek show up sent a boulder crashing through his confidence, and he hasn't been the same ever since. Every time we talk, every time I see him, there's an air of anticipation in our conversation. He's determined not to make another move until we talk about The Kiss, but just when I think I've worked up the courage to tell him how I feel, I decide against it. Besides, the cooking competition is this weekend, and I don't want to mess up his concentration or focus.

At least, that's what I keep telling myself.

The day before the competition I get up with the sun. After a quick jog in the park, I shower and get ready for the day. Tara's plane gets in at two, and I have a bunch of errands I want to run before I have to meet her. Just before I head out the door to drop off some books at the library, my phone rings.

"Hello?"

"Miss Cunningham?"

"Yes, this is she."

"Hi Miss Cunningham, this is Roberto down at Benny's Auto Sales. How are you today?"

"Oh, hi. I'm doing fine, thanks."

"Glad to hear it. Listen, I don't know if you're still looking for a Volkswagen Beetle, but we just got one on the lot and I have a note here to call you if that happened."

I suck in my breath. "You have a Volkswagen Beetle? Like the other one?"

"Well, it's not exactly like the other one," he says, hesitant.

"Does it have a sunroof?" I ask, biting my lip.

"No, not a sunroof—it's a convertible."

The poor man probably thinks I'm possessed because I practically scream with excitement. "I'll be right there," I say.

———

"Tara!"

I wave, calling her name from the other side of baggage claim.

"Ames! There you are. I was about to call an Uber," she says, walking up to me.

"Sorry, I got held up," I say, giving her a quick hug. My face hurts from smiling so much and I'm practically vibrating with excitement. She gives me a strange look.

"What's the deal? You're buzzing like a bee in a flower shop."

"You'll see. It's a surprise."

We chat as we walk out to the parking garage, about her flight (the guy next to her wouldn't shut up), her work (she just got promoted—huzzah!) and what Jeremy plans to do while she's gone (play video games and eat way more pizza than he should). The further into the parking garage we go, the more excited I become. When she realizes which car I'm heading toward, she stops.

"You got a Bug?" she cries.

"Yes! Just this morning. That's why I was late."

She squeals, and both of us start talking at once. I tell her all about the car and how I came to get it. We climb inside, and she helps me unlatch the roof and open up the top. "Wow. A convertible Bug. You've wanted one of these for forever."

"I know. Wasn't it nice of Derek to get it for me?"

She laughs. "Better than that rock that was dragging you down, that's for sure."

We talk the whole way to her parents' house, catching each other up on anything we may have missed between our texts and phone calls. Her parents live in the Valley now, so it's a forty-minute drive from the airport. We take her bags inside, and I plop down on the guest bed while she unpacks a few things.

"Thanks for being willing to drive back to Vegas with me," I say.

"Of course. It'll be just like old times."

"Yeah, only this time we'll have a more reliable car to get us there."

"Thank heavens for that," she says. "When do you want to leave?"

"Sunday, if that works for you."

"Sure. I can only stand my parents for about three days anyway, so I'm good with that."

My phone pings and I pull it out of my pocket. I grin when I see Jason's avatar on my lock screen. Tara looks over at me.

"Who's that?"

"Jason," I say, swiping up to read his message.

JASON

Want to come over tonight? I'm making meatballs

AMIE

Can Tara come too?

JASON

Tara's in town?

AMIE

Yup. She just flew in today. 😊 She's going to drive back to Vegas with me

JASON

Sure. Come over anytime

"Want to go to Jason's tonight for meatballs?" I ask, looking up at Tara.

She grins. "Absolutely. I've been dying to see the two of you together."

"Tara, we're only friends," I say, deliberately *not* thinking about all the little moments that felt otherwise.

"Mm-hm, *friends*," she says, drawing out the word into two syllables.

I roll my eyes at her. "You're as bad as my mother."

"Amie, Jason's been crazy about you since junior high. And judging from what you've told me about the summer, he's still crazy about you."

My mouth drops open. "What? Tara! How do you know he liked me back then? How come you never said anything?"

She shrugs. "For the same reason I didn't say a lot of things to you. I didn't want to put the idea into your head that maybe you liked him, too. I figured if you didn't realize it, you must not have feelings for him."

I stare at her, and she laughs. "Come on, Ames. I know you. I was just looking out for you, that's all."

"It's not that you didn't tell me about Jason," I say with a frown. "It's that... well, you had me figured out years before I even realized that about myself. What does that say about me?"

"What does it say about *me*, you mean. It says that I'm the best friend a girl like you could ever have, because I love you enough not to tell you things so that you can make up your own mind about them."

I get up from where I was sitting on her bed and give her a hug. "Tara, you really are the best."

She grins. "I know. Now come on, I'm starving. Let's see if Jason is as good a cook as you say he is."

———

When Tara and I arrive at Jason's, there's Italian opera music blasting through the house. Jason is singing along with gusto, but he turns it down when we come in. We help him roll the meatballs, talking and laughing like old times. Jason makes the spaghetti and sauce from scratch, of course, with fresh tomatoes and basil and garlic and all sorts of ingredients I wouldn't know what to do with. Of course it's delicious, and I eat and drink so much I think I might burst.

It's an amazing night.

"Jason, if you ever get tired of cooking for yourself, you're welcome to come cook for me," Tara says, after finishing another helping of pasta.

Jason smirks. "And how would your husband feel about that?"

"Jeremy? He would welcome it. Believe it or not, I'm not such a great cook."

"Believe it," I murmur to Jason. He grins, and I doubt the flutters in my stomach are due to indigestion.

"Come to think of it," Tara says, ignoring me, "with what we pay for takeout each month, we could probably afford to pay you a private salary."

"Tempting," Jason says, "but I'll have to pass."

"Darn. Well, what if Amie wanted a private chef? You know she still hasn't found another roommate since I got married and moved out..."

"Tara!" I laugh-choke at her, my face flaming red. She winks at me and goes off again on what a phenomenal cook Jason is and that he should totally come to Vegas and work as a chef.

I seriously want to strangle her.

Jason looks pink around the edges, but he's laughing like a good sport. He probably wants to strangle her, too.

We help clean things up, then sit down in the living room to talk for a bit.

"Are you nervous about tomorrow?" Tara asks.

Jason shrugs. "Not really. I'm more excited than anything. I'm not doing it to win, so I'm not really vested in the outcome."

"Wait, you're not trying to win? What's the point, then?"

He smiles. "The point is getting feedback from the judges. I want to know how my cooking compares and what I can do to improve."

"That doesn't sound like as much fun as winning," Tara grumbles.

"The winner gets admission into the cooking school and the first semester's tuition," I explain. "But Jason's not planning to go to culinary school, so he doesn't need to win."

"You're crazy, Jason," Tara says, shaking her head. "But I guess you know what you're doing."

By the time we say goodnight, it's almost eleven. Tara and I wave and head back down the street to my house, where her parents' car is parked.

"So when are you going to tell Jason how you feel about him? And don't pretend that you don't know what I'm talking about. I was watching you all night, Ames. You're crazy about him."

"You know, I could kill you for what you said back there," I hedge.

"What, about a private chef? Come on, Ames, you can't tell me you haven't thought about it. He could be making you breakfast in bed!" She waggles her eyebrows, and a nervous laugh bubbles out of me.

"Geez, Tara, get a grip! It's *Jason*."

"Exactly my point. It's Jason. So what gives? Why haven't you told him how you feel? You used to tell him everything—except the stuff you only told me."

"I don't know. I've been trying to figure out what to say to him. How do you tell one of your best friends that you're in love with him?"

"You say, 'Jason, I'm in love with you. Let's runaway together.'"

I smirk. "Just like that, huh?"

"Or you could kiss him. That would probably get the point across, too."

When I don't say anything, she stops and stares. "Wait. Amie! Have you already kissed him?"

"Um, sort of?"

"What do you mean, sort of?"

"I mean yes, we've kissed, but I don't know if it was me that kissed him or him that kissed me. It just sort of happened."

"Why didn't you tell me? Amie! I need to know these things!"

I laugh self-consciously. "It was awkward, ok? I don't even know how it happened."

"Tell me everything."

So we stand outside in the dark, Tara leaning against the car and me pacing the sidewalk in front of her as I relive the picnic with Jason. When I'm finished, she pushes away from the car and places both her hands on my shoulders.

"Amelia Francine Cunningham, you are the most adorable idiot I know."

"Thanks," I say, rolling my eyes.

"I'm proud of you for not letting Jason speak up first. That shows a lot of growth. But Ames, he's got to be going crazy, waiting for you to talk with him. Go put him out of his misery already."

"What, like right now?"

"Yes. You'll both be happier. Trust me." She gives me a little shove back in the direction we came. "I expect to hear all about it tomorrow," she calls, climbing into the car as I head around the corner.

I put one foot methodically in front of the other, retracing my steps back to Jason's house. I try to think about what to say and how to say it, but the more I focus on the words the more panicked I become. Pretty soon I'm standing on his porch, still not sure what I'm going to say, but I knock anyways. *Breathe, Amie. You got this.*

The door opens and Jason stands there, light spilling out from behind him into the cool night air.

"Oh, hey Amie. Did you forget something?"

"No, I just... um... well, I wanted to tell you something."

He leans against the doorframe, waiting, but in the quiet darkness my confidence evaporates. Suddenly I'm afraid. I'm afraid of what Jason will say, or what he won't say, when I tell him how I feel. I'm afraid of how it will change our friendship, or what will happen if he doesn't feel the same. I'm afraid of what it will change for the future and what it will change for the past, and I'm afraid of not knowing what to do about any of it. And I'm terrified of being hurt again, especially by Jason. I squeeze my eyes shut, taking a deep breath.

"I just wanted to say... good luck tomorrow. You're going to do great."

For a minute he doesn't move, then he slowly straightens

up. I stare at him, a capital C for coward plastered on my forehead.

"Is that really all you wanted to say?" he asks, his eyes searching my face.

"Yes," I say, though it comes out a little shaky.

He waits, watching me. Then slowly he smiles. "You know what the best form of luck is?"

I swallow. "What?"

He reaches up, brushing away a strand of hair, his hand coming to rest on my cheek. His eyes never leave mine as he leans in, letting me know his intent before our lips ever touch.

"A kiss," he murmurs, gently pressing his lips against mine.

Kissing Jason in the park was an electric shock—all fireworks and red flags and explosions. But this kiss is like being submerged in lava—a slow burn that never seems to end.

Too soon he pulls away. I don't want to open my eyes, but at last I do. His look says everything I wish I had the courage to say myself.

"Thanks for the luck," he says.

Chapter 28

J ason's scheduled time slot is three o'clock. He's one of the last contestants to go in front of the judges before the announcement of winners at four. I sent him a text this morning wishing him luck (again). His reply makes me smile whenever I think of it.

JASON

You gave me all the luck I need last night

I haven't felt butterflies like this in years, and I don't ever remember feeling them for Derek. It's wonderful and strange all at once, and even though I haven't come out and told him, I think Jason knows how I feel. It certainly seemed that way last night.

"I still can't believe you didn't tell him," Tara grumbles as we arrive at the school.

"I didn't want to mess up his concentration today," I lie. Tara rolls her eyes, seeing right through me.

"But you're going to tell him today, right?"

"Yes, after the competition."

"You better," she mumbles.

Trois Fourchettes has a large campus, so we follow the signs to the banquet hall, where the auction and judging will take place. We pay for our tickets and enter the building, filling our lungs with the delicious aroma of gourmet food.

The cakes are lined up on long, narrow tables along two sides of the room. Some of them look quite amateur, but many are Pinterest-worthy creations. I scan the tables, looking for Jason's cake.

"Over here, Ames," Tara calls.

I make my way over to where she stands, in front of a cookie-laden creation sprinkled with edible confetti. My mouth waters just looking at it.

"Wow, someone's willing to pay $400 for Jason's cake?" she says, scanning the auction form attached to the table.

"Doesn't surprise me," I say. "Just look at it!"

"I'm trying not to," Tara says. "Or I might bid on it myself."

We check out the other cakes, and glance over the stanchions at the first course entries. We didn't pay for the salad bar portion, but seeing what's available makes me wish we had.

A little before three o'clock we head over to the rows of chairs in front of the judges' podium and take a seat. Three adults and three children are seated at the tables on the stand, each of them eating a cupcake as a young woman waits nervously for their reaction.

"This is just like one of those cooking shows," Tara murmurs.

The judges give their feedback, then the woman thanks them and walks offstage. Jason is announced as the next contestant, and he comes through a doorway which I assume leads into the back kitchen. He's wearing a white chef's jacket, black pants, and a nervous smile.

"Amie! Can we sit with you?"

I look up to see Jason's parents walking quickly down the aisle.

"Of course!" I say, waving them over. "They just called him up."

Paula takes a seat next to me and Brian sits beside her. They wave a quick hello to Tara, then we all turn our attention back to the podium.

"Tell us about your salad," one of the judges says, as an assistant places bowls of colorful fruit in front of each of them. The kids grin, and one of them cries out that she loves blueberries. Jason smiles, looking relieved.

"For my first course, I created a classic fruit salad with an almond lemon glaze."

"I like the choice you made to cut the fruit into shapes," the only woman judge says, spearing a tiny cantaloupe rocket. "Definitely kid-friendly."

"The glaze is delicious," the man to her right says.

The last adult judge—Chef Ivan Marić according to the placard in front of him—says nothing, only tastes the salad and makes a few notes on his form. I can see a flicker of uncertainty in Jason's face, which makes my stomach twist with nerves. He told me earlier that of all the judges, Jason values Chef Marić's opinion most.

I'm not sure which entrée Jason decided to enter, because I know he was practicing several. When the assistants bring it out, the elementary judges shout for joy.

"It's pizza!" one yells.

"Cheese pizza!" another cries. "My favorite."

I share a confused glance with Tara. "He just made plain cheese pizza?" she asks. I shrug, not sure.

The adult judges say nothing, until Chef Marić takes a bite.

"It is margherita pizza," he says, his surprised voice slightly colored with an accent.

"I thought it was cheese," the woman says. She takes a bite and smiles. "Very well done. It's delicious."

"Quite imaginative. Can you tell us your reasons for making it upside down?" the other judge asks. I think he's the head of the school.

"I conducted a poll and did some research," Jason says, "and found that most kids prefer cheese pizza over any other. But cheese pizza can be a bit plain, so I decided to make it a margherita pizza, only I hid the fresh basil and tomatoes underneath the cheese."

"Very clever," Chef Marić says with a smile.

The judges make notes, and soon the cupcakes are brought to the table. The full-sized cakes were viewed and judged before the doors were opened to the public, so this is just the taste test. Jason was worried about his cake being too plain-looking, but I reminded him about all the requests for sprinkles, and the gender divide that colored frosting created. He ended up making what he called a Confetti Cookie Surprise: chocolate cake with a cookie crumble center, white buttercream, and lots of colorful sprinkles.

It's hard to gauge what the judges think of his cake; their comments are polite but generic, and Chef Marić says nothing. I can see the disappointment behind Jason's smile.

There are two contestants after Jason, and a short break before the announcement of winners. More people show up as we wait—friends and family members of the various competitors.

"I was afraid we wouldn't make it," Paula says as we wait for the awards ceremony to start. "We got pulled over for a burned-out brake light just as we got off the highway."

"I still think that cop was just looking for an excuse," Brian grumbles.

Paula opens her mouth to say something, but the emcee starts speaking and drowns her out.

"We'd like to thank all of the entrants for sharing their talents with us, and for all of you who have joined us today," the woman at the microphone says. "Thanks to your efforts, we helped raise over sixteen-thousand, four hundred dollars!"

While the crowd applauds, the contestants file in and line up along the back of the podium in two long rows. I crane my neck, searching for Jason in the sea of white coats.

"We'd also like to thank all our judges for their expertise and advice. Our elementary judges Kimberly, Brennan, and Zak, as well as our adult judges: Ms. Olivia St. James, Chef Frank Laurent, and Chef Ivan Marić."

The crowd applauds again. "Do you see Jason?" I ask Tara. She shakes her head.

"And now, we know that everyone is anxious to hear who our winners are, so without further delay, Chef Frank Laurent will announce them to you."

The judge who liked Jason's salad glaze takes the podium amid polite applause. "Thank you, we are delighted that so many entered this year's competition. As you know, the theme this year was Kid-Friendly Foods. Contestants were judged against an established rubric with standard categories for presentation, skill, and taste, as well as a few additional categories strictly for our younger judges. Kids are, after all, the best judges of what constitutes kid-friendly food."

The crowd applauds again, and I finally locate Jason among the contestants. I catch his eye and he winks at me.

"Now, we have some wonderful prizes to give out, starting with our third place winner." Chef Laurent pauses, making sure he has the attention of everyone in the room. "Cammie Harrison has been awarded third place, as well as a two-hundred dollar gift certificate to Williams Sonoma."

The crowds cheers as a plump young woman with ebony skin and gold-tipped braids comes to the front to accept her prize.

"Our second place winner, and the recipient of a complete set of Chef Marić's stainless steel cookware and hand-forged cutlery, goes to Felix Mattheson."

The young man who steps forward is lanky and blonde, and looks about fifteen years old. I'm impressed that someone so young can cook well enough to win. He takes his certificate, shakes hands with the judges, and stands beside the woman who placed third.

"And now for our grand prize winner," Chef Laurent says. The crowd falls silent, and Tara grips my arm.

"For the first time in the nine years we've been holding this competition, we have a tie for the grand prize winner."

An excited hum fills the air, the remaining contestants murmuring to each other on the stand. The judge waits until it's quiet to continue.

"After consulting with the rest of the educational board, it has been decided that both grand prize winners will be offered admittance into next year's incoming class, as well as the first semester's tuition."

The scattered applause is short. I think everyone is as impatient as I am to hear who won.

"The grand prize winners of this year's competition are Sydney Harris and Jason Henley."

I scream, jumping out of my seat along with Tara and Jason's mom, applauding wildly. Jason steps out from the crowd of contestants, making his way to the front of the stage.

I'm laughing and crying and jumping and screaming as Jason shakes hands and poses with the other winners. He's wearing the biggest grin I've ever seen, and judging from how badly my cheeks hurt, so am I.

"Again, congratulations to our winners!" the emcee says, taking the microphone again. "We'd like to invite everyone to join us for drinks and hors d'ourves to celebrate, prepared by our current students."

Tara and I join Jason's parents as we move to the reception area. Most of the contestants are already on the floor, talking with and hugging those there to support them.

"Do you see Jason anywhere?" Paula asks me.

I shake my head.

"Let's wait for him over there," she says, pointing to a relatively empty corner of the hall.

We start moving that direction when my phone buzzes in my pocket.

JASON

I have to talk with Chef Laurent. Are you with my parents?

AMIE

Yes, we're waiting for you in the corner, back behind the drinks bar

JASON

K, will you let my mom know? I'll be
there asap

AMIE

Sure thing

We make it to the corner and I turn to Jason's parent. "Jason said he's going to talk with Chef Laurent," I tell his mom.

"What about?"

"I'm assuming it's to let them know he won't be accepting the admission and scholarship package."

"What? Why?"

"Jason's not going to accept?" his dad asks.

Oh dear. I thought Jason had already spoken with his parents, but apparently not.

"Um, well, I don't think he was planning on it."

"Then why did he enter the competition?" his dad asks, almost angrily.

"Brian, I'm sure Jason will explain everything when he finds us," his wife says.

"What will I explain?" Jason says, coming up behind me. We all turn to look at him, his mom reaching out to hug him.

"Oh honey, we're so proud of you!"

"Thanks Mom."

"Way to go, son," his dad says.

"Thanks Dad."

"Jason, I was drooling from my seat," Tara says. "I still think you should come back with us to Vegas."

Everyone laughs, and Jason turns to me. My face hurts from smiling, but I can't seem to stop. I stretch up on my toes, throwing my arms around his neck and planting a kiss on his cheek.

"Thanks for being here, Ames," he says.

"I wouldn't have missed it."

"Now, what's this I hear about you not accepting the grand prize?" his dad asks as we step away from each other.

"Don't worry, Dad. I didn't enter expecting to win, and I didn't plan to accept if I did. I won't be leaving the carwash."

His dad frowns. "Why not? Weren't you accepted to the school?"

"Well yeah, but—"

"And doesn't it come with a scholarship?"

"Yes, but—"

"But what? Wouldn't you rather be a chef than manage the carwash?"

Paula puts a hand on Jason's arm. "Honey, why aren't you taking the scholarship?"

Jason looks back and forth between them. "Who's going to run the carwash if I do?"

His dad laughs, clapping a hand on his shoulder. "Jason, managers come a dime a dozen, but there's not many that can cook like you. You have to live your own life. The carwash is yours if you want it, but if not, I respect that. No sense wasting your life doing something you don't enjoy."

Jason wraps him in a bear hug. "Thanks, Dad. You don't know how much that means to me."

"How long have you felt this way, sweetheart?" his mom asks.

Jason blows out his breath. "A long time."

"How come you never said anything?"

He shrugs. "I didn't want to disappoint Dad. I know how much that carwash means to him."

His dad shakes his head. "I'm sorry, Jason. I never should have put so much pressure on you. I had no idea you didn't want the carwash." He stops, looking thoughtful. "You really love to cook, eh?"

Jason grins. "More than anything."

More than anything.

A few weeks ago, Jason said he was ready to give up the carwash and his life here if I wanted him in Vegas. But would he give up this chance to follow his dream? It's not really a question, because of course he would. That's Jason. But can *I* allow Jason to give this up, for me?

That one's not as easy to answer.

His parents move away to get some food. Tara throws me a wink and follows after them, leaving us alone. I smile at Jason, reaching for another hug.

"I am so proud of you," I say. He holds me close—closer than before—and doesn't let go even when I start to pull away.

"None of this would have been possible without you," he murmurs, his lips at my ear. His breath tickles my neck, sending shivers coursing through me.

"You mean without Veronica," I tease.

He laughs and steps back, but keeps his hands around my waist. "Yeah, I guess I do owe Veronica a thank you," he says. "But I'm not sure I want to hear her gloat. I'd rather give all the thanks to you."

Jason looks happier than I've ever seen him in my life, and that makes me happy. He takes my hand to lead me away, when Chef Marić walks up to him.

"Mr. Henley," he says, his deep voice thick with the flavor

of a foreign language. "Chef Laurent just told me that you have refused the grand prize. Is this true?"

His bushy gray eyebrows are drawn down in displeasure, making him look a bit like an angry Santa Claus.

"Yes, it is, but only because of a misunderstanding," Jason says.

The older man's face lights up. "Ah! So you will accept the scholarship to *Trois Fourchettes?* You will study at the school?"

"Yes, I was on my way to find Chef Laurent just now and explain everything."

"Good, good, that is good. When he told me, I was very upset. I came to find you and convince you to come cook with me, if you were not going to take the scholarship."

Jason's eyes widen. "You were?"

"Yes, yes, I want you to come cook with me. But take the course first. You have talent, Mr. Henley, and I want you in my kitchen."

He shakes Jason's hand again, smiles at me, and turns back into the crowd. Jason looks at me, incredulous.

"Did that just happen?"

My face splits into a grin. "It did."

"Chef Marić wants me to cook with him?"

"Yup. And something tells me that's not an offer he made to the other winners."

Jason laughs, running a hand through his hair. "This can't be happening. I can't believe this is happening."

"Believe it, Henley," I say, giving him a playful nudge. "Your life is about to get a whole lot more delicious."

———

Jason's parents don't stay at the reception long, and Tara leaves shortly after they do. Since she was my ride to the school, Jason offers to drive me home. He tells me all about his day on the way back to my parents' house: about meeting the other contestants, what the school kitchens are like, and how he almost forgot the cupcakes back at his place. I drink in the sound of his excitement, not wanting to tell him what I know I have to.

He pulls up in front of the house and cuts the engine. "Does it feel real yet?" I ask.

"Not really. I still can't believe Chef Marić wants me to work with him."

"I believe it."

He flashes me a grateful smile. "And I can't believe my dad is ok with me leaving the carwash." He shakes his head. "I should have told him a long time ago. But I was so worried about his response, so afraid I would disappoint him."

"But you didn't. And now there's nothing standing in your way." I smile at him, and he quirks an eyebrow at me.

"I'm not so sure about that."

His look ignites my pulse, and I force my heart back down into my chest. I can't lose my head. Not tonight. I have to keep my wits about me, and pretend that I don't love him.

I can't let Jason give up his dreams for me.

Because I know if I tell him how I feel, he might throw it all away and follow me to Vegas. I can't let that happen. I *won't* let that happen.

He reaches across the seat, brushing a hand across my cheek, and as much as I *want* to lean into him and fall into his kiss, I force myself to pull away. He stops, that small dent forming between his brow.

"I've been doing a lot of thinking," I say, looking anywhere but at his face.

"About what? About us?"

"About everything."

He sits back, waiting.

"You know what happened with Derek," I say, measuring my words. "We'd been together for three years, and when he told me it was over, it broke me. I came home in pieces. I was so broken I didn't even know how to think on my own." I pause, giving him a small smile. "But then I ran into you. And you've been so great. You've helped me so much."

"You've helped me too, Ames."

"I'm glad I've helped you. But I'm ready to go home."

His eyebrows shoot up. "Home? I thought you said this was home."

"It is. But Vegas is my home, too." I swallow, looking down at my hands. "I finally know what I want to do with my life. I'm already enrolled at UNLV, and switching my major will mean a few more years of school. Vegas is where I need to be. It's where I *want* to be. My future is there. And your future is here."

He turns away, putting both hands on the steering wheel and leaning his forehead against them. We sit in the dark for several minutes, the silence growing thick with unspoken questions.

"What about us?" he says at last. "What about the picnic?"

I swallow. "What about us?"

He blows out his breath in a false laugh. "I guess that answers my question."

I can hear the hurt in his voice, and I want so badly to open my heart and tell him how I really feel. But I can't. Not now that he can follow his dream.

I reach for the handle, opening the door. "Thanks for being such a good friend, Jason," I say, trying to keep my voice even.

"Only a friend?" he asks.

I can see it in his face and hear it in his voice—he's reaching, hoping, begging me to tell him he means as much to me as I do to him. And he does. He means so much to me that I have to do this.

I nod, turning away. "Only a friend."

Chapter 29

I t takes sixteen hours of nonstop driving to get from Spokane to Las Vegas, and we start before the sky is fully light. It's a typical road trip with Tara, consisting of really loud music, really bad junk food, really good conversation, and really empty gas tanks.

At least we didn't have to hitch-hike to the nearest station this time.

By eleven pm we hit the outskirts of Vegas, and I can feel the thrum in my veins as we drive past The Strip. The lifeblood of the city pulses with neon expectation, calling to passers-by to stop and stay awhile in a city that never sleeps. I didn't realize how much I'd missed it until this moment.

I want to drive through town with the top down, but it's still 98 degrees outside, so we keep it up and blast the a/c instead. At last I pull off the highway, turning down a few streets until we arrive in a typical Southwest suburban neighborhood. Rocks and palm trees grace the handkerchief-sized front lawns, while beige stucco houses butt up next to one another so close you could lean out your window and play patty-cake with your neighbor.

"Welcome home," Tara says as we pull into her driveway. "You're staying tonight, right?"

"Yeah, I think I will. Can you help me at the apartment tomorrow?"

"I can in the morning, but I've got a cut and color at two pm that I can't reschedule."

"That's fine. It shouldn't take too long to get things squared away."

Jeremy is there to welcome Tara with a kiss and me with an awkward hug. Hugging Jeremy has *always* been awkward because Jeremy himself is awkward, but he gets points for trying.

"Good to see you, Amie," he says, swinging his arms gently at his side.

"Thanks, Jeremy. Good to see you, too."

"Are you guys hungry? I can order us some pizza," he says, turning to Tara. She makes a face.

"Ugh, no thanks. I'm so sick of cheesy, fatty food. Besides, I'm exhausted."

"Me too. I think I just want to call it a night," I say.

"You know where the guest room is," Tara calls, already heading down the hallway.

I put on my pajamas and climb into bed, pulling out my phone to text my mom.

AMIE

Made it safely to Vegas. Love you

She's already in bed so I don't expect a response, but I stare at the screen, arguing with myself. Part of me wants to text

Jason as well, to let him know we didn't drive off the road or into a cactus or something, because with Tara in the car, you never know. But now it's different between us, and somehow that feels like crossing an invisible line. So instead, I put my phone down and turn off the light, wondering if I made the right decision after all.

———

We stop at the grocery store on the way to my place in the morning. Thankfully Tara cleaned out my fridge and cupboards after I left in June, for which I am eternally grateful. The last thing I want is to walk into my apartment after three months and smell rotting potatoes and rancid milk.

I restock the fridge while Tara empties the bags. "It's been lonely here without you," she says.

"Whatever. You've got Jeremy and a job you love—I bet you didn't even miss me."

"I did *too*. When he's not at work, Jeremy is a hopeless homebody and I was desperate to get out. I had to sneak over here and watch *Gilmore Girls* by myself on more than one occasion."

"Well you're the one that made me go, so you've only got yourself to blame," I say, putting away the last of the groceries.

"That's true, but I can't say I'm sorry." She studies me for a minute. "You've changed."

I gawk at her. "You're *just* now noticing my hair?"

She laughs, hitting me with a towel. "That's not what I meant and you know it."

Grinning, I grab the towel and toss it on the counter. "I know, I know. Just teasing."

"It's good to hear you laughing, and I'm glad you went. It helped. A lot."

"Thanks for making me go," I say with a wry smile. "I feel like a completely different person than I was three months ago."

She smiles. "What else are best friends for?"

"For helping clean up the mess after a massive breakup, for one thing," I say, putting my hands on my hips. "Ugh. This place has Derek written all over it. Time to take it back."

We start by pulling all the pictures off the walls and tossing them in the trash. I launch the two extra-large frames into the dumpster and grin in delight when I hear the glass shatter against the bottom. Tara collects the odds and ends lying around the living room—useless decor that Derek bought in an attempt to make my 2-star apartment feel more like a 5-star penthouse. It helped bring it up to maybe a 3.5-star level but that's about it.

Tara heads for the bedroom while I go into the office, collecting notes and cards and photos and dumping them in the trash. After a few minutes she comes to the door, holding up my Pottery Barn duvet cover. "Mind if I keep this? I've always liked it."

"Go for it. Take the rug from the front room, too."

"Sweet, thanks."

It takes a couple hours, but at last we manage to remove every trace of Derek from my apartment—even the fancy jar of *White Caviar Crème Extraordinaire* in the bathroom. Tara's car is filled to bursting with items she'll either keep or sell, and I've got a load to take to Goodwill in mine. The walls and floors of my apartment are strangely bare, but I smile as I think of how fun it will be to decorate the place in shades of Amie.

"What about your dress?" Tara asks, pulling out a bottled water from the fridge.

"I'm going to sell it. It cost nearly as much as my ring so I should get at least a couple semester's worth of tuition out of it."

"Have you decided what to change your major to?"

"Early Childhood Education. I sent an email last week, but I have to meet with a counselor in person to make it official. I'll go in tomorrow to do that and enroll in my new classes."

"Wow. Can't get much farther from pre-law than little kids, I guess."

"It's not just about doing something totally different, Tara. I'd really like to work with children. I loved helping at the library this summer."

"That's because you don't have any younger siblings," she says, making a face. "If you had to live with my sisters growing up, you'd never want to see another snot-faced little hoodlum in your life."

I laugh, and we finish loading up the last of the items from the house. I wave as Tara heads home with her treasures, then climb into my car to drop off my donations.

I drive down the parkway for a while, passing through six-lane intersections and a whole lot of traffic before finally arriving at the Goodwill on Twain. A nice young man in a blue vest helps me empty the car, hauling away the last few remnants of my old life.

It feels good to wash my hands of Derek, once and for all.

I flip on the radio as I pull up to a red light, glancing out the window at the businesses on the corner. There's a strip mall at the back of the parking lot, and beside it is a small building with a bright yellow awning. A sign above the double doors reads "Sunshine Valley Preschool" in rainbow-colored letters, and below that, hanging in the window, is a large sign that says HELP WANTED.

For a moment, I imagine myself sixteen again, shaking the Magic 8 ball in my room, wondering if I should stop and take a chance or keep on driving. The old Amie would have needed that little black ball to make the choice, because there's no one else around to make it for her. She would have looked back at the stoplight and waited patiently for it to turn green, then driven sedately back to her little apartment. But I just left the old Amie in half a dozen garbage sacks at the back entrance of a thrift store. *This* Amie is going to take chances and plan for her own future, one little choice at a time.

The light turns green and I smile, turning into the parking lot.

Chapter 30

TARA

So? How did it go??

T ara's text is waiting for me after my interview the next morning.

AMIE

I got the job!

TARA

Woohoo! 🎉🎉🎉 Way to go Ames!

AMIE

Thanks. I'm super excited.

TARA

When do you start?

AMIE

As soon as all the paperwork is done. I have to get a background check and fingerprints and training and all that first. But soon.

TARA

So proud of you

I stare at the phone for a long time, then finally stop arguing with myself and flip through my messages to text Jason.

AMIE

Guess what?

I wait, hoping for a quick response, but nothing comes. He's probably at work, tying things up before he passes the torch to a new manager.

AMIE

I took a giant leap of faith and applied for a job at a preschool yesterday. They wanted to interview me right away, and this morning I got the job!

I wait, but there's still no response. Feeling deflated, I send one last message before stowing my phone.

AMIE

Anyways, just wanted to share my good news. Hope all is well.

My apartment is completely bare, now that Tara and I have cleaned it out, so instead of going home I decide to do some shopping. The Frugal Fanny in me wants to steer the car toward IKEA, but I resist, reminding myself that I have plenty of money left over from selling the ring to afford some fun, unique items for my apartment instead.

My favorite home store smells like a cross between cinnamon bears and lavender lotion, which is surprisingly pleasant. I grab a cart and laze through each department, stopping to admire and ogle things on every shelf in every aisle. After two hours I've collected enough bedding and linens and art and decor to furnish a small hotel, so I finally check out and take my treasures out to the car.

The home store is located in a large strip mall of big box stores, sandwiched between a pet store on one side and an electronics store on the other. There must be an adoption event going on, because the parking lot immediately in front of the pet store is roped off with banners and balloons.

I've always loved animals, and being home for the summer made me realize how much I've missed having a cat. Tara doesn't care for cats so I never got one when we moved here, and Derek didn't like getting fur on his clothes. But since neither of those are an issue any longer, I decide to take a look at what's available.

There is a litter of puppies more adorable than anything, but while puppies are cute, they inevitably grow into dogs, and I'm a bit frightened of dogs. I love cats, though. Cats have personality, and they're the perfect companion to curl up with me on the sofa while I read.

I wander through the front of the store, looking into a dozen kennels and crates until a fluffy ball of orange fur catches my eye, and I pause. It's a marmalade cat, curled up on a hammock slung across the cage, watching me with lazy gray eyes.

"Hey ginger," I say, "what's your name?" I look at the label attached to the side of his cage. "'Sam.' Really? Huh. That doesn't seem to suit you at all."

He lifts his head, trilling a meow at me.

"I would have given a handsome boy like you a more regal name, like King George. Or Reginald."

He stretches, then climbs down from the hammock to sit on the floor of the crate, looking up at me.

"Do you like either of those names?"

He meows, cocking his head.

"I completely agree," I say with a smile. "But don't worry—we'll find the perfect name for you."

In less time than it usually takes me to decide what to have for lunch, I've adopted a large tabby cat with intelligent eyes and a decidedly twitchy tail. I buy everything I need for him—including a carrier—and haul it all out to my car. I have to rearrange some of the items purchased at the home store, but eventually I find a place for everything and head back home.

———

"I thought you were going shopping for stuff for your apartment?" Tara says, her voice echoing. She must have me on speakerphone.

"I was. And I did get stuff for my apartment." I scratch the orange tabby on my lap under his chin and he starts purring. "I got new bedding and curtains and throw pillows, and some new things for the bathroom."

"And a cat."

"What have you got against cats?" I ask, the subject of our discussion humming like a lawnmower in July.

"Nothing," she says. "I just didn't know you planned on getting a cat is all."

"I didn't either. It just sort of happened."

"Have you given him a name?"

"Yup. He's a handsome guy and deserved something sophisticated, so I've settled on Mr. Knightley."

I can hear the laughter in her voice as she responds. "Well, I'm excited to meet him, but for now I've got to go. I'll talk to you later."

"See ya."

I hang up the phone and look down at the animal in my lap. "Should we set up house, Mr. Knightley?"

Mr. Knightly stretches out, kneading my leg with his paws. I ruffle his fur affectionately and move him gently off my lap and to the couch. He looks at me reproachfully for a minute before proceeding to bathe himself.

"Good idea. You take a bath, I'll set things up."

I don't get very far before my phone chirps, alerting me of a new message. I see Jason's face and swipe the screen, suddenly nervous.

JASON

That's awesome! Way to go, Ames. I'm really proud of you.

Guess we both get to follow our dreams now

My vision gets blurry and my throat tightens up as I read his texts. I've tried so hard not to think about Jason for the last three days (has it really only been three days?) but it's practically impossible. Just like everything used to remind me of Derek, now everything seems to remind me of Jason. I sigh, putting away my phone and drying my eyes. I've made my proverbial bed, and now I'll have to lie in it.

I just didn't anticipate the mattress being so hard.

Chapter 31

The next few days pass in a blur. I stop at the police station to get fingerprinted for my new job, as well as sign up for the mandatory first aid and CPR classes I'll need. I meet with a guidance counselor about my reasons for changing my major and get the transfer approved. After registering for classes, I order my books online (thank goodness for two-day shipping!) and make sure I have what I need. By Sunday night I have everything ready for the new semester, which starts in a week.

While I've been busy running around preparing for school and my new job, it's been easy to keep my mind off Jason. But now that everything is in order and I have time to relax, I'm terribly lonely. It's been eight days since I last saw Jason, and two days since his last text. I keep thinking about the summer, and how easy it was falling in love with him. Although I guess I fell in love with him a long time ago. I just needed reminding.

Mr. Knightley rubs against my legs, and I bend down to give him a scratch. "Hey fella," I say. "It sure is nice to have a roommate again."

He trills a meow and settles down on my lap while I flip on the tv. BBC is running a special of all the Austen film adaptations they've ever done, so I settle in to watch Pride & Prejudice. With a purring lapwarmer, Mr. Collins spouting soliloquies, and the sun dipping lower in the sky, I finally let myself relax. Only one thing could make this more perfect, but he's over a thousand miles away.

———

KNOCK, KNOCK, KNOCK.

I jolt awake, the pounding on the door startling Mr. Knightley, who bolts into my room. It's completely dark outside so I'm a bit disoriented—how long have I been asleep? A glance at the tv (which is still on) shows Lydia hanging on Wickham's arm, so I can't have been sleeping for too long. I rub my eyes, trying to focus.

KNOCK, KNOCK

Ugh, that's right. The door.

"I'm coming!" I call, wondering what time it is and who could possibly be knocking at my door on a Sunday night. I unlock the door and swing it open with far more force than necessary, glowering at whoever is on the other side.

"Finally. I thought I was going to have to break in."

I stare at him. "Jason?"

He grins, dimple and all. "In the flesh."

"What are you doing here?"

He smirks. "It's good to see you, too."

I laugh. "Sorry, I'm just so surprised! Come in, please."

I step back to let him in, just as Mr. Knightley arrives to

investigate. He wraps himself around my legs, mewing plaintively.

"Who's this?" Jason asks as I shut the door.

"My new roommate," I say, reaching down to pick him up. I carry him back into the living room, and Jason follows. He looks around.

"Nice place," he says. "It suits you."

"You think so?" I sit down on the couch with Mr. Knightley. "It's all new. I had to exorcise Derek from the premises when I got back."

He chuckles, sitting next to me on the couch. I lean back, and he reaches over, scratching Mr. Knightley behind the ears.

"What's his name?" he asks.

"Mr. Knightley."

"Mr. Knightley? Like from Jane Austen?"

I nod.

"Well hello, Mr. Knightley. Aren't you a lucky kitty to be roommates with this amazing woman?"

My heart is racing, his words and his closeness sending fire through my veins. I clear my throat, wishing I could clear my head just as easily.

"So... what are you doing in Vegas?" I ask.

He sits back, looking thoughtful. "I came to talk to you about the picnic."

I laugh nervously, more to dispel the anxiety building inside of me than because anything about this is funny. "Didn't we already talk about that?"

"No, we didn't," he says, crossing his arms. "You only said that your future was here, and my future was there, and you wouldn't even answer me when I asked about us. So here I am, and I'm not leaving until I get a straight answer from you."

"Couldn't you just have called?" I say wryly.

"You could have hung up on me if I called. This way I'm sure to hear you out."

"I would never hang up on you, Jason."

He quirks an eyebrow at me. "Oh no? And why is that? Tell me, Amie. Please."

His look is earnest, and it tears at my heart. How can I say no to that face? How can I say no to my heart?

"You really want to know?" I say quietly, looking down at the orange tabby in my lap.

He laughs humorlessly. "Do you think I would have come all this way if I didn't?"

I look up at him with a tentative smile. "Probably not."

"Then tell me, Amie. Tell me how you feel about the picnic, about the kiss, about us. Tell me everything. Please."

I look down again, wondering if I'm brave enough to open my heart to him. *Don't be afraid,* I tell myself. *It's Jason.*

He waits, watching me.

"I'm in love with you." The words come out more strongly than I imagined, and hearing them spoken aloud gives me courage. "I think I've loved you ever since we were kids, but I didn't know that's what it was. I didn't know it was love because it was so comfortable and felt so right, and it didn't scare me. I thought love was supposed to scare you. I thought it was supposed to make you think and feel in crazy new ways that weren't normal. Does that make sense? I thought—"

"Amie—"

"—that love was something you went looking for, not something that grows inside of you when you're with someone who knows who you really are and likes you anyways."

"Amie—"

273

"Just hear me out," I say. "I love you, but I didn't want to tell you. I didn't want you to give up the opportunity of going to culinary school and becoming a chef, not for me. I didn't want—"

His lips are on mine before I even realize that he's moved closer. One hand wraps around my neck and the other around my waist, and my mind goes blank. All I can register is the feeling of his mouth on mine, the warmth of his body so close to my own, and the heady feeling of being kissed by the man I love.

"Amie," he says, breaking away. "You are the most ridiculous, frustrating woman I have ever met."

I blink. "What was that?"

He laughs, cupping my face with both hands so I'm looking directly into his eyes. "All summer long," he says, "you worked at figuring out your own heart. I saw you struggle and I heard your frustrations as you realized your people-pleasing, chameleon-like attitude had cost you your own hope and happiness. But I saw you change. I saw you work and grow and become, and it was amazing, Amie. *You* are amazing.

"But then," he continues, "just when I was so sure you were never going to put your own happiness in jeopardy again, just to make someone *else* happy, that's exactly what you did."

I laugh, and the tears that were filling my eyes spill down my cheeks. "I guess I did, didn't I."

"You definitely did," he growls. "But by the time I realized that's what you were doing, you had already left. I knew that if I called you, you would deny it, and it would be a lot easier for you to pretend that you didn't care for me in that way if you knew I was a thousand miles away. I assumed it would be harder for you to keep up the charade if I came to see you in person."

"And here you are."

"Here I am."

"Even though I'm ridiculous and frustrating?"

He laughs. "Did I say that? What I meant to say was that you're perfect."

A laugh bubbles out of me at his words. "Me? Perfect?"

"Yes, you," he growls, sweeping my hair out of my face. "You are perfect for me, and I don't intend to let you out of my sight again. The last week has been torture."

"I don't understand. Are you moving to Vegas?"

He grins, and I gasp. "Jason! You're moving to Vegas?"

"Yup. Soon as I can find a place."

I launch myself at him, throwing my arms around his neck, laughing and crying and kissing him all at once. Mr. Knightley darts away, his hair standing on end.

"So, if you're moving to Vegas," I say, wanting to hear him say the words, "does this mean you love me?"

He rolls his eyes. "Of course I love you. I've loved you almost my whole life." He leans over and kisses me, soft and slow. "I didn't know if you'd ever feel the same way about me as I felt about you."

"How come you never told me?" I ask.

"I tried, remember? At the homecoming game. But I know I didn't try very hard, and I didn't do it very well. I didn't want to influence you. I didn't want you to think you felt something for me when you really didn't. I saw how you adapted yourself to others, even as a kid, and I didn't want that. I wanted this. I wanted *you*."

"I wish I would have known," I say, burrowing into him. "It could have saved me a lot of heartache."

He kisses the top of my head and I feel the fire spreading through me, settling into my bones. I turn my face upwards, which is all the invitation he needs to kiss me again.

I don't know how long we spend wrapped up together on the couch, because time doesn't seem to matter anymore. All that matters is that Jason loves me, and I love him. There is nothing that feels more perfect than the rightness of being in his arms and knowing that it's where I belong.

When the passion of our kisses dies down, and Jason's lips are soft and tender on my own, I pull away to look at him. His eyes are bright, reflecting the joy I can only imagine he sees in my own eyes. I lean forward and kiss him on the tip of his nose, and he laughs.

"What about culinary school?" I ask.

He grins. "You'll never believe it, but I'm already enrolled at a school here."

"What? How?"

"It turns out that *Trois Fourchettes* has a sister school here—The Sweet Spoon. Once Chef Laurent understood that I only wanted to quit because I was moving to Las Vegas, he transferred my enrollment and scholarship here. I start next month. But dang, I had no idea how big Vegas was. It's going to take some getting used to."

"Oh that's right, you've never been to Vegas before."

"Nope. You'll have to show me around."

I stand up and reach for his hand. "Well, first things first. I'm taking you to my favorite restaurant. Come on."

———

"You're taking me here?"

We climb out of the car and I raise my eyebrows at him. "You got a problem with that?"

He laughs. "No, but Amie, we're in *Las Vegas*. Some of the best restaurants in the country are in this town! Aren't these," he gestures to the brightly lit In-N-Out in front of us, "all over the California coast?"

"There's a reason for that, you know."

"Because Californians have the nation's worst drivers *and* worst taste buds?"

I shove him playfully in the shoulder and he laughs, grabbing my arm and pulling me close. His lips are on mine before I realize what he's doing, and my entire body instantly reacts. My arms reach around his neck and I press myself into him, savoring the warmth of his lips on mine.

We're standing in the middle of a crowded parking lot with dozens of onlookers, but I don't care. Jason is here, and he loves me. *Me.* Not the me he wishes I was or the me he hopes I become someday, but me as I am right now. I shiver, pulling him closer.

A catcall from a group of teenage boys pulls us apart, and Jason looks over at them. "Mind your own business," he yells.

"Get a room!" comes the reply.

"You know, that's not a bad idea," he murmurs, kissing me on the jawline.

I laugh. "You're just trying to get out of eating the world's best hamburger."

He scowls. "I'm trying to come on to you, and all you can think about is food?"

"Yup," I say, grinning as I break away from him. He groans,

and I take his hand, dragging him with me. Because that's where he's going to stay.

With me.

THE END

Other books by Shaela Kay

*If you enjoyed the book, please consider
leaving a review!*

Acknowledgments

I'm always in awe when I finish a book. So much goes into the writing of it that it feels impossible to recall everyone who has helped me along the way. Primary thanks go to God, for blessing me with the ability and desire to write. Without Him, I would be nothing and could do nothing. I am grateful everyday for the life my Heavenly Parents have given me.

For my wonderful and supportive husband, John. There's a little bit of him in all the heroes I write, and I am grateful everyday to share my life with him. Thanks for your constant encouragement and unfailing support, my love. You're my favorite.

For my local writer friends and besties: Queenie, Madge, Sachiko, Bawb, and Xena. I don't know what I would do without you! Thanks for all the encouragement, brainstorming, and sprint sessions, and for listening to me moan and groan about this book when it was driving me nuts. You guys are seriously the best.

For Sally (Britton) Treanor, because I couldn't do this writing thing without her. I'm so grateful for modern technology that 1) introduced us to each other, and 2) makes it possible to communicate every day, even living thousands of miles apart. She has blessed my life in countless ways, and I am so glad to have such an amazing woman and talented author to call my best friend.

My heartfelt thanks go to Krista Jensen, whose wonderful book *Kisses In the Rain* first sparked my desire to write a contemporary romance, and whose continual encouragement and critique were invaluable to me. I'm constantly in awe of what a talented writer and thoughtful friend she is, and I'm so grateful for her influence in my life.

Much love and gratitude go to Rachel Runge for her airline expertise, and to Rachel Hawks for providing the knowledge (and samples) of homemade macarons.

My mother-in-law, Maxine Odd, is a fantastic proofreader (she's got serious skills, y'all) and a wonderful support. Love you!

For all the wonderful readers and friends who have read my other books and enjoyed them. You guys keep me going. I'm not a career author, but you're the whole reason I put my sweet little stories out in the world instead of keeping them to myself on my computer. Thank you for your support.

My kids are fantastic and I love them to pieces. My little girls Audrey and Mira tell me I'm the best author ever (even though they're too young to have read my books, haha) and their hugs and kisses and encouragement mean the world to me. My eldest daughter Elina finally read some of my books and *gasp* actually liked them! Thank you, Butterfly, for your love and support. Caleb, my oldest, has been a rockstar. I can't count how many times he helped his sisters or did extra chores or fixed meals so I could work. He has been a huge blessing in my life, and I don't know what I would do without him.

To all the friends I've made along my writing journey, thank you. All the retreats and conferences and writing sessions with you have lifted my soul and made me want to be a better person, a better woman, a better writer. Thanks for being awesome.

About the Author

Shaela Kay was born and raised near Seattle, WA. She studied Theatre and English at Brigham Young University-Idaho, but left her studies in order to be a wife and mother. When she isn't reading or writing, you can find her quilting, crafting, or working as a graphic designer. She and her husband John live in the Pacific Northwest with too many hobbies and not enough bookshelves.